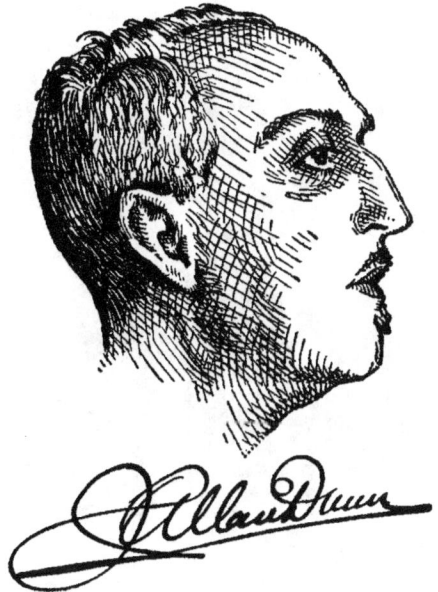

The CRIME MASTER

THE COMPLETE BATTLES OF GORDON MANNING & THE GRIFFIN

VOLUME 1

J. ALLAN DUNN

ALTUS PRESS • 2014

EDITED AND DESIGNED BY
Matthew Moring

INTERIOR ILLUSTRATIONS BY
Joseph A. Farren

PUBLISHING HISTORY

THANKS TO
Gordon Dymowski, Joel Frieman, Monte Herridge, and Everard P. Digges LaTouche, and Ray Riethmeier

TABLE OF CONTENTS

JOSEPH ALLAN ELPHINSTONE DUNN was born on 21 January 1872 in London into a wealthy Irish family. The son of Joseph H. Dunn and Elizabeth Elphinstone (Miall) Dunn, he was educated at Winchester Public School and went to New College, Oxford, where he got his Bachelor of Arts degree in 1893. Subsequently, he also received a degree of Bachelor of Science. He was a tall (6'1") and handsome man.

Interested in travel, adventure and writing, Dunn became a journalist, which allowed him to journey around the world. He covered the Spanish-American war of 1898 in the Caribbean and the Philippines, and the Russo-Japanese war of 1904. He was a friend of Jack London, and during the Russo-Japanese war they witnessed the battle of Port Arthur and nearly got shot.

He traveled the China Sea, Hawaii and the South Pacific, and was one of the first white explorers in New Guinea, claiming to have faced death from hostile tribes there:

> White man's magic saved the day. I traced the tribal totem—a tortoise—on my arm with a stick of soap. Then I set fire to jungle bark fibers with my burning-glass, rubbed the ashes over my arm, and lo, there was the turtle's outline, showing my kinship with the tribe. Soon I was pressing on, my most thrilling adventure safely behind....

Ending up in Hawaii, he became the associate editor of Austin's *Hawaiian Weekly* for a period. During this time, he

married Grace K. Buchanan on December 15, 1900 in Honolulu. While in Honolulu, he inherited around £4,000 from his
uncle (the equivalent of half a million dollars to-day). With
this newfound freedom, he built his own yacht and sailed the
seas, circumnavigating the world thrice. A description of him
at the time from an actor friend of his who visited him:

> Dunn lives in a little house, on the outskirts of Honolulu,
> that was once occupied by the late Robert Louis Stevenson.
> This is not remarkable, because, according to the Hawaiian
> landlords, everything on the island was once the home of the
> famous Scotsman. Dunn has a big wicker chair on his veranda
> that he occupies most of the time. His writing materials, paint
> boxes, cigars, canvases and prompt books are piled around
> within easy reach. He wears, in the privacy of his home, a
> costume that is a combination of the native dress and certain
> portions of the Shakespearean wardrobe that he used while in
> Janet Waldorf's company. He writes a bit, paints a bit, acts a
> bit and altogether enjoys himself mightily all the time.

By 1904-05, he moved to San Francisco with his wife, and
was a member of society there, staging and acting in plays with
his society friends. He was the editor of *Sunset Magazine* from
1906-07, and advertising manager for the San Francisco rail-
road. He continued to be a close friend of both Jack and Charm-
ian London during this time, staying at their home frequently.

In January 1913, he was caught after having pawned stolen
jewelery from his friends and hosts, though no one prosecuted
him. His thefts included some pajamas from Jack London! He
claimed that he committed these thefts because the magazines
for which he wrote had delayed payments and he had run out
of money.

He divorced his first wife the same year, remarried in Sep-
tember 1913, to Gladys Courvoisier, and moved to Greenwich
Village, New York. It was Gladys's third marriage; both prior
marriages had ended in divorce for cruelty. He started his
writing career the same year, starting with a couple of articles

in the *Saturday Evening Post*. His writing career took off, and he was on his way to producing a million words a year.

He and Gladys had a son on March 13, 1916.

On August 11, 1918, he and Gladys quarreled, and Gladys threatened to kill herself and the child. She rushed to her room, took out a gun and held it to her head. When Dunn called to her, she turned around and discharged the revolver, killing their son.

During the trial, and later, Dunn stood by her side, and she was sentenced to a year in prison. They were separated by 1926 and Dunn was paying her $600 a month alimony.

Dunn was a member of the American Expeditionary Forces in France during World War I, and was thrice decorated for his actions, reportedly attaining the ranks of major and staff officer.

Dunn may have married for a third time, as there was a news report of his disappearance in 1927 and of his wife's search for him. The trigger for the disappearance seems to have been a telegram Dunn received: "Book ordered stop. Not received. Awaiting instruction." It was signed "Given," and without a return address. Dunn went away the same night, without waking his wife.

He married one more time, on October 30, 1936, to Loyola Lee Sanford, who was his agent.

Dunn was a director of the Explorers Club, member and vice-president of the Adventurers Club, member of the Circumnavigators Club and the Advertising Club. He published more than forty novels, and more than two thousand stories in all.

J. Allan Dunn died on March 25, 1941.

THE CRIME MASTER

"One of Us Is Going to Win," the Griffin Warned Investigator Manning. "That One Is—Myself!"

THERE WERE no windows to the curious room, elliptically shaped, the high walls in one continuous curve with no visible sign of a door. Diffused and mellow light flowed in from unseen mysterious sources. There was ample ventilation. From somewhere, diminished, rather than faint from distance, music sounded, music orchestrated in the ultra-modern school that some call decadent. Music that stirred the physical emotions rather than exalted the mind or stimulated the spirit. Not the strident, strenuous phases of jazz, but insinuating melodies, rhythms that seemed to suggest exotic landscapes, the glidings of great, gorgeous snakes, the flight of rainbow-plumaged birds, the fall of crystal waters—lovers watched upon by lurking, creeping ape-men.

The walls were tapestried in two shades of gold, dull and burnished, in a pattern that did not obtrude yet made itself manifest. The carpet, ankle deep, was of rare weave, matching the walls. There was a hint of incense, of burning amber. And a strange atmosphere of evil, an influence that abused beauty and harmony, twisted them to its own malignant purposes.

Those walls back of the golden tapestries were of steel. The place was at once a sanctum and a stronghold. The ceiling curved in a shallow dome. On its background of dark blue, certain constellations were accurately inlaid in gold. Two signs of the zodiac, in conjunction, and their attendant stars.

Here and there were divans, deep cushions on the floor. A

high chest of black wood, with inlays of pearl and ivory, actually a safe of the most modern construction. A chair, carved, like a throne, back of a carved table. On the table a strip of ancient woven silk, once the back of a Manchu princess's robe; a crystal globe, slotted at the top with openings for air, three-quarters filled with water into which streamed constantly a jet of compressed air. Emerald weeds waved and contorted goldfish swam solemnly through the subaqueous jungle.

There was a disk of smooth copper-gilt suspended in a frame of ivory. On either side of this smaller replicas. A tablet of white porcelain, illuminated from beneath, on which a man was making notes and calculations with a stylus of agate tipped with lead.

The whole place was bizarre. It might have been the abode of an astrologer, a mystic. The seated figure should have worn a pointed cap, a robe inscribed with cabalistic characters, a long beard.

Instead, there was a clean-shaved man in modern dress. His face was the most arresting thing in the room. At the moment

Behind his paper he watched the
man with the brief case.

it was calm, cold, rigid, almost, as an ivory mask and nearly as colorless. But the eyes gleamed like jewels; hard, brilliant, the eyes of a fanatic or a madman whose brain, while erratic, still retained control. It was in the eyes that the malignant influence of the room seemed to concentrate, perhaps to emanate.

The features were, in their way, beautiful, but they were stamped with a predatory cast. The lips were thin, cruel, the nose a finely chiseled beak, the whole face dominating. The ears well shaped, but the ears of a faun, pointing up to crisp hair, silver-gray that did not give so much the suggestion of age, but of virility that lacked pigment. The only lines were two scores that ran from nostrils to the ends of the mouth.

This was the man who called himself the Crime Master. He might, as he looked, have been a fallen archangel, hurled from Heaven, intent upon revenge. He was an arch-enemy of society, of the world of finance, nursing injuries that, in his warped brain, had mounted until he was a foe to all established foundations of modern civilization.

A gong sounded, with a light, sweet note. The music ceased. A voice thin but distinct came from the smaller disks, synchronized. He listened intently, a smile that lacked all kindness, deepening the brackets about his mouth.

He spoke into the big disk. His voice was smooth, silken-smooth, but forceful, exultant, mocking. He gave swift instructions. Then, as the music once more crept in, he erased, with a moist felt, all that had been on the tablet of porcelain, now transferred to a memory of intense energy and reception; made another note—a date, and regarded it with the same smile. His long, thin fingers folded themselves about each other. Then, with a swift movement, subtle rather than sudden, he brought heavy paper from a drawer, dipped a quill pen into violet ink, held in a well of onyx whose lid was the head of a griffin, the mythical winged lion, and wrote quickly, still smiling; folding the letter with a chuckle that suggested the soft gurgle of an eddy on the Styx, or of the sacred river of Kublai Khan, running through caverns measureless to man, down to a sunless sea; addressed the envelope, sealed it.

"So," he said softly. "It appears we have a worthy opponent. The real game commences."

He pressed a silver button in the desk-top. From a deeper drawer he drew out a mask that seemed made of gold-leaf, pliant but distinctive, changing his features to the semblance of an Egyptian relief of the Hawk-God. Now he looked not unlike the griffin lid of the inkwell, the device that was on the scarlet seal that closed the letter.

The gong sounded twice. With his foot he pressed on the heavy carpet and a section of the wall slid noiselessly aside. A man appeared, a valet, his sign of service the wasp-striped waistcoat he wore, a human automaton, expressionless.

"See that this is mailed at the Grand Central post office by four this afternoon."

The Crime Master felt in the pocket of his coat, brought forth a tiny box of gold, damascened, enlivened with small, sparkling and exquisitely cut gems. In it was a green paste—hasheesh.

Five minutes later he was at full length on a divan, the phantasies of the hempen extract mingling with the music that now played more and more faintly, lulling him to sleep and dreams. His features relaxed, but they did not lose that stamp of enmity.

II

THE WISE old trainer, owner of Garrity's Gymnasium, looked with professional interest and approval at Gordon Manning, coming out briskly from the needle shower after his daily handball game.

"There you have a man who keeps himself fit," said Garrity to a new and somewhat paunchy patron. "Always *has* kept fit, if I know anything, and there's not much in the line of athletics he couldn't get away with, if he put his mind to it. As it is, there's worse boxers an' wrestlers swaggerin' round, thinkin' they're champs."

"He doesn't look such a marvel to me," said the other, watching Manning closely, a little enviously, as the latter came striding naked from the shower cabinets, lean and lithe. "You wouldn't call him much on muscle."

"You wouldn't? Next time you git a chance, you take a look at the limbs of them chimpanzees out to the Bronx Zoo. You won't *see* much muscle on them. They're skinny, those chimps, they look stringy, but they can take apart a man twice their weight an' size.

"It's quality that counts. Know anything more muscular than a snake? One of them big boas? See any muscles bulgin' on them? Manning is built the same way. His muscles are like first-class rubber bands. They've got resilience. His brain's the same way. Watch him play handball and you'll get what I mean. Coördination."

"What does he do? Anything?"

"He's some sort of a lawyer. I know he's got offices down on Liberty Street. I know he was the youngest major in the A.E.F. where I was top sergeant. An' I'm dead sure he don't loaf. He couldn't, not his sort, any more'n quicksilver'll stay put."

The listener was impressed, almost against his will. There *was* something out of the ordinary about Manning, his poise, the carriage of his spare person, the lift of head and chin, a certain pride that was not offensive, a suggestion of proved efficiency. Perhaps the trainer had not exaggerated, after all.

"Now you, sir," said Garrity bluntly. "You've got a nice body, but you've abused it. You want to take it easy at first. I'll start you off with the medicine ball. There's a class of gents ready to start in a few minutes."

While the pudgy, somewhat puffy patron turned toward the gym, Manning dressed rapidly, left the place and walked the few blocks to his office, lithe as an Indian, though with a freer tread, swinging his cane. His face was thoughtful.

That was a curious cane he carried, heavier than it appeared. It was made of rings of leather shrunk about a steel core whose end made the ferrule, while the head was capped with a plain gold band bearing the initials G.M. in modest script. A weapon, rather than a cane. The only weapon Manning carried, as a rule, no matter how dangerous his errand, but one that, in the hands of a skillful and powerful man, was formidable, deadly. And even Garrity did not know that Manning was an expert fencer.

He came to his office building, tall though not one of the latest, sandwiched in between others on a strip of land that ran between two streets. There were four elevators, one of them an express, stopping first on the seventh floor, where Manning had his office suite. One car was temporarily out of order, as announced by the card on the grille. The starter gave Manning a military salute. Manning answered it in swift gesture of authority, now discarded yet still recognized by a few.

The car shot up, stopped. The operator opened the door with a friendly grin. They didn't know much about Manning's affairs in the building, but any public servant gets to be a good judge of people he sees every day.

On the outer door of Manning's suite his name appeared above the two words that seemed to designate his profession.

GORDON MANNING
Advisory Attorney

But there was only one man in New York, anywhere, besides himself, who knew Manning's true vocation. So he believed. And hoped.

There was an intelligent-looking red-headed youth in his outer room, two women stenographers in the next, deft, deferential, businesslike. His personal office was well but not luxuriously furnished. In one corner stood a circular safe of ultrahardened steel, practically impregnable—and empty—though no one knew that but Manning.

It seemed all it was intended to represent, the obvious repository of secrets. It would take experts hours to get into it. And it was only a lure. Manning kept his secrets accurately filed in a trained memory, supplemented by a condensed file in a cypher that he had improved upon from many he had studied. That file was in his desk, ingeniously concealed.

Manning never appeared in court. He had clients, though they were not so numerous as important. He oftener refused advice than gave it. His fees were large, but his cases, turned over to other attorneys for action, did not occupy all his time. Yet, to those who took occasion to comment on him, he was a man of little leisure, of comparatively few friends though many acquaintances. None knew him intimately. He was cordial enough but reserved, although he was not considered an enigma.

He took seat in his desk chair, gazing out to the towers of Manhattan, lining the busy river, with its spidery bridges, its teeming commerce. The window was open, the sounds of the metropolis blended in a symphony of achievement.

His dark eyes were like those of a hawk, or an eagle, made for the fathoming of far perspectives, far-seeing, eager, with a certain fierceness that came into them now. His body lounged, at ease, relaxed, but his mind was centered on a desperate and dangerous quest. He sought a man, a universal enemy of the powers that had built up the city he loved, the greatest city in the world, New York. He sought him in secret and stern resolve, the man who had mocked, was still mocking, at the police—looting, murdering at will, head, without question, of a band that was not only devoted to him, or linked by rites of deviltry, but infinitely resourceful under the direction of their head. The Griffin.

Manning frowned. He admitted himself worried. It was never known where, when or how the Griffin would strike, and he had never failed. Mad perhaps, with a species of insanity that might some day burn out his inflamed brain, but, meanwhile, made it that of an evil genius.

He swung his chair to the desk, always clear of papers not

under immediate consideration. He had been set to the trail, but he could find no starting point, no scent toward the following of it, the solution of the mystery that gripped him. The Griffin left no traces, save those of devastation. No clews.

Manning was fresh to the trail, but there was a long count against the offender—the man who had no name that is to say, no name unless it was revealed in a device he used, embossed on—ovals of heavy paper, cartouches he affixed as tokens of his presence—of his absence from the scene of crime—or token that he was the master-mind who originated it.

A device that was the head of the mythical creature known to heraldry as a griffin, stamped in scarlet.

It might, Manning fancied, be a clew to the surname of the man, who seemed more fiend than human. But that was only a fancy and he wanted facts.

It was a waiting game he was forced to play and that harassed him. The hideous certainty that the Griffin would reveal himself, stagger the city with some fresh crime that would come like a bolt from the blue, stagger the very foundations of law and order, without warning, without trace of the offenders.

These acts were like those of the fictional Frankenstein, shaped like a man, minded like a fiend. A fiend of frightfulness and inordinate cunning, of illimitable daring and deviltry, heading an organization growing ever bolder with success.

Manning signed some letters, summoned one of the stenographers, dictated, ran through typed documents, digesting their contents, arriving at solutions. But all the time his brow was furrowed.

His subconscious brain busied itself with the main issue for which his business was only a camouflage. It held a presage of impending trouble that he was powerless to prevent, though he must trace its source. He knew he was up against no ordinary opponent, but one as resourceful and relentless as any he had encountered in his duties in the war opposing the Boche Secret Service.

He finished up the correspondence, gave a word of praise to the girl and got his car from its parking space, easing the powerful but unostentatious machine through the traffic, driving with automatic accuracy, his mind ever prescient of impending calamity, out to Grand Concourse, through the park, on to his home in Pelham Manor, a bachelor establishment catered to by his picked Japanese servants, perfect if remote.

All the way his eyes, that saw the traffic, the lights, were conning with their eagle gaze for an elusive quarry, a fabulous beast, a scarlet griffin.

III

A S MANNING picked up the square envelope with its bold superscription in violet ink, he had a premonition, perhaps of the quickened senses, a positive emotion or reaction; that here was something evil. He did not analyse such matters. He believed that all hunches were based upon actualities, that so-called luck was merely the blossom, or the fruit of seed some one had sewed where perhaps he might not pluck.

But he had seen many curious things in his time. In the war, when he was detailed on Secret Service though ostentatiously merely a brass hat. In the Orient and the far-off places he had traveled since the war. He would not have disputed that vibrations for good or wickedness might not persist, did not cling, as some subtle odor, to objects handled by persons of strong vitality and will.

And here was evil. As if the envelope had been defiled by a malignant touch. He opened it without hesitation, abruptly.

My dear Manning:
Allow me to exchange congratulations with you upon your acceptance of the post you have just taken over. I take it that, with myself, it is not entirely the pursuit of—shall we call it crime?—that interests you, whether to achieve or prevent it; but that the adventure of the chase appeals.
It does to me. I trust we shall share many interesting and

thrilling episodes. I am complimented, spurred by having such an adversary. It inspires me to further efforts. I fear that we shall never meet. I may, ultimately, have to make sure of that. In the meantime, until you push me too hard, and I grant that possible emergency, I shall thoroughly enjoy playing the game with you.

It is like playing chess with a skilled opponent. A game in which, however, you labor under a handicap. I always make the first move. Let us pit our resources against each other. We might perhaps both be called Crime Masters. But it will be no stalemate. One of us is going to win. Myself. For, if you seek to master crime, I am its master.

You will hear from me soon. Very soon. I much prefer to dealing with you direct.

There was no signature, only the embossed griffin's head, with its rapacious beak, its rampant attitude, stamped on an oval of bright red, scarlet as blood.

IV

IT WAS a shock, an unexpected blow from an unseen adversary; rather, not so much a blow as a flick of insult, a challenge.

The man known to the police as the Griffin had, attested the mute evidence of his scarlet seal, committed many crimes. He had robbed, he had at times killed with what seemed mere, diabolical wantonness. His coups were always coupled with great gains, carried out with a precision that bespoke an evil genius in conception and preparation.

He might, Manning reflected, be well termed the Crime Master, juggling the words to make the meaning suit his successes, though, as he had written, they could be twisted to have an opposite interpretation, one that Manning meant to make apposite—to himself—as one who mastered crime.

It would be a hard-fought game, not played in the open, with the quarry always well away. The letter told one thing. The Griffin was a man of education, of sardonic humor, with a brilliant, if warped, brain. The use of the seal already indicated that.

The writing, Manning was sure, would lead nowhere. He did not doubt the other's ability to write several distinctive hands, carefully studied. He had shown an infinite capacity for taking pains.

As for the paper and the postmark, if a clever criminal was careful, they were useless as clews. Only the amateur, the person of one, sudden crime, forgot details. The Griffin was a professional.

Every little while, at intervals of weeks or months, a crime tagged by the seal was perpetrated. Every little while, press and public clamored for the police to apprehend him. They suspected Centre Street of concealing the use of the seals in certain cases—and they were not away from the truth.

The chief commissioner, with his newly appointed squad of secret police, could do nothing with the Griffin. He worked alone, he was not a gangster, a racketeer. The commissioner had called in the aid of Manning, enlisted it, a willing volunteer. They had held, so far, no communication, would hold none until Manning had tracked this beast, run it to earth, destroyed it, or been destroyed himself. Yet, the Griffin had discovered his employment. It was something close to magic, which is merely the mystery of the unknown.

Manning accepted it as a fact. There was no use taking time to determine what indiscretion had freed the information. A harassed man might mutter in his sleep. Gossip flies far and often its links are intangible.

It was not himself. He slept soundly. He slept apart. The thing was out. The Griffin had learned of the appointment and, in his bizarre fashion, it had given him greater zest to prove his own powers, to show himself the Crime Master.

"A form of grandiose dementia," Manning diagnosed it. There was nothing to do but wait for the fulfillment of that promised "very soon," to wait for that "opening move" which would be fraught with inevitable tragedy, too late to remedy.

The Griffin might overplay his hand. He might not be playing chess so much as hurling boomerangs. So far, none had swung back to destroy him. He was like a wolf, captain of a lupine band, swooping down on defenseless, unsuspecting sheep. And Manning was the shepherd.

He ate dinner by himself, waited on by the imperturbable Japanese who had been with him for years, devoted, impeccable retainers who would protect him if he needed them, who maintained the little house Manning had built from his own plans, secure from intrusion.

After the meal Manning read a review, smoking a pipe. His hoped-for encounter with the Griffin might prove only a battle of wits, but, if it ever came to handgrips, with him or any of his followers, the man would need all of a maniac's strength to cope with Manning.

V

IN MANNING'S private office the next day the telephone rang crisply, imperatively. It was a private line, unlisted, unconnected with the general office instrument. As he lifted the receiver he was conscious, almost as if he had received an electric shock, of the same sensation he had experienced with the letter he had received from the Griffin.

A question, doubtless, of vibrations, himself tuned-in, receptive, expectant, his whole being, body and brain, a coherer.

Manning did not consider the voice disguised. It was resonant, but not harsh, cultured, tinged with maleficent humor, mocking.

"Manning," it said. "It is within a few minutes of eleven o'clock. I trust you have standardized time, so you can check the moments. They are quite important.

"Don't try to trace this phone call. It cannot be done. I told you you would hear from me very soon. This is the first move, now in the making. It will be accomplished by eleven o'clock, precisely.

"Then you can get busy and solve the problem, if you can. To use a vulgar idiom, this is being pulled off under your very nose, Manning. I have chosen the man because of his close proximity to you. In a measure, you are responsible for his selection and his demise, his most untimely and unforeseen demise. Not entirely. He has other qualifications, naturally."

Manning glanced at the clock on his desk. It was accurate to a second. He felt that the Griffin—there was no question of his identity—was talking against time. He knew that he could not trace the wire. Others had tried to do that. The Griffin had some method of using the telephone service without automatic cut-in. He was equally sure that the crime now being predicted would be carried out.

The mocking voice kept on.

"I am afraid, my dear Manning, that you are powerless to prevent my coup, but I shall take precautions. We have another seventy odd seconds. It would be too late for you to take advantage of the occasion by buying certain stocks for a swift fall, as I have done. I have no especial enmity against the man chosen, but his death will be very profitable to me. I have an expensive organization to maintain.

"He dies by a new method I have recently perfected. I shall be interested in your failure to uncover it—and me. It will exercise your ingenuity. And the name of the man—"

The clock on Manning's desk began to chime the hour.

He heard his caller chuckle as the strokes went on to four—to five.

"The name is Richard Ordway. Two floors beneath you, my dear Manning. And quite dead by now, I assure you."

Richard Ordway! Private banker, promoter, financier, manipulator. Manning knew him. They were members of the same club. He often saw him in the building. Stocks might well go into turmoil when Ordway died suddenly. There would be a panic on the Exchange, the Curb. Sales that could not be traced in the mad scramble.

And the Griffin, scattering his orders, using his organization, could not be detected. Yet, because of that quirk in his brain, he had thrown down the challenge to Manning.

Manning's wits worked fast. The supreme impudence, the insolence of the call, sent a surge of hot blood through him. His resolve might hardly be strengthened, but it rose within him. And the Griffin, for all his cleverness, had given out something that might yet betray him.

His voice was distinctive. Manning would not forget its inflections. He had landed more than one spy because of certain shadings and intonations, slight accents. He might never hear it again, but—if he did?

He leaped into action, wasting no time. He knew he could not save Ordway, but, before the last stroke had sounded, he was out of his side door into the corridor, hat on, cane and gloves in hand.

The Griffin had, he fancied, overlooked one other matter. He pressed the button, caught the express descending, stepped into the car. On the third floor they overtook the local. When the latter arrived Manning was lounging at the cigar and news stand. He had bought an impromptu but effective mask that he had used before—a newspaper. Like many other individuals in the district, he buried his face in it, seemingly seeking market news.

He had marked the indicator of the other local—the third still out of order. It was at the top of the building. Four people stepped out of the one that had followed his express car. A young clerk, a girl, a man he knew and another man who carried a brief case, well dressed, self-assured, walking swiftly, but showing no especial signs of hurry.

Manning had certain qualities that make up the born detector. He had studied many things. He did not absolutely believe in physiognomy, but there were certain features he considered evinced undeniable traits. He acted now like a hound that has caught the scent.

He was assured that Ordway, up on the fifth floor, was dead. He could not aid him. He was not anxious to uncover himself in any capacity of investigator until he had to. But he followed the man with the brief case, realizing that, if he was a member of the Griffin's organization, he might, would, know him by sight.

Manning knew the tricks of shadowing. At Wall Street and Broadway the man dived into a subway entrance. Manning followed, running to make the express, seeing his quarry enter, two cars ahead. The man kept in the train until Forty-Second Street, and Manning trailed him, up through Grand Central to Madison Avenue.

The man swung aboard a surface car. Manning followed in a taxi, telling the driver what he wanted. A New York taxi driver is surprised by nothing. He scented a hot tip. Above Fifty-Seventh he stopped and Manning saw his man turn a corner. He left the driver grinning over a two-dollar bill.

The hotel was one that harbored all sorts and conditions of people, both men and women, who did not obviously work. There was a lobby and a desk, facing two elevators. Between the cars there was a long mirror, used by the lady guests for a final overlook.

Manning found a pillar, stood back of it, seeing his man in the mirror, marking the pigeonhole from which the clerk gave him his key. He made sure of it as he asked an idle question about an imaginary registration, and then left.

Fifteen minutes later his carefully relayed message got through and was responded to by Rafferty, detective of the old-school, but to be relied upon in ordinary routine. Rafferty had an intimate description of the man, knew the number of the room. It was sufficient.

Manning's instinct told him he was on the right track, but he had to go warily. He was dealing with no ordinary opponent.

There was no reason for him to arrest his suspect, many reasons not to. Manning did not forget the Griffin's boasted "new method" of killing. He acted on inspiration, based on experience. The Griffin would not have expected him to dash down to the lobby of the building to trace the man. At least, he did not think so.

VI

THE DEATH of Ordway was a sensation. When Manning got back down town it had been long discovered by his secretary, who had been immediately hysterical. All had happened as the Griffin must have hoped. On 'Change the news spread like wildfire. Fortunes were made and lost, matters were still in the balance as Manning arrived.

The police were there. Detectives from the homicide squad. There was nothing to show that Ordway had not died from natural causes. He was slumped over his desk, without mark of a wound.

But an alert reporter had been on the spot. He had seen, pasted on the dead man's blotter, conspicuous, flaunting, the scarlet seal of the Griffin. Already the press was reeling off sensational stories. This time Centre Street could not cover up. The Griffin had struck again.

Newsboys proclaimed it. The Street was in disorder. The panic spread through the length of Manhattan.

And Richard Ordway lay on the operating table while experts tried to find out how he died.

Manning read the report of Rafferty, on a flimsy, sent by ordinary messenger service to his office.

Suspect traced to Hermes Hotel, room 637, registered as David Sesnon. Checked out at 1.20. Took Yellow taxi 3748, name Alekko Kalimachos—driver has good record. Two bags. Checked in at Hotel Clarence at 1.30, under name of Daniel Sievers. Same initials. Probably careful of laundry marks. Went to barber shop. Shaved off close-clipped mustache and had hair cut. Looks different, but could identify. Took taxi to Pennsylvania Hotel stockbrokers, watched market. Am continuing shadow.

R.

There was some delay at the Morgue. Manning insisted on a special autopsy. He believed he had circumvented the Griffin, but he was not congratulating himself beforehand. Sesnon— Sievers, was still under observation, but they had nothing on him, and the Griffin was not to be caught easily.

The observation of the market, powerfully "bear," suggested that the man he had trailed was more than ordinarily interested, but it did not prove it. The latest editions carried the announcement of the police surgeon that Ordway had died of heart failure, but they hinted at other, more sinister reasons.

The grim operation of autopsy was under way. There were two surgeons present, one distinguished specialist supplementing the regular official, by request of the chief commissioner. Assistants in the laboratory searched the organs.

A third man stood with the surgeons. He was accredited, had proved his identity, shown his knowledge of their craft. He made no suggestions. It was Manning, but he was subtly altered. His skin was darkened, his lean cheeks were plumped, his body was cleverly padded. His voice was altered, his movements slow and deliberate. Glasses veiled his eyes, though their eagerness pierced the lenses.

There was nothing, after long investigation. No sign of a weakened heart, only the body of a man who regularly visited his doctors, who had recently passed a practically perfect test for a vast sum of additional insurance. Dead, he still commanded millions by his demise.

No sign of bullet, of knife. None expected. No trace of known poisons. No unusual traces in any analysis.

Manning had said nothing of his telephone call. This affair was his own. He would conduct it in his own fashion. It could add nothing to their thorough search. The scarlet seal proclaimed that murder had been done, but the men of science stood baffled.

There were no bruises, no discolorations on the body. A blemish or two, a mole, blotches that looked like slight eruptions, lesser pimples, such as might appear on the skin of any man.

A ghastly spectacle, though the proceedings had been conducted with dignity.

Manning moved closer, under the powerful overhead light. He looked at the reddish marks, one in particular.

He knew of poisons in the Far East, largely vegetable ones that, even when introduced into the blood, would be absorbed within an hour or so by the tissues, leave no trace by any reactions known to Occidental science, if to Oriental.

"Would you mind examining this mark closely?" he asked the surgeons. "It looks like a half-healed eruption, there seems to be a slight trace of what might be pus. I have a theory it may not be."

His credentials and his manner, his knowledge, made them deferential. They were willing enough to try anything, perplexed, weary.

An incision was made, the pallid and bloodless flesh removed about the spot, the specimen taken off for minute observation.

Manning was examining the dead man's coat when they got back, regarding critically a slight stain, almost invisible, on the sleeve.

"We find no trace of anything toxic," said the specialist. "But there has been a parting of the tissues, not by any sharp instrument, hardly discernible. The curious thing is that stearine, wax of some sort, seems to have been injected. We have not yet determined its exact composition."

"Exactly," said Manning. "And the mark, as you will see, was on the shoulder, beneath this spot on the sleeve. I think you will find your stearine also there. It should show slightly on his shirt. His undervest was sleeveless."

They gazed with animation, energetic to follow his theory, though they did not see what it would prove.

The stain on the fine weave of cloth, on the linen of the shirt, swiftly yielded results. A waxy substance was held in the fibers.

"It passed through," said Manning. "A pellet of wax that has almost dissolved, but not so thoroughly as its contents. You may know that a candle can be fired through a board from a gun. This capsule, loaded with virulent poison, was probably discharged from an air pistol. Probably at close range.

"That, I think, is the cause of death. As for the poison, there are several, not classified, their source in doubt, that I have met with in the Malay peninsula, Borneo, and other places. Unless you can think of some reason why stearine should have been injected through the coat, the shirt and shoulder of such a man as Ordway, immaculate, precise.

There was no such reason and they knew it, all of them, standing about the riven body.

"Damnable!" said one of them. "Damnable! No doubt as to who did it. That fiend must be found."

"I agree with you," said Manning.

"We are much indebted to you," said the specialist. " I wish I knew more of you. Your name."

"I am afraid," said Manning dryly, "that that pleasure, my pleasure, surely will have to be deferred, doctor. I am known only by my finger whorls. You gentlemen need me no longer. You will bring in your findings without me."

"Those findings are indefinite enough to be losings," said the official surgeon ruefully. "Convincing enough to us. But—"

He shrugged his shoulders. Manning bowed to them and went out with his slow, assumed walk.

"You'd almost think he knew what to look for," an assistant ventured.

"That's nonsense, Edwards," snapped the specialist. "We don't know who he is, but his credentials are irreproachable. But, my

God, what a devilish device! And advertising his crime with that red seal!"

"The Griffin, if it ever existed," said his colleague, "is extinct. I only trust this one will be soon exterminated. They ought to set this man who was here to-night, whoever he is, on his trail. He might cope with him."

VII

M ANNING SAW that the key to Sesnon's new room in his new hotel, under the name of Sievers, was in the box and he, presumably, in his room.

Manning had already heard Ordway's secretary, in a calmer mood, confirm the arrival of a man with a brief case, giving the name of Sesnon, who had an appointment with Ordway.

That appointment must have been gained through excellent credentials, which may have been manufactured. The main bait had been what he could offer Ordway. Of that, save that it had something to do with an asbestos mine near the Pennsylvania-New Jersey line, the secretary knew little. Ordway kept such profitable matters to himself until he was ready to use them. Long-fibered asbestos in any place easily reached was a thing men had long looked for.

A second appointment had been granted in which, presumably, Ordway would have the tests of the asbestos. Sesnon would give out the exact details, and an expert would be sent secretly to investigate. It was all a blind, and Ordway, trying to make money with himself on the big end, had lost his life.

With his death the pool that he was manipulating was drained dry. His own estate suffered, but many, forewarned, henchmen of the Griffin, made money. Money was the cold-blooded motive for the Griffin's selection of Ordway, coupled with the fact that the "first move" since Manning had taken hold, took place beneath the latter's nose. If anything could have urged Manning on, this semiresponsibility did so.

So far Sesnon was tied up with his arrival in the lobby after the murder. Manning's intuition, his judgment, had been correct. Now the trail led to the Hotel Clarence, and Manning followed it, alone.

The case was far from complete. That trace of stearine in cloth and flesh was not conclusive. The poison had been assimilated. But, if Sesnon—alias Sievers—could be found with poison pellets in his possession, with the air pistol that fired them, they had him. With the vision of the chair facing him he might well talk about the Griffin.

Manning had arrived in a cab, with a kit bag. He registered, looked at Sievers's signature casually, got his own room and followed the boy with his kit bag. He was not on the same floor as Sievers, but that did not matter. He knew the number of the latter's room. It was a sweltering night and the heat suggested a plan, not too novel, but efficient.

He got Sesnon's phone through the hotel exchange. The answer brought a grim smile to Manning's face. He had run the quarry to earth. Sesnon was clever, but Manning did not think he believed himself in any danger, though he had taken precautions of changing appearance, shifting his hotel, taking another name. The rub came in the question as to whether he had got rid of his lethal weapon and ammunition. That would soon be known.

"Did you want a fan?" Manning asked the man at the other end of the wire. "This is the engineer. I can have one sent up right away."

"I didn't order one," the answer came back, "but I could sure use one. You must have got the wrong room."

"Sorry, sir. I'll shoot one up to you."

Two minutes later Manning knocked on the door. As it was opening he spoke his piece.

"Here's your fan, sir." Then he was inside. He had no fan. He had no gun. But he wore his hat, and he carried his cane. He had sprung a surprise, but he had one given to him. There were two men in the room, both with their coats off. There was a whisky bottle on the table, with ice and soda water. Both rose to their feet as Manning strolled in. And both evidently knew him.

The amazing thing was that they might have been twins. Hair cut, general features, coloring, height, weight, and make-up were startlingly similar. Suits and ties were similar.

One was Sesnon, one his "ghost." His appearance was prob-ably brought about for use in drawing off a "tail," if there was any. In all likelihood routine instructions, rather than alarm, for Sesnon regarded Manning coolly enough. It showed the quality of the Crime Master's brain, the action of the expert player, looking moves ahead for all possible plays and contingencies.

Again Manning acknowledged the Griffin's resourcefulness. The man's methods were bold and subtle. He was like a slippery eel that, even when seemingly caught, slides through the hand and leaves only slime behind.

Manning knew which was which.

"What do you want?" asked Sesnon. The presence of his seeming twin did not actually involve him. He might or might not admit that he had called on Ordway. It was not necessar-ily criminal to share or shift his hotel. He knew nothing of the results of the autopsy though he might now suspect he had been trailed. He was still confident.

"I want you, Sievers, or Sesnon, for the murder of Ordway. I myself traced you from his office. Also I know how he was killed."

Sievers did not flinch. His eyes narrowed slightly.

"Which of us are you talking to?" he asked.

"You. When you made your changes, Sesnon, you forgot to put in different sleeve links. There will be no question about your identity. I'm taking you both. I have two men in the lobby to take you down. Stand still, the pair of you."

He saw their glances meet, shift quickly and obliquely to the window. It gave out to a narrow alley. Not the best room in the hotel, but it had one advantage for their kind. It was a fire exit.

Sesnon's double moved silently and swiftly. His right hand swung up—inside his partly open vest. The wrist halted, his fingers clutching for a gun. There would be a good tale for the Griffin. The latter had impressed them with the cleverness of Manning, and here they had him. The gun was muffled. There was nothing to it. Let the two dicks stay in the lobby. They would get clear.

Then he grunted—and then he gasped.

The steel ferrule, with a flick of Manning's wrist, had hit and paralyzed his own, as the end of the snaky, but heavy cane struck a carpal bone where the radius joined it.

The cane circled, shot forward, stabbed him in the belly. It lifted in a *sabreur's* sweep and tapped him over the ear. He lost all interest in the proceedings. It took but a second.

But, in that second Sesnon had hurled himself upon Manning, striving to throw him, to knock him out. He had no weapon on him, from sheer precaution, a carefulness overdone in this case. He was powerful, trained, and imagined easy conquest, astounded to find himself grasping a body that was sheathed in muscle and hard flesh, that turned his attack to defense.

He had grasped Manning's right wrist and Manning let his cane fall. He held a private satisfaction in tackling this murderer with his bare hands.

He tied Sesnon in the fierce clinch, held him, and flung him loose, bewildered at the expert handling—loose for a moment—then Manning's upper-cut traveled from his hip and connected.

It was all over. Sesnon fell like a length of chain, his coördination unlinked.

Manning went over him, went over the "ghost" and found little of value, save money, with which both were plentifully supplied. Then he called the office, spoke crisply to the clerk:

"Two men there in the lounge. They're from headquarters. Send them up here, right away."

He had two of Griffin's men in the toils, but there was not
much to hold them on, save suspicion and limited circumstan-
tial evidence for Sesnon, a Sullivan act charge for his "ghost."
No jury was going to convict them of murder. There was no
positive evidence that Ordway had died of anything adminis-
tered externally. Only opinion, and a scanty showing of grease
that an expert lawyer would laugh off. They would undoubtedly have the best legal advice. Unless Manning found the
stearine pellets and the gun, found them soon, in Sesnon's room
they would be out on bail.

Yet he could hardly have arrested Sesnon on his first hunch
that he was the murderer. Now he almost took the room apart
and found nothing. The pair were taken away. They would get
a good sweating, a rousing third degree. Sesnon, nursing a sore
jaw, affected to be jaunty. The "ghost" was still feeling too sick
from the jabs and strokes of Manning's cane to say anything.

"We won't be there long," Sesnon boasted.

Manning relayed through to Centre Street, asking to have
the two held as long as possible, but he did not doubt that the
Griffin would soon get busy. Because of his minute examination
he should be certain the poison pellets and gun were not in the
room, but he was not satisfied.

He went over the search again. Then he retained the room
for himself. It was midnight when he once more got through
to the commissioner. He had found his evidence. Sesnon had
hidden the pistol with a cunning worthy of the Griffin himself.

He had wrapped it in black cloth, a small parcel, for the gun
could rest in the palm of the hand. He had wired it underneath
the grating of the fire escape, close to the building. It was practically invisible and might have stayed there for months, though
no doubt some stranger would have visited that room later,
another of the Griffin's emissaries, and removed it. It was a
marvelous piece of mechanism, loaded with a tiny capsule of
wax, ready for deadly action.

If Sesnon had been able to use it on Manning, the duel for

crime mastery would have ended then and there. He had evidently found Sesnon almost ready to leave, not wishing to destroy the gun, not caring to chance carrying it with him any longer.

Strenuous efforts had been made to admit them to bail. Big Jake himself, most famous—and infamous—of mouthpieces, had left guests and tried to spring them. Politicians had been busy. Any amount would have been put up. The Griffin had scored heavily in the falling market. Bail money would be negligible compared to his profits.

But they were still held. Sesnon would have to stand trial for murder. Yet they were faithful. What hold the Griffin held on them could not be shaken. Promises, bullying, long hours of "degree" got nothing out of them. They knew nothing of the Griffin. Nothing. Then or afterward.

Manning drove home to Pelham Manor in the small hours, well satisfied though tired. He ran the car into the garage, went, patent key in hand, to his front door. The inlet of the lock was covered with a scarlet cartouche, red as blood, the head of a Griffin stamped upon it.

The Red Griffin, Master of Crime,
Strikes Again, and a Grisly Form is
Left In a Millionaire's Bedroom

A GONG SOUNDED, sonorous but mellow. The faint strains of music ceased. Perfume of amber drifted through the big room, with its curved walls that showed neither door nor window. A voice came clearly from the brazen disk that was suspended on the elaborately carved desk between two smaller ones.

The Griffin, the mysterious malefactor whose crimes baffled and alarmed the police, the press and public of the greatest city in the world, listened intently, his hand curved beneath his chin. His face held a half sneer of malevolence, of contempt.

It was his habitual expression. The outward semblance of a man who hated much, loved nothing, a man bereft of humanity, waging war against humanity, against society, and law and order.

In a letter, nothing short of a challenge, to Gordon Manning, special and volunteer investigator, late of the Secret Service, youngest major in the American Expeditionary Force, the Griffin, who was otherwise nameless, had styled himself the *Crime Master.*

He had admitted the possibility, though not the probability, of Manning twisting the meaning of the phrase, of proving himself the *master of crime.* There was a subtle distinction there, like a chuckle. It was just a jest to the Griffin. Manning took it seriously.

The Griffin's brain was askew. It was possessed by a diabolical urge of revenge against the world. It nursed a grudge and nurtured it in an intellect that was keen beyond the ordinary imagination. His hate was archaic, primitive, possessed of monstrous ego, but his methods were modern.

As the voice continued, his sneer changed to a slight smile of satisfaction. He gave a few crisp orders in return. Then lit a Turkish hookah pipe, in the bowl of which hasheesh was mixed with the tobacco, a stimulant rather than a drug to the Griffin.

Manning termed his attitude grandaisse dementia. That was the nearest medical term. What madness lurked in the brain cells had not rotted them, but stimulated them for evil to the nth degree. Some day, perhaps, this excitation would destroy him. Now it destroyed others.

He was like the monster Frankenstein, let loose on the earth in the shape of a man, lacking a soul. One might imagine him having sold it to the devil, or think him some true Satanic spawn set free to engender wickedness and wreak wanton destruction.

For a while the rose water bubbled in the container of the hookah, the outblown smoke-twists were drawn away by the perfect ventilation of this room that was like a fortress, its walls of chilled steel, back of the rich brocades in blending shades of gold, the pattern woven like the visions in the Griffin's brain.

Then he drew up heavy paper, dipped his exquisite pen in violet ink held in a stand whose lid was the carved head of a golden griffin.

MY DEAR GORDON MANNING:

For you are dear to me. It seems as if you might be a very worthy opponent. Once we have clashed, and you have won two pawns of mine. You found them faithful pawns, I think. They are off my board, but I have not forgotten them. Now the game is set anew. And, as ever, the first move is mine. I choose my own gambit.

You were very ingenious in your discovery. There was, of course, a slight flaw on my part. I have not the time to sufficiently experiment. Let us see how you can solve my next problem. It is, at least, ingenious.

I do not put it beyond you. I am keenly interested to see what you will make of it. You may even capture other pawns. I trust not. But they will be only pawns. You will still be playing with an invisible, an intangible opponent.

I shall let you know when, to use the French phrase, "the fact is accomplished." But, do not take too many of my pawns. I can spare them, but I do not relish their capture. And, should you advance to the possession of more important pieces, I may, however reluctantly, be compelled to forego this tilting of ours, for all its invigoration, and proceed to—I choose the word with care—eliminate you.

Antagonistically yours.

For signature he made a clever drawing of a griffin's head. He addressed the envelope, sealed it with a scarlet cartouche, an oval of thick paper embossed with the same design, the emblem he left always to proclaim his identity with what Manning called crime, and the Crime Master reprisal, stamped it, summoned a servant.

Before the man came the Griffin donned a mask fine as

A section of floor revolved, revealing a gaping hole.

goldbeater's skin. It made him look like the facial simulacrum of a long buried Egyptian monarch on the outside of the funeral coffer, save for his glowing eyes.

"This to the mail," he said. "At Grand Central. Send up the man who is waiting.

II

THE MAN who came through the opening in the softly sliding panel looked like an ideal English upper servant, not the stage type, but the real thing, reserved and dignified. He bowed, keeping his distance from the strange, commanding figure at the desk.

"Your credentials have been checked, Jennings," said the Crime Master. "On both sides of the ledger. Your term at Dartmoor left you with a desire to change your country. I congratulate you on your manner of entry. You are, as a convicted criminal, an undesirable adjunct—but I also am, technically, a criminal.

"You have now entered my service—"

"I beg your pardon, sir, I—"

"You have entered this room," said the Crime Master. "That suffices. I shall take care of you under all circumstances, even if you blunder. But not if you try any tricks, Jennings. Not if you try any tricks. Would you mind stepping back slightly? Thank you. This is merely an object lesson, in the first primer, the kindergarten. So—"

The ex-butler's face turned from ruddy red to the hue of cigar ashes. In front of his feet the floor revolved with a slight whir. It left a circular gap, with polished sides that were lost in shadow. But there came up a hissing, gurgling sound of running water that was soul-racking. It closed.

"Merely a parallel," said the Griffin. "Or a parable. Translate it as you will. I have other methods. To those who serve me—"

He opened a drawer, took out a rouleau of gold pieces, double eagles. Jennings's somewhat protruding eyes bulged. The Griffin pushed the stack over.

"Call that a retainer. Obey me, to the best of your ability, which I judge, now and after performance, and you need never want. Whatever you may temporarily suffer I will make up to you and shorten the suffering. But I should advise you to follow instructions closely. *Very* closely. They have a habit in the United States of punishing severely any one who—let us say—kills and bungles. Most unpleasantly. The electric chair. They are not so merciful as in England. They shave your head the night before for the electrodes. It is not an incentive to sleep. You can smell yourself burning. And they tell me you leap like a hooked trout against the belts."

He laughed as Jennings blanched again. Added another stack of the gold pieces to the first. It was plain that he enjoyed the other's terror.

"You will not come to that. The last time you killed you were quite clever. That is why I sent for you. Now, you are to go to this address. It is on Long Island, the home of a man who has battened on the credulity of the ignorant, swallowed the savings of the widow and the orphan. A rich man, but growing old. With a young wife—the fool! Jennings, you must be careful with your women."

"I've learned my lesson, sir."

"You think so, but you have not changed your nature. When you look into a woman's eyes, remember the tube you saw just now. Let it be a symbol. Later on, Jennings, when you have served me, you may make a fool of yourself, but never of me. Now, or later. You understand."

"Yes, sir."

The ex-butler was standing on a thick rug when he felt that he was incapable of movement. His blood tingled, tingled until it was agony. He was in the clutch of some mysterious power that brought the sweat out all over him. The golden mask of the Griffin wrinkled with a silent laugh.

"Right! This man has applied for a butler. You will receive a slip from the agency to which he wrote. They will be told that the vacancy has been filled, and remitted a fee. I want from you, within twenty-four hours, a report of the household, a plan of the floors, every detail of the service under your control. *Every* detail. Now, come close and listen."

There was sweat again on Jennings's face when the Crime Master ended his instructions. Not alone of fear for himself. He felt as if he had been conferring with Apollyon. He was a crook, he held no scruples, the gold he had pocketed was his gold, but he acknowledged the Crime Master, whose wickedness, whose devilish ingenuity permeated him. He gasped, his cheeks like gills, rising and falling, mottled like headcheese.

"By God!" he exclaimed. "You're a marvel. It's bound to work."

"And you'll be rewarded. But, don't invoke God. There is *no* God. I, who am your master, your paymaster, am not omnipotent. But I'm powerful enough to handle you, or throw you to the dogs. Worse than the dogs. Did you ever think of being gnawed to death by rats in a sewer, Jennings?"

"No, sir."

"Then, think of it. I have a better imagination and a better method for those who betray me. Obey orders. And look out for a fatuous fool named Gordon Manning, a man of some parts, who may bamboozle you. You have the gold. Go! I will give you ten times that amount if you succeed."

The Crime Master had given some secret signal. An opening showed. Jennings bowed himself through it, backward, bowed as he might to Satan.

III

GORDON MANNING was in his own house, the house he had himself designed, at Pelham Manor. It was close to dinner time. One of his trusted Japanese servants had just rubbed him down, nude himself save for a loin cloth, after a bout at jujutsu, for which Manning had supplanted his usual game of handball at a down town gymnasium, due to a rush of business.

Aside from his detective proclivities, invoked by the desire to come to grips with the Griffin, to destroy him, Manning was an advisory attorney. He did not appear in court, but his counsel was accounted valuable, his fees were all sufficient.

Toyata grunted as he surveyed his master, handed him his dinner clothes, valet as well as trainer. His own body was stalwart, muscular. Manning's was lean. But he had given Toyata a hard quarter of an hour. He kept fit, body and mind. And he did not despise the wisdom of the Orient, physically, mentally and psychologically, in which he had traveled.

"Little more, you too smart for me," said Toyata. Manning patted him on his brown shoulder.

"You teach me," he said. "Some time I need. Some time, maybe, I need you."

"You need us? All same you find us," said Toyata. And meant it. Manning had brought his three Japanese overseas. They were devoted to him. If the Griffin had his fortress, Manning's house held its secrets and it held three devoted retainers. No Romio of Old Nippon was better served.

To-night, as always, when he touched the envelope, Manning felt a crepitation. It was as if a slug crept down his spine. He did not have to look at the bold handwriting to turn and see the scarlet seal. He was not afraid of the Griffin, but he knew that this missive was a death warrant. Before he could enter the field a man had gone out into the void, suddenly, unshrived. Sometimes he felt as if the Crime Master was half justified. There were scoundrels and scoundrels, but the Griffin was the greatest of them all. He held no power of judgment. The man was a fiend who must be wiped out of existence, or social order was in constant peril.

While Manning believed he had to deal with a maniac that did not mend matters so long as the Griffin was at large, using his infernal cunning. Manning had nothing of the ordinary thing called fear in his composition. His war record proved that. Fear was one thing, it was another to believe that the odds were too great, to believe one could not win out. But a man could face such an issue with courage.

This was different. He had not been able to face the Griffin. He knew the tones of his voice, their subtle inflections, the mockery that underlay all he said. Some day he hoped to recognize him by that voice, where he could come to grips with him. Meantime he was up against something intangible, invisible.

A man's writing meant nothing, unless you tied up the two. Paper and postmarks led nowhere when a superbrain covered the details. But even a superman or a superdevil might slip. And Manning hoped for the benefit of that margin of error.

He had been on the trail of his quarry once. He had taken the active perpetrators and they had been found guilty, but nothing could break down their determination to cover the Griffin. One man was condemned to die in the chair, but he revealed nothing. The Griffin's influence was uncanny, it held a hint of the supernatural. Manning believed it *was* the latter, from the standpoint that a madman was not controlled by the laws nature designed for man.

IV

MANNING HAD the resources of Centre Street behind him. None but the chief commissioner of police had known of his appointment, and he had meant to keep under cover, but the Griffin had found out about it. If the Griffin did not show himself, if he merely played the game, moving pieces on the board; so Manning must pit wits against him, but he could not longer count on concealment. The Crime Master had more than the one advantage he boasted of—the first move. He knew where Manning lived, in Pelham Manor; he had set one of the scarlet seals on the lock of Manning's front door after the last coup in which a man had died and the Griffin gathered riches.

Manning felt now that he was watched, that he would be trailed if he worked in the open, yet that hardly seemed a necessary procedure so bold was the Crime Master in his invitations. It seemed as if he at once invited Manning to take part in the game and laughed at him with the assurance of an expert who, with his chosen opening assured, is sure of winning. Once Manning took up the trail, however, he might well have to disguise himself, to approach as an unknown if possible. That would not be easy. The Griffin would be expecting his arrival. It depended, of course, on the sort of crime committed, the circumstances, the environment.

When the telephone rang he knew who it was, sure before he heard that voice, educated, refined, save for the mockery in it, allied to the utter wickedness of the man's ego. That suave voice, silken yet merciless, like a bowstring, seemed to dominate the room.

Manning knew it was useless to try and trace the call. The Griffin had perfected some manner of induction that prevented that. This time he did not even trouble to warn Manning.

"You got my letter, Manning? This is the Crime Master. I believe you have also named me the Griffin, I suppose because of my little souvenir. You have a clew there, Manning, if you only knew it, but I am afraid you are on the wrong trail.

"However, let that rest. You will see that souvenir again before long. This is Thursday. To-morrow will be Friday, which some think an unlucky day. You rise early, perhaps. I shall call you when the thing is accomplished. It is really an act of justice. But I fear you won't agree with me. And the method I have used is really quite ingenious—and quite new. I dislike old-fashioned ways. They are usually crude.

"Good hunting to you! Pleasant dreams."

The voice ceased. For a moment Manning fancied he heard faint strains of music, the echo of an amused and tolerant laugh.

It set his blood tingling with the sheer impertinence of the man, the colossal conceit. He could guess why he had been called so soon, warned to expect another call, sardonically wished pleasant dreams.

The Griffin wanted to demoralize him, to keep him awake with worry and impotence. It did not quite accord with the Griffin's professed pleasure at a worthy antagonist. It was not fair play, but that could be expected.

Manning had slept too often waiting for the zero hour. He called his favorite setter and took his cane, the only weapon he carried, formidable enough, with its rings of leather shrunk over a steel rod, its sharp ferrule.

He smoked his pipe on his walk, returned pleasantly tired physically, read for a while, rolled to slumber and awoke fresh, taking exercises and then a needle shower. But now his mind was active, it responded to apprehension, and though he ate his breakfast it was with no great appetite or enjoyment. He was waiting for the inevitable ringing of that bell.

Meantime he mused. The Griffin's hint of his name holding a clew had occurred to Manning, Those scarlet symbols had been placed to identify the man who planned the crimes, even if he did not actually commit them, for months before Manning volunteered as special agent. That was one thing.

Another was the Griffin's boast of new methods. Untried, they might, it was likely they would, be imperfect. And he must find that flaw. *Must.* As the hour of seven chimed he found himself pacing up and down. He filled his pipe, and the hand that applied the match shook ever so slightly.

"Pshaw!" he exclaimed aloud. "I'm getting nervous."

Then the phone sounded. It meant that some one was dead, by foul means, that the Griffin had struck again. It jangled in his ears, then he was cool again. He had to be so, with such an adversary.

"The name is Severy Hastings, Manning. The address Pebble Manor, Stony Ridge, Long Island. There are plenty of trains,

or you might take your little car. You may even arrive before
the family knows what has happened.

"Hastings sleeps late. He is not as young as he might be—he
was not as young. Perhaps his conscience troubled him of nights.
It should. He made his millions through manipulating other
people's money, and kept it all. Of late he had posed as philanthropist. He contributed to charities, to institutions and popular
appeals. Always publicly. Perhaps he thought that advertising
below might help him get through the needle's-eye gate of his
old-fashioned heaven."

Manning contained himself. He must not lose a word. He
wanted to perfect his impressions of that jibing voice.

"He will sleep well now. Sleep till he *rots*."

For an instant the voice lost suavity, it was the voice of an
unleashed beast, wild and feral.

"He married a young wife lately. She may mourn him. There
is one thing she *will* mourn. A choice collection of uncut stones
that Hastings kept in a so-called safe in his own room. That
was the only taste of his that I approved. I like uncut gems. He
saves me the trouble of gathering them. You'll hear from me
again. *Au revoir!*"

Silence, save for that faint suggestion of music, though
Manning had put up the receiver.

Manning lost no time. In five minutes he had got his roadster and was letting it out to top speed, losing not a second
when he got into traffic, careful to avoid trouble, intent upon
arrival.

"Severy Hastings!" It was a name to conjure with! Manning
knew little of the way in which he had acquired his great wealth,
save that he wondered whether at some time the Griffin had
lost money through those manipulations he spoke of. He felt
sure that revenge for injuries, fancied or real, was at the bottom
of this madness.

But Hastings never failed to respond to any call for money.

He was now retired. Had married a widow, comparatively young compared to himself. Played golf. Now he was dead.

Manning wore no disguise. It did not seem needed at present. He carried his cane, a curious accessory for a car. Later—

V

PEBBLE MANOR was a stately place, apart, on rising ground overlooking the Sound, set in gracious and spacious gardens. The name manor belonged to them, rather than the house. That was nondescript but beautiful, largely Italian.

As Manning drove in through the gates, catching sight of a lodge-keeper running out of the little building there, he knew he was too late to bring news. There were other cars at the door.

It was opened by a butler, tall, dignified, dressed in his morning semi-livery. Back of him, Manning saw scurrying maids, one hurrying up the stairs, another disappearing toward the back with a scared look over her shoulder.

"My name is Manning," said the special agent curtly. "I have come from New York, on an investigation."

"Ah, yes, sir. A most distressing occasion. You will be wanting to see the local authorities?"

The man was precise. Birth, death, no occasion would flurry his trained composure.

"I shall want to see Mrs. Hastings," said Manning.

"Yes, sir. I am afraid you will have to wait. She is quite prostrated. The doctor is with her. A severe shock."

A man came bustling out of a room on the right. Manning placed him, officious, cursed, rather than blessed, with authority.

"What do *you* want?" he asked.

"I'll tell you privately," said Manning. "Let's go where you came from." The butler opened the door of that room, closed the front one.

"Too damn smug that man," said the local officer. He looked

at the special credentials Manning showed him with respect, but he was still dubious.

"I've phoned New York," he said. "There'll be men out here soon."

"Then I'm glad I got here first," said Manning evenly. "They'll know these credentials of mine, or you can telephone again. I would suggest the chief commissioner. *If* you please."

He was in no mind to wait until others arrived. He wanted a preliminary investigation, to find his own clews. Centre Street detectives were sometimes primitive clumsy.

"I'll stroll round the grounds," he said. "Mrs. Hastings is really too ill to see?"

"Doctor gave her a shot of hop. She's out. I reckon you're all right. Plain case of murder. Strangled. Cord round his neck now. I ain't touched a thing. Wall safe's open, but those wall safes are junk. It ain't empty. I saw papers there."

Manning nodded and went outside. The butler came out from the back as Manning strolled around.

"Anything I can do for you, sir?" he asked.

Manning eyed him. The man seemed to take him for granted as some one of importance and authority.

"You can show me Mr. Hastings's room from the outside," he said. "Is it here, or in front?"

"In the rear, sir. Up there. The front gets the morning sun, you see, sir. Mr. 'Astings didn't like it in the mornings."

"I see."

There was a loggia, a portico, set into the walls, arched. On the second floor.

"That's all," said Manning. "What's your name, by the by? I'll want to talk to you later."

"Jennings, sir. I've not been in Mr. 'Astings's service long, but he was a fine gentleman and a good master. Very considerate. A terrible thing to 'appen, sir."

"Yes," said Manning curtly. "That's all."

Jennings bowed and left. A bit of a hypocrite, Manning fancied, but his job called for it, he supposed. Maintaining the regret of an old retainer, a little nosey, a little reluctant to leave. Manning saw him watching from a window of what might be the butler's pantry.

He looked for signs beneath the portico, but hardly expected to find them. The Griffin would not bungle. But that strangling cord was nothing new.

A ladder would reach there easily enough. There was a four-car garage, elaborately equipped. Stables, with riding horses in the stalls. Doubtless Mrs. Hastings rode, perhaps Hastings. No chauffeurs, no grooms. They would all be in the house, in the servants' quarters, gossiping.

A small building that was locked. It held garden tools. It was designed in Italian fashion, with a lean-to under a tiled roof. There were ladders here—two of them, on wall hooks. Manning appraised them. There were vines on the house, and they would be used for trimming them and the trees in the orchard.

He tore a handkerchief in two, wrapped the halves about his palms, and took down the shorter ladder, carrying it back into the orchard, sliding it in a slight depression where the long grass hid it.

He was back at the tool house when he saw the butler hurrying toward him. He stood nonchalantly regarding the view, filling his pipe.

"The constable, or whatever he is, sir, says it's perfectly all right, sir."

"Then I'll come in."

The detectives from New York had not arrived. The local man was apologetic.

"The commissioner said you were to take over," he said.

Manning nodded.

"I want you to come over the house with me, Jennings," he said. "We'll see Mr. Hastings's room first."

The body of the multi-millionaire lay on his bed in his

pyjamas, his head on the pillow, his body partly underneath the clothes. The doctor had seen him, a police surgeon would presently appear.

Manning did not disturb him. He saw the cord tight about his neck, sunken, the flesh bulging. The eyes were closed. The jaw had fallen. He saw the opening of the wall safe, a circular door. It had not been jimmied, but that meant little. A man expert with a microphone could have listed the combination in a few minutes.

There was a gun on a bed table, by a lamp. A treatise on star sapphires lay close to the shaded light.

There was a button in the frame of the bed, placed handy for an alarmed man to touch.

"Did Mr. Hastings fear burglars?" Manning asked Jennings.

"I wouldn't say *that*, sir. He was cautious. Had a lot of stones in the safe, I'm told. And, for an elderly man, he was active. Quite. It's hard to understand how he got strangled without turning in an alarm, even if he could not get at his gun. That button sets off a gong that would wake the dead. But we heard nothing."

Manning glanced at the open window, a door that might lead to a dressing room, another to a bath.

"Slept with the window open?"

"Always, sir. It was open when I brought him his coffee and toast."

"You served him?"

"Yes, sir. He preferred it that way. Didn't like a maid in his room."

"All right. Have you a telephone directory?"

"Yes, sir."

"Bring it."

The moment the butler left, Manning raced through the suite as his own setter might search the brush. The tiny colonnaded portico made for privacy. The bathroom window was large enough to admit a man, but it was fast locked, with a patent catch. So was the one in the dressing room. When Jennings came back Manning was gazing reflectively at the safe.

"We'll go over the house," he said. "Top to bottom."

"Excepting Mrs.'Astings's apartment, sir?" Manning nodded.

There was nothing of luxury lacking in the house. Manning passed through the servants' hall, crowded with excited help, through the kitchen, through the cemented room that held the big frigidaire. He asked for ice water and got it, Jennings pulling out a tray of cubes.

"You run this?" he asked.

"I try to, sir. Would you like some breakfast?"

"I've eaten," said Manning. "Now show me where the help sleeps. All of you."

"I'ope, sir"—Jennings dropped intermittent hs—"you don't think this is an inside job?"

"Inside or outside, you want to know who did it, don't you?" he challenged Jennings.

"Of course, sir."

"All right. I've had my breakfast. I'll stroll about outdoors again until the others get here."

He had seen two telephones in the garage. One looked like a house connection. The other might be direct. He made sure he was not overlooked when he tried the second, got a "through," named his number.

VI

THERE WERE a police surgeon, a detective sergeant, and two aides, three reporters. Manning let the sergeant take charge.

The sergeant looked through the safe, found in some steel drawers morocco cases that held necklaces, other jewels.

"One drawer empty," he said. "May or may not mean a thing. I'll dust for finger-prints. I understand Hastings had a collection of uncut stones. Looks like they were after them. Might have been in here. There's some bits of wadding."

"Strangled!" said the police surgeon. "Died of suffocation. Look at this cord. Yellow silk. Oriental. Any Japs or Chinks in the household?"

"None," said Manning laconically. "He strangled, but not from the cord. You'd better have an autopsy."

"Why?"

"Because a man who dies that way has bulging eyes, his tongue shows. Look at that bed-clothing, look at that pillow. Strangle a man, and he struggles, writhes. This one died in his sleep."

"How?"

"I'm not sure yet. But I think you'll find sulphurous oxide in his lungs."

The surgeon looked at Manning. He knew the authority he held. He looked at the pillows and the spreads upon the bed.

"We'll do that," he said.

The sergeant surveyed the open window, looked through the arches of the portico.

"Came in this way," he announced.

"Yes, and no," said Manning. "You'll find no traces."

The sergeant regarded him with the superior glance of a professional toward an amateur as he rated Manning.

"You got it all faded?" he asked, superciliously.

"Just a hunch," said Manning. "Call Jennings."

The butler came.

"You wanted me?" he asked.

"I wanted you," said Manning. "These gentlemen have got their own theory about what happened. I don't agree with them. I'd like a chat with you, in your own quarters. Confidentially."

He watched the butler closely, winked at him.

"Very well, sir. Come this way."

Jennings had a tiny suite for himself. Sitting room, bedroom and bath. There was a telephone—two phones—in the sitting room. Manning took a comfortable chair. The butler stood until Manning asked him to sit down.

"They think it's a Jap or a Chink," said Manning. "Tell me, have you seen any round here, probably Chinese, though it might be a Hindu?"

"Why, come to think of it, sir, there was a dark complexioned man on the same train with me the other day. He got off at the same station. Wore a cloth wrapped round his head. I took him for one of these chaps that give what they call seances in the old country. But I've seen nothing of him since. I've not been away from the house. I've been getting things organized and in running order, sir.

"Do you think it was some one like that who strangled the master and took the stones, sir?"

Manning shrugged his shoulders. He was not yet ready to express himself.

The telephone tinkled. Jennings answered it. It was one of the extensions of the outside service line.

"It's for you, sir," he said respectfully. He stood close to Manning, outwardly deferential. He must have heard, whether he intended to or not, the message. It contained one word after Manning's voice had identified himself.

"No."

Manning hung up. For a moment he stood silent, tapping the floor with his cane.

"Shan't I take your cane, sir?" asked the butler.

"No, thanks; it doesn't matter. I shall be leaving soon."

He was sure now he had his man. Absolutely certain that one of the Griffin's pawns stood in front of him. To prove it was another matter. But he had one card to play. The rest stood on intuition, blended with logic, and one or two things he noticed that seemed to interlock, like the pieces of a jigsaw puzzle. There were many missing, but these joined, they gave a glimpse of pattern.

44   J. ALLAN DUNN

"You say you came recently into Mr. Hastings's service, Jennings? Through an agency, I suppose."

"Yes, sir." For the space of a swift breath Jennings had hesitated.

"Which one was it?" Manning's voice had taken on an edge. The self-contained butler looked at him with eyes that strove to read his mind—eyes that gazed straight for one glance and shifted. His red and white complexion was patched.

"I don't really remember, sir. I registered at several. You see, I've not been over on this side long. I'm not acquainted. But Mr. Hastings was well satisfied with my references."

"I'm sure of that. It doesn't matter much. Let's see what the rest are doing."

Manning turned to walk from the butler's sanctum. He heard back of him a suppressed sigh of relief. He had his man now, he believed, but he would still have to bluff, to force the other's hand. He could arrive by more tedious and lengthy ways, but such methods did not go well with the tactics of the Griffin. If he had alarmed Jennings the play might fail.

There are scores of employment agencies in New York, yet there are only a few, less than six, catering to the extremely select. From the garage phone Manning had sent in inquiry concerning Jennings, asking if he had been on the books of the twenty most flourishing concerns, and the answer had been *no!*

But Jennings had lied when he said he did not know from what agency he had been sent—or he had not come from any. And lied again about the Hindu.

A bluff, in Manning's opinion, was just as good as the man who made it. The setting also helped.

VII

MRS. HASTINGS was still under the merciful influence of the drug. The body had not yet been removed for autopsy. The police surgeon and the detectives were waiting the arrival of the proper conveyance, the grisly accessories of the coroner's and undertaker's rites. They were in the dead man's room, investigating, questioning the servants, brought to them one by one by the housekeeper. Understanding of human nature led them to hold the inquisition where the murdered man lay stark, his face covered now, a mute witness that might force some sign from any guilty person. Precisely for this reason Manning took Jennings with him. He was not going to lose sight of him.

He believed that the only reason Jennings had not disappeared was because to do so would have aroused instant suspicion and a too close hue and cry.

The police surgeon nodded to Manning.

"I found this on the dead man's chest," he said. "His skin is smooth, and this was pasted right over the sternum bone."

Manning did not have to look at it. It was the scarlet seal of the Griffin, the symbol of slaughter.

"You think he was killed with the cord?" he asked. "Jennings here says he saw a Hindu, at least a man with a turban, traveling in the same train with him some days ago, getting off here. Some of them practice Thuggee."

"Whoever did it," interrupted the sergeant, "must have climbed to the porch, come in through the open window, killed, got the gems, and gone out the same way. Simple enough, though he was foxy and wiped out prints. They always do these days."

"Sometimes they overlook a thing or two," said Manning. "They smooth out the marks of the ladder, clean their shoes, but, after they put the ladder away, they might forget to clear *that* of prints.

"At the same time," he went on, eying Jennings covertly, "I don't agree with you. I don't think any one came in through the window at all. The man who tied that cord round Hastings's neck, opened the safe and got the jewels, came through the door."

"You mean an inside job?" asked the sergeant.

"You haven't answered my question yet," Manning told the surgeon. "Mr. Hastings's own physician thought it strangulation."

"The cord is sufficient to cause death. There are certain signs of suffocation."

"Of suffocation, yes," said Manning. "But some are missing. That cord was tightened after Hastings was dead. The eyes should have been bulging, the tongue protruding. I doubt also whether even a strong and active man could have subdued the deceased without his turning in an alarm. Hastings was well on in years, but he was still physically active enough."

"Then what killed him?" demanded the sergeant incredulously.

"A weapon that has now become invisible, vanished, save for the effects it left, that the autopsy will reveal in the lungs. Traces of sulphurous oxide or cyanogen. I am not certain which, until I have examined the frigidaire more closely. But the man who killed Hastings knew his ways, knew of the alarms, knew he slept with his window open, the others closed. There is a fireplace here, but it has its throat shut by a damper during the summer.

"A man climbed to the porch, set in through the window a cake of the compound used for the extra refrigeration, a special accessory to cabinets of the elaborate type used here. He closed the window and left it to evaporate, to give off its deadly fumes, leaving no trace. Then, two or three hours later, he opened the window again. You will see it has been treated to slide very freely in the steel frame.

"When the room was clear again, he entered—through the door. He may have opened the damper for a time to insure a draft, he opened the safe, and, for a final flourish, an attempt to provide false evidence, to set us on a wrong trail, he twisted that cord about the dead man's neck. Suffocated, but not strangled.

"That is not theory, gentlemen, it's facts. That ladder you used, Jennings, reeks with your finger-prints!" he said.

The butler's patchy complexion had turned white, but it was the pallor of desperation rather than fear. His dignity fell from him like a cloak. Manning was between him and the door. He crouched like a trapped beast, his features a mask of snarling hate as his hand shot toward his left shoulder under the morning coat he wore. This was the face of a man who had worn the clothes marked with the broad arrows of bleak Dartmoor, the face of a killer.

The detectives reached for their weapons as Jennings got to the butt of his, held in a clip.

"Damn you, I'll get *you!*" he cried. For a moment his fury was so great, his convulsed face so demoniac, that Manning half wondered if this could be the Griffin himself.

He had been leaning, lightly, casually, on his cane. Now he flicked this from right to left, back again, more sharply. The heavy rod struck Jennings's shins, the ferrule ripped the cloth of his trousers, went through to the bone with a nerve shock that could not be offset, a blow bringing agony, halting all nerve coördination.

The butler's hand was checked, the gun in it, but still beneath his coat, for a single pulse beat. Manning's right fist shot hard to the other's jaw. It was a blow that would have dropped most men. But, like the extra smash that sometimes actually restores a fighter on the verge of a knockout, it failed of its purpose, and the next second saw them closed, wrestling to get possession of the gun while the officers hovered, afraid to shoot.

Jennings literally gnashed his teeth. Foam flew from his lips, and then he tried to close his jaws on Manning's neck. His teeth grazed the skin.

Manning got his right hand free, his left still grasped the other's wrist above the pistol, the muzzle jerking here and there. He stepped a little to one side, devoting all his attention to the butler's right arm. Thumb and two fingers sought and found a spot close to the biceps, viced down in a jujutsu grip. He stepped back. The gun had fallen. Manning shifted holds a little. His left arm went back of the murderer's elbow, his right now at the wrist. He put out pressure, there was the crack of snapping bone, and Jennings went down in a writhing heap.

Instantly, the detectives swarmed over him, jerked him to his feet, regardless of his broken arm.

"No sense in beating him up," said Manning. "He isn't the Griffin. We've got him for murder, anyway."

"You haven't proved it yet," gasped the prisoner.

"I think we will. We haven't searched you yet, or your quarters. And there's the ladder. You came here under false presentations, to begin with. You overplayed the game. I rather think that cord was your own idea. Ah! You should have got rid of those, Jennings. That was clumsy."

The butler wore a chain of heavy gold links. A watch on one end, on the other the little contrivance known in England as a sovereign purse. There were none there, but there were two of the Griffin's scarlet seals.

"That takes you to the chair, my lad," said the sergeant. "Now, what did you do with the gems?"

VIII

JENNINGS, LIKE a true bulldog, refused to aid them. It was Manning who found the package at last, in a false bottom of the butler's suitcase. He did not need now to see if there were finger-prints on the ladder.

But, with the evaporation of the chemical—the death invisible—the case might have been incomplete. There was the cord, but the condition of the flesh beneath it showed it was not the cause of death; that it had been applied long after life had fled and the blood had ceased to circulate.

They could get nothing out of him.

"I can't tell you about the man you call the Griffin," he said.

"I have never seen him. I don't know where he lives. I don't know anything."

"If he ever actually interviewed him," said Manning, "he might have been taken there blindfolded. What were you going to do with the jewels? How were you going to deliver them?"

"You've got me," said the butler. "I suppose you'll burn me. I tell you I wanted them for myself."

His head rolled from side to side. He was in pain, and the inquisition had not been a light one. That end of it was not Manning's affair.

Manning hid his chagrin. Again the Griffin had eluded him. Hastings was dead.

The recovery of the jewels was a hollow victory. The tool would die, but the Crime Master was still free.

They could not promise Jennings any immunity. He must pay the full penalty. And Manning believed him when he vowed he could not tell them anything to lead them to the Griffin. That diabolical assassin still lurked in his secret den, plotting fresh horror.

"Better set that arm of his," he suggested to the police surgeon. "You might examine that ladder for prints to tie up the case. You'll find it in the orchard, under some grass, in a little ditch. It was not, after all, a perfect crime. But he may have overstepped instructions at that."

He picked up his cane, which he had dropped in the fight, got his hat and went out to his car. In his ears he seemed to still hear those faint strains of music, an echo of the Griffin's mocking laugh. Once more he had failed—and he felt depressed.

He stepped into his car, started to switch on the ignition, and went rigid. The control button of his horn was in the center of his wheel, and on it, neatly affixed, was the crimson cartouche, the red seal, red as blood, with the head of a griffin embossed upon it.

TUNED OUT

The Griffin Strikes Again, and a Blaze
of Green Flame Leaves a Baffling
Riddle for Inspector Manning

T HE MYSTERIOUS individual known as the
Griffin, to the police, the press and public of New York;
his ill fame swiftly spreading nation-wise; the man who mockingly announced himself as the Crime Master; sat in his thronelike chair in the strange room with curving walls.

Music, rare music, not the chance selection of a radio
program, sounded faintly and melodiously in that curious
chamber with its bizarre appointments. The scent of burning
amber permeated it. There were no signs of ventilation, no
windows, no visible entrance. The walls were of steel, back of
the tapestries of woven gold, the floor of steel beneath the
priceless rugs.

The Griffin wore a robe of heavy silk brocade. He had just
set aside the jade mouthpiece of a hookah pipe. On the desk
were a gazing globe of crystal, three suspended bronze discs,
the central much larger than the others, a vase of Ming dynasty
in which there was a single golden-flecked orchid of deepest
violet, looking like a poised butterfly, an inkstand of rare onyx,
whose lid was a griffin's head, in gold.

Immediately before him was an astrological chart, a list of
names, names prominently known, each with a date of birth
beside it. Two names had been scored through with a crimson
pencil. There was also a pad on which the Griffin had been
figuring.

His was an almost perfect face, from the sculptor's standpoint, yet it was marred with an expression of evil, the face of a fallen angel. The cranium was that of a person of high intelligence, but it was perverted. Here was a man who might have achieved the heights but had deliberately preferred the depths. His profile was falconlike, the brow high above the outstanding, finely chiseled nose. The well-shaped lips, a trifle thin, yet sensuous, were set in a mocking curve. The eyes were cruel, cruel as those of a tiger waiting for its prey to pass, as those of a boa expectant of a victim.

He studied the chart. His intention was to find a name whose birth stars now showed conjunction with the evil sidereal influences. He did not believe in astrology, he did not believe in god or man or devil. The stars decorating his dome were set there from a whim of fantasy, largely for effect on those who served him. His present occupation was, for him, a means of choosing his next victim. He held no doubt of the result. His strike was deadly. That it accorded with the predictions of the chart was his own doing. He would use the coincidence for his own ends: to cater to the superstitions of his underlings, to give himself in their eyes the mystery and awe of supreme wisdom, of infallibility.

A madman who was not a maniac. A brilliant brain gone astray, its intent set to a revenge multiplied and distorted by the malignant growth of his insanity, his grandiose dementia. A genius, with the instincts of a fiend, without humanity.

He chuckled as he made his final selection, ticked a mark with a crimson crayon against the name. He rolled up the chart, the list of names about it, tore off the leaf of calculations and set fire to the fragments in a bowl of bronze, putting away the roll in a deep drawer.

He renewed the tobacco in the bowl of the hookah, lit it, drew it to a glow and settled back to smoke, musing as the rose water in the container bubbled, cooling the smoke that passed through it. The music rose and fell, exotic, modern, yet infinitely primitive. Debussy's *L'Après-midi d'un faune*. It was seductive, sexual; but, to the Griffin, there was another interpretation. He had nothing to do with women.

Presently he touched a button.

A section of the curving wall slid noiselessly aside. Out of the opening appeared a strange creature, more like ape than man, an ape with the mange. The figure was naked save for a loin-kilt of red cloth, a high turban of the same. His skin was black as ebony and black hair grew on his chest, and on his misshapen shoulders. The lower part of his arms was so long that his hands reached below his knees. They too were hairy. But his face, distorted, set in a leering grimace, was without whiskers. The low brow was furrowed, deep lines ran from nostril to mouth on either side; the eyes were small, like jet, monkey's eyes, shallow, shifting perpetually.

Between his shoulders there rose a great hump. He was a dwarf, a kobold, sub-intelligent but shrewd; voodoo-bound, brought from Haiti, worshipping the Griffin, his dog. He fawned like a dog. He looked like a page in Hades, sent from the infernal regions to become the familiar of the Griffin.

The face of the Griffin was now covered with a mask that gleamed like goldbeaters' skin, plastic, molded to his features but changing them. Through it gleamed his pitiless eyes.

The dwarf bowed until his turban touched the ground, remained so, crouching. The Griffin took a lump of translucent Turkish sweetmeat from a cloisonné casket and tossed it to him, as he might have tossed a scrap of meat to a favorite hound. The hunchback retrieved it, sucked it greedily, squatting, his beady eyes fixed on his master.

"Quantro," said the Griffin, speaking the Creole of Haiti, "Who is God, the Supreme? The Lord of Life and of Death?"

"You, O my worshipful Master."

"You would die for me?"

"Willingly."

"You are prepared, always, to protect me?"

The misshapen being gobbled the last of the sweetmeat, stood up. The glow in the room, that seemed like daylight but could not be, heightened the plum-black of his skin. From his kilt there flashed a curving blade out of a scabbard of sharkskin. He held it aloft. Its shining steel showed dark along the edge, rimmed with deadly venom that also stained the point.

"Those who would harm you kill me first," he cried.

The Griffin gave him a nod and a grim smile. The greeting and its answer was a formula but he knew the value of its repetition. The dwarf was his, body and what soul he possessed, but his mind was shallow, his memory deficient.

"Quantro, the stars proclaim the time for another vengeance. Let us verify it. You have a white cock ready? Then you shall guard me later while I speak with others whom I do not trust as well as I do you."

The dwarf's eyes glowed like polished obsidian reflecting fire. He chuckled horribly, gibbering.

"Ready, O Mighty One."

To the pressure of another button, a new section of the wall responded. Master and man stepped into an automatic elevator

"Put that candle down,"
Manning demanded.

that bore them swiftly down a steel shaft, landed them in a cellar hewn out of the rock foundations, squared, laid with cement. In the middle of the chamber there was a block of stone, dark-veined with red in the purple matrix. Light glowed from some invisible source.

The dwarf disappeared through a vaulted exit. The Griffin took the only seat. The divination did not touch him, save that he was sadist enough to like to see the flow of fresh blood, the struggles of the victim. It was an ancient rite—Hebrew, Greek, Egyptian, almost universal, one of the occult "mysteries."

The Griffin realized that some day he might well need the devotion of a bodyguard like this. Quantro was as strong and active as a chimpanzee, for all his hump. His loyalty was fanatic. He returned bearing by its legs a white cock, squawking abortively, sensing its fate.

With incredible swiftness and dexterity Quantro slit the fowl's throat, cut the sinews of the flopping wings and split the struggling body with his keen blade. The sign was favorable.

"It is well," the Griffin said. "Wait here for me."

He disappeared through a second arch, down a passage where the murmur of a dynamo sounded, where green lights flickered and there was the sound of hammering on metal.

II

G ORDON MANNING flexed and reflexed his lean, strong body under the tingling spurt of needle shower in the down town gymnasium where he kept himself fit with handball, once a day. His body glowed, his eyes sparkled with health as he went mechanically through his rubdown and the donning of his clothes. His mind was occupied with an ever-present problem, the capture or destruction of the Griffin. It was open war between them.

Manning had been the youngest major in the A.E.F. Ostensibly a brass-hat of the staff, he had actually been in the secret service. Now he had volunteered as a special agent of the New

York Police Force, with secret appointment from the Chief Commissioner, baffled and worried with the failure of the department to get rid of the man who, for months, had committed a series of terrible, far-reaching crimes.

Manning's ostensible profession was that of advisory attorney. It brought him sufficient income without use of more than half of his time or energy. The balance he devoted to coping with the Griffin. Twice he had partly thwarted him, not in time to save life, but to capture the tools of the Crime Master. Nor could any confession be extracted from these men to implicate the Griffin, to give a hint of his whereabouts.

To Manning, the Griffin had issued open challenge. Though Manning's appointment was supposedly secret the Griffin had learned of it, greeted the other in congratulatory terms that were tinged with sardonic scorn, styling him a worthy adversary while he warned Manning that he was handicapped, since the Griffin would always make the first move in the game they played, alluding to that contest in chess terms.

His comparative failures, the knowledge that the Crime Master, as he had first named himself in his letter to Manning, was plotting other diabolical coups, undermining society, commercial industry, mocking the law, was beginning to wear on the special agent. At any hour the mail might deliver a letter in the characteristic writing of the arch-criminal, the telephone ring and his mocking voice come over it to announce his latest deed, timed so that Manning could take up the scent while it was fresh, but after the act had been accomplished.

There were times when he questioned his own capacity, but he knew that, like a highbred hound, he would pursue to the bitter end; he believed that some day he would come to grips with this inhuman monster.

Always the Griffin's coups were marked, as his letters were sealed, by the presence in some conspicuous place of a cartouche of scarlet, an oval of heavy paper embossed with a griffin's head.

Red, the color of blood, was the symbol of the Crime Master, grim and significant.

What next, when, where would the strike come, out of the unknown? At moments Manning could have believed that the Griffin was as fabulous as the mythical creature whose head he used for crest; save for the warnings, the evident fact that none of the men he had captured, the first ever caught in connection with the Griffin's crimes, could have plotted such coups. The voice of the Griffin, as he had heard it, educated, refined but infinitely and subtly evil, was always in his ears. Some day he would come face to face with the owner of that voice. That he was assured of, even, in his most despondent moments.

The Griffin had promised him that, if he sufficiently interfered with the Griffin's affairs. He could force him out of cover at last, if he annoyed him enough. Meantime, the Crime Master was free to go ahead with his diabolical schemes of what he called reprisal against a rotten condition of social and civic affairs.

Manning walked to his office, swinging his cane of leather rings shrunk on a rod of steel, a weapon he had often used to prime advantage. He was a good fencer. With a turn of his wrist he could cripple a man, and had.

Arrived, he attended to the matters prepared for him, then swung his chair toward the window, gazing out on the tall buildings, hearing vaguely the busy noise of street and river. It was the very foundation of all this that the Crime Master threatened.

Already the conservative papers had reached the point where they could not ignore the matter in their editorials, counseling against panic. The tabloids and the sensational press made the most of the tragedies while they clamored for the capture of the Griffin.

There was only one thing that held Manning in his offices. He had a premonition that the afternoon delivery of mail would bring him a communication from the Griffin. It was not nervousness, not apprehension, but the outlet of some sixth sense, or that of his subconscious brain, constantly digesting that vexing problem, tuned-in to the evil vibrations emanating from the Crime Master. Such things were fantastic to the precise scientist, but they had happened before.

In this very building the Griffin had struck, and notified Manning over his own telephone of the murder before the body was cold. It was uncanny because the man was uncanny, abnormal.

His secretary brought in the mail. Manning did not need the look on her face to tell him that his hunch was right. He knew it was there, had known it was on the way, that envelope of heavy paper, the bold writing in violet ink, the scarlet cartouche sealing it. The girl knew that seal. All of Manhattan knew it. Manning could trust her, trust all his employees, including the red-headed lad in the outer office. He knew they must fear for him, perhaps for themselves.

He held up the letter.

"This is extremely confidential, Miss Reynolds," he said. "And entirely personal."

"Very well, sir.

She was not a pretty girl, but she was very efficient, not to be stampeded. Manning respected her abilities. He had a heart affair of his own, not too forward but promising. The girl he hoped some day to marry had been abroad but was now on the way home, the ship due in a few days. He had been glad she was away. She would not, he thought, have understood his volunteered adventure, appreciated it from his standpoint. But, until he had gone through with it, until the duel between him and the Griffin came to the final issue, he must put all thoughts of that kind from him; he must try to make her understand that, without divulging his mission and his risks.

He slit open the envelope with his desk paper knife, took out the sheet enclosed. Despite himself, his hand trembled, slightly. It was the same eager tremor that a thoroughbred hunting dog shows in the blinds before the ducks come in; but Manning frowned. Then his pulses dropped to normal and he read:

DEAR MANNING:

It will be some time in the near future. I am concluding the necessary preliminaries and I shall advise you at the crucial moment.

You have somewhat annoyed me. You made away with my spoils, my legitimate loot, on the last occasion. And took another of my pawns. The hoard is reset. This time there are no spoils, only, to me, the satisfaction that the world is rid of a supreme charlatan.

Your discovery of my previous methods marks you as the man I hoped you were. This time the *modus operandi* will be purely automatic. The victim—I believe you call them victims—will coöperate. A semi-suicide. That is hint and stimulus enough for you. This time there will be no pawns for you to capture, but I know you will be interested in solving what you describe as crime, and I call a beneficent vengeance. For the man I have marked is a liar, a rogue, a cheat!

As an adversary, I salute you! You play a better game than I thought you would. But don't prove too dangerous. I may call checkmate, in so many moves. I may even give you a hint of what you can expect in the near future.

I can tell you this much beforehand of what I have planned. The man whose demise, not untimely, is forecast lives not very far from you—or from me.

Antagonistically, but sincerely,
THE CRIME MASTER.

Manning put down the letter. It held the elements of madness, of illusion. He believed a part of it lies. How much he could not tell. It was the cunning of dementia. The Griffin was a supreme egomaniac. He seemed to consider himself pledged to remove men he had marked down under the plea of their villainy. And he had chosen upright, valuable citizens. It was another proof of his warped mentality.

Here was another doomed. And there was nothing to do but

wait. To wait, and control himself. The communication was cunningly devised to undermine Manning's resistance.

He did not believe the phrase about there being no more pawns in this game. The Griffin might have devised some devilish means of death that did not call for an actual assassin, but someone would be there. He knew that he would surely find that scarlet seal conspicuously affixed on the scene of crime, on the body of the victim probably, as he had himself seen it, had found the taunting symbol on the wheel of his car, on the lock of his house-door. The Griffin was not supernatural.

If he was given time he would have a cordon ready to surround the place. *If* he was given time. He acknowledged the cleverness of the man who styled himself Crime Master. To Manning there were two readings to that phrase. If he won *he* would be a Master of Crime. He meant to be so far as the Griffin was concerned.

There came a rap on his door. The secretary reëntered. This time a radiogram.

It was from the girl he had begun to love. A sentiment he must now deny himself. The Griffin had forced him into the open. He was a marked man. He must carry on alone.

> Arriving Renalia Wednesday next via Cherbourg and Southampton. Hoping to see you soon.
> ELEANOR.

Manning folded the message into a spill. As the Griffin had destroyed his calculations, so Manning burned this, down to the last half inch, crumpling the char into his metal waste-paper basket. He washed his hands, took hat and cane and went out, his face grim, drawn.

He got into his swift roadster and drove swiftly homeward, out to Pelham Manor, where he owned the house built under his own plans. There three Japanese attended him, faithful retainers, devoted. It was a little sanctuary of its own. But, as he drove, he dwelled on the phrase in the Griffin's letter, that the next crime would take place not far from his house, not far from where the Griffin himself lived in secrecy. If he was not lying again.

Would he come this time into contact with the Crime Master in person? The thought, the hope, spurred him, eased the terrific strain of inability to check that opening move, to devise means of coping with it beforehand.

What did the Griffin mean by semi-suicide, by automatic *modus operandi?*

III

D EEP IN the rocky bowels of the foundation of his lair, the Griffin, masked, watched an experiment arriving at completion and, he hoped, perfection. This was his laboratory, a series of stone chambers hidden from all sight, buried beyond betrayal.

He was masked. So were the two men who worked over the devilish contrivance. So were all his men save Quantro. Nothing could disguise his hideous misproportion. He accentuated the Griffin's mystery and power. Those who labored here, some servants, some specialists, were all nameless, numbered. They preferred to be so. On each arm was a brassard bearing the numerals of their identity, known only to the Griffin.

He was no scientist by training but his brain, inflamed though it might be, was capable of comprehension of all they did. It was his mind that conceived the modes of death he dealt out, each one different, mysteries until Manning's acumen had solved the last two.

He might solve this. But he could not prevent it. Its ingenuity was satanic, devised to meet the conditions of the victim's habits, long since studied and spied upon by the Griffin's orders. He had a servant of his own now in the unconscious victim's employ.

Wires crossed this chamber, wires insulated, vibrant with

charges from the purring, unseen dynamo that provided the Griffin's lair with light and heat, with ventilation and power.

On a stand there stood a radio set of the latest make, its loud speaker attached. The universal dial for reaching given sending stations was missing. Its gap yawned.

There were two telephone instruments attached to the strung wires.

The loud speaker announced the beginning of a program. A man in working overalls threw a switch. The wires became less active. They had been fairly throbbing with power which still flowed through them in diminished volume.

Before the program started the Griffin took up one phone, the man who had thrown the switch the other. The Griffin spoke in a low, clear tone and the other answered. The line was in order.

Now the program started, a violin solo. Another switch was thrown. The chamber was suddenly aglare with high voltage. The experiment was at its height, concluded.

Under his mask the Griffin's face was triumphant. Its rare beauty blurred. It became the face of Apollyon, deriding Heaven.

"So," he said quietly, "it will work. Continue the tests. There must be no slip. You understand! Number Nine, Quantro will bring you up to me in an hour. I have instructions for you."

Number Nine, gaunt, his hair prematurely gray above his mask, turned toward the Griffin as if to expostulate. He saw the Crime Master's eyes and gave a gesture of capitulation.

When the hour was up he appeared in the upper chamber. Quantro stood on guard beside the chair of the man he hailed as Supreme Lord. He could not understand what was spoken but his small eyes glittered, he watched intently, for sign of treachery, for some dim comprehension of what might be in hand. He knew it would end in death, in victory for the Griffin.

The Crime Master spoke swiftly, distinctly, giving directions that were technical, some of them, all simply set forward.

"There must be no mistake," he emphasized. "You understand

that? I shall be close at hand. All will be arranged for you, your credentials will not be challenged but, if they are, I shall take measures to have them credited. You know the place, the time. See that your watch is set to standard time, within a second. I will provide that. You will be paid for success, a thousand dollars. For failure—"

His pause was more pregnant with threat than spoken words. The dwarf edged forward, his hand on the hilt of his weapon, sensing some sort of crisis, hoping to be employed as executioner. The Griffin sat like a statue.

Number Nine tried to speak, cleared his throat, found a husky voice.

"You said I would be employed only as an expert electrician."

"That is how I am employing you."

"But this is murder."

"That is a word too often foolishly employed. You have your orders—there are alternatives. You know what I can do with you. If you spend your life in the prison from which I rescued you, and your sentence, at your age, would mean just that, I am afraid your family will suffer. There is another way out, if you choose to take it, but that would leave them in the same distressing circumstances. You have no insurance. That is all I have to say. You will do as I order—or suffer consequences that will, I assure you, not be pleasant, that will extend to that family of yours, for whom you still retain a foolish responsibility. Now go."

The gaunt man seemed to shrink in stature. He threw out his arms, dropped them listless to his sides. He was trebly a prisoner now, to the Griffin, to the consequences of previous weakness, to his family. It was the Crime Master's last hideous threat that conquered his limited resistance, not the reward, given for being accomplice and accessory to callous crime.

"Take him down, Quantro," said the Griffin in the dwarf's language. "You need not return to-night, save to your usual post."

Alone, the Griffin refilled his hookah bowl but did not light it immediately. His face became convulsed, he rocked with devilish laughter, out of his usual control.

"You sought to smirch me," he chuckled. "Now, my dishonorable and learned friend, I shall tune you out—out of the Universe into the Everlasting Void!" His mirth echoed from the starred dome, the curving walls. He spat blood from his lips where he had bitten through his cheek. It calmed him. He took out a flagon of silver and a small silver goblet from a drawer, measured himself a draught and sipped it.

Then he lit the hookah. The smoke bubbled through the scented water. Music sounded faintly, insidiously. He took off his mask and sat relaxed, the mocking sneer fixed on his lips.

IV

MANNING SAT in his own study on Tuesday evening. He dared not leave town, whatever emergency might arise, though he did not doubt that the Griffin would find means to communicate with him; he was certain that the emissaries of the Crime Master kept close touch with his whereabouts.

To-morrow morning the Renalia docked. He meant to be there to meet Eleanor Severn. He could not break off intimate relations so abruptly, he hoped to renew them. But now, with that mysterious hunch, that same sense that warns the adventurer of lurking foes, of oncoming, unseen danger, he feared he might not meet the steamer.

Tuned in as he was to the activities of the Griffin, sensitive to the vibrating emanations of that tainted but powerful mind, he felt that the time for the next crime was close at hand.

He had, to what extent he might, provided for it. Four picked men were ready at the local police quarters, equipped with motor cycles, armed. He could do no more for the moment. He could not tell in which direction the blow might fall. The detectives had been there within a few hours of his receipt of the Griffin's letter.

He forced himself to read. Zero hours had not found him wanting, but he was conscious of a certain internal nervousness, an irregular rise and fall of his diaphragm. At least the enemy on the front were tangible. Known to be there. He knew the tremors would cease with action, but he could not be human and remain unmoved when, at any moment, a man might be foully slain.

At last the telephone rang. He heard the voice of the Crime Master, clear, with that mocking inflection that always made Manning's blood tingle, caused imaginary hairs to lift at the back of his neck where his atavistic forebears had worn them.

"Manning, look at your time. Mine says nineteen minutes of nine. At nine precisely, very precisely, the affair will be arranged. I am giving you what is termed a sporting chance. There is a bare possibility that you may arrive in time, not, I think before the blow falls, but in time to perhaps resuscitate my man sufficiently to hear his last words, his farewell wishes. Perhaps.

"You should arrive close to nine. Those four men of yours will be a little late, I fear. They are farther away from the spot where they are quartered. Now, listen intently, while I tell you where the house is situated. Not very far from you, as I promised. Not very far from me. I may even observe your efforts."

Manning had taken out his watch. It coincided with the time given by the Griffin, within a few seconds. He longed to speak with the inhuman brute but he knew it useless.

"The gentleman's telephone is temporarily out of order, Manning. It is not listed, anyway. Neither will those of his neighbors be in commission, if you want to waste your time trying to get the numbers. Are you ready for the directions?"

They were terse and succinct. The Griffin took pains to make them clear, to indicate the swiftest route. Manning knew the house, though he did not know who lived in it. An old survival of Colonial days, up a dirt road half a mile from the highway. He had glimpsed it among the trees. He permitted himself to answer.

"I know the place," he snapped.

"Good!" The tone of the Crime Master was infinitely condescending. "At nine sharp—the fireworks! Now for the name, my dear Manning. I would like you to know it now. Jeffrey Ferguson. I fancy you know it. Ferguson the charlatan! That's all. I may see you later. You may even glimpse me. Hurry, Manning, hurry."

For a second Manning sat as if turned to stone though he heard the faint echo of a mocking laugh, of far-off music.

Jeffrey Ferguson! The preëminent psychiatric! Retired now from active practice, living in seclusion to devote his time to writing. A man who had done more for nervous ailments than any other in America, who had devoted his gifts free of charge to shell-shocked soldiers after the war, holding a clinic that included the most skillful of his colleagues; establishing a foundation, giving up his wealth.

God! This arch-fiend seemed intent upon destroying the best and noblest. Ferguson had many useful years ahead of him. The solution flashed through his mind, a possible solution, even as he called the number to get his four men started.

Was it possible, was it not plausible that Ferguson had known the taint in the Griffin, that he might, in the past, have declared him insane, dangerous, in or out of court?

The line was dead. The Griffin's sporting chance was a jest, save perhaps for Manning. He summoned his butler, left instructions for one man to continue to try and get the line, for another to take his second car and hurry to the waiting four, with directions where to go. He knew he could rely upon his Japanese.

Then he started his own roadster, raced down his drive, struck the highway, sounding his special Klaxon. The local patrolmen knew its note and its authority. The eight pistons rose and fell in perfect rhythm. The car quivered as the indicator showed the speed on the dial. Forty, fifty, sixty, seventy! It quivered at ninety, and then Manning had a little in reserve.

He skidded into the dirt road at almost that speed and called upon the engine for all it had for the final spurt.

The house was to the left. High banks hid it. Then trees. Now came a picket fence and he saw the residence, two lights in the back lower story, more brilliant illumination on the second floor.

Manning swung his searchlight, looking for the gate. It was open, as if in invitation. He slackened and then lurched through on two wheels, grazing a post.

His car clock was a good one, in time with his watch. It was exactly nine o'clock. Suddenly the house was dark. Then a vivid flare of green light shone through the upstairs window, flashed on a great elm near it, died.

He was too late!

He leaped from the car, flash-torch in one hand, spraying the path, his cane in the other.

Manning sprang up the steps to the porch, tried the front door, half expecting it to be open. It would be like the Griffin. But it was closed and he hammered on it with his cane.

A light appeared through the glazed side-panels. A man was approaching, slowly, with a candle.

He opened the door.

"What do you want?" the man asked. He seemed half stupid.

"Your master, Mr. Ferguson! Something has happened. Stand back, you fool!"

"Yes, sir. The lights went out, all of a sudden."

Manning barely listened as he sprang up the curving stair-case, his ray lighting him. He knew how these old houses were planned. This one had been restored but he went direct to the door of the room where he had seen the green flare, opened it.

V

JEFFREY FERGUSON sat in his library, going over the notes for his next chapter. Now and then he glanced at the old but reliable clock that stood in the corner. He had received a telegram an hour before. A long message, signed by the secretary of the Ferguson Foundation. It said that John Hayward, whom Ferguson looked to as the most brilliant of the younger men of his own branch of the profession, would speak from WRAK at nine o'clock on Medical Jurisprudence. It was a subject dear to Ferguson.

His radio was in perfect order. The man who had called that afternoon to overlook his telephone installation, which came in on the roof, had told him that he had repaired a slackness in his aërial. A tall, gaunt man with gray hair and an anxious look. Ferguson had thanked him, given him a glass of medicinal port. The man had choked over it, he remembered, but drained the glass.

The old clock started its preliminary whirr before striking the hour. Nine! Ferguson glanced at the memorandum he had made of the proper setting of his dial to bring in WRAK.

He twirled it, seated before the set. As he made the combination he suddenly tensed, rigid. He seemed enveloped in green flame. His veins were filled with scalding fluid. The dial burned like molten lead. Only his finger tips touched it, and then he fell sideways from the chair—electrocuted.

Tuned out.

The door burst open at two minutes after nine. Ferguson lay stiff beneath the beam of Manning's torch. There seemed to be a blotch of blood on his forehead. Manning knew what that was. The Griffin's seal.

The lights stayed out. The radio was silent. All through the house fuses had blown out. He heard the ticking of the clock, its mechanism undisturbed, as he knelt above the dead man with the cartouche on his forehead. There was no chance of resuscitating Ferguson. He had been tuned out.

But—someone, some human agency, had placed that seal on his brow. The man with the candle appeared in the doorway.

"Is anything wrong?" he asked.

"Put that candle down," said Manning. He knew there was no use to call aid with the telephone, that it would come too late, for Ferguson. He listened in vain for the beat of motor cycles coming up the hill. But, as he guessed what might have happened, threw his ray on the devastated set, he meant to hold this man, at any cost. There might be others.

The man advanced, looking at the dead, stiffened body. Then he blew out the candle and kicked at Manning's torch.

Manning swung the cane he still held, swung it viciously. He heard the other groan. His torch had struck some piece of furniture, gone out. The next moment someone sprang at him.

Manning grappled with his antagonist. They swayed about the room, they stumbled over the writhing body of the man he had struck across his throat. They tripped over the corpse of Ferguson.

Was this what the Crime Master meant by a demonstration of what might happen to Manning if he interfered too closely? Manning thought not. His opponent fought desperately but he seemed to have no weapon. He clutched Manning's wrist above the hand that gripped the cane, for a while he matched him. They reeled through the open door, on to the dark well of the spiral staircase.

It was a grim wrestling match. Manning strove to free his hand, to launch a blow with his cane. They were in blackness. Both were hard pressed, but he could feel the other yielding, slowly, with dynamic bursts of energy that lessened as they floundered in the dark. At any moment the other man might come back into it.

Then he heard, above their panting, punctuated by the steady ticking of the clock, the sound of motors, striving up the hill. His men were coming. His opponent seemed to hear it, too. He put out a gust of strength, he bent Manning backward.

Manning set his crooked knee back of the other's leg. He thrust forward. He got one arm free at last, his left, and struck fiercely. Knuckles to bone. The man's clutch gave way. He fell, vanished, and Manning heard him falling, striking, tumbling down the stairs, himself on the verge of them, clinging to the bannisters.

The squad came in. Their torches sprayed through the gloom. Two of them stooped over a prostrate form. Two charged up stairs. The library was vacant of anyone save Ferguson's body. The man with the candle had revived and gone.

Nor could he be found. A rear door was wide open. There were some marks of footprints, faint in the torch light, indeterminate.

"That chap at the foot of the stairs, his neck is broken," said one of the detectives.

Manning looked at him, at his shell. A gaunt man with gray hair. A man who had mistrusted, at the last, the Griffin's promise of protection, had, perhaps, exceeded his instructions, perhaps tried to win higher reward by killing the man who had so unexpectedly interfered.

It might have been done for the sake of his family, might have been in desperation. The Griffin might not have told him his private duel with Manning. It was a secret locked behind his lips, silent for ever. His neck was awry, his head limp on that broken stem.

And Ferguson was dead. Manning gave his orders. They ransacked the house, found extra fuses, restored the lights. Manning, with an idea of what had happened, after his inspection of the ruined radio-set, the remembrance of the Griffin's suggestion of automatic death, went to the roof.

The telephone wires had been shifted. They ran close to the aërials. A supercharge over them would leap to the latter. Their insulation was scorched.

Once more the Crime Master had eluded him. One of his tools lay broken, silent forever. Another had escaped.

He went down to his car, his clothes torn in the struggle with Number Nine. The four took charge of the rest. There was little to do. Ferguson was dead. Once more the Griffin had triumphed. The loss of a pawn was nothing to him.

Defeated, Manning took seat in his roadster. He started the engine and went coasting down the hill. As he turned into the highway, powerful lights enveloped him and he kept to his side of the road. A machine surged by him. He held sight, for an instant, of a face that looked out at him, the face of a devil, surely. He caught the sound of a laugh, the indetermined syllables of a voice that was familiar.

Furiously, he turned his car, swept in pursuit. But he could not gain on that crimson rear light, fast as he drove. It seemed to jeer at him. It seemed, to his exasperated fancy, to look like the seal on the Griffin's letters, the seal he had seen set on the forehead of Ferguson. His car reeled, swayed as he held the bucking wheel. Then they came to a place where three roads met. There highways, all cemented, holding no trace of cars. Two of them curved. He tried one and, coming to a straight stretch, saw no red light. He had lost again.

VI

THE RENALIA docked at ten. Manning paced up and down the wharf. He was bruised and shaken, physically and mentally, by his experience of the night before, but more stubbornly resolved than ever upon the elimination of the Griffin. His night had been racked with recurrent glimpses of that indeterminate face in the rear of the car that had outraced his own, memories of the mocking laugh, of the twisted face of Ferguson, of the red blotch of the Crime Master's seal on his forehead.

And he was more resolved than ever to shut out Eleanor Severn from his life until he had run to his last covert this supreme criminal. It meant nothing that one gaunt body lay in the Morgue. It had not been identified. Yet it might be, might hold some clew.

He doubted it. Someone might claim that relic of a man but who could tie it up with the Crime Master!

The papers carried the news of the latest achievement of the Griffin. He had done his best. But had the Griffin done his worst? What did he hold in hand? What ghastly deeds?

The liner came proudly in. Manning forced himself to the moment. He saw Eleanor Severn waving to him. He waved back, goading himself to the immediate occasion.

Presently she came down the gangway. There were others to meet her from whom he had kept aloof, but now mingled. He felt the grasp of her hand, saw her astonished gaze.

"Are you ill, Gordon?"

"No. But I have been very busy. You look wonderful. Let me help you with your baggage."

Her relations acknowledged his methods. The customs man chalked her trunks, unexamined, after a word from Manning, a glimpse of a badge he wore.

"You'll come up to the hotel?" she asked him.

A messenger pushed through before he had time to answer. "Miss Severn?"

He proffered a florist's box. The girl took it while Manning tipped the boy.

"Did *you* send these?" she asked, her eyes aglow.

Manning shook his head. He should have thought of it—but he had not.

There was a great spray of orchids, elaborate, expensive. Eleanor Severn sought for the envelope, opened it.

"Why, how funny!" she said. "I wonder who could have sent them?"

The envelope contained a card, blank of writing but with a scarlet seal affixed, a seal that bore a griffin's head. Manning knew.

"Number Fourteen," Under Torture's Stress,

Aids the Griffin in a Terrible Plan

T HE BALL rebounded at eye-dazzling speed, glancing again at sharply varying angles, went hurtling back again. The skin of the two players was varnished with the sweat of their lean, athletic bodies; they seemed like a pair of wing-heeled Mercuries as they bounded about the court, evenly matched.

The decisive point was scored and Gordon Manning, breathing hard but unwinded, shook hands smilingly with the man who had defeated him—for the first time. They went off to the showers together and the old trainer, owner of the down town gymnasium, who had been watching the game from the balcony, shook his head slightly.

"Manning seemed off his game. A bit stale perhaps," hazarded the man beside him; a successful stockbroker who believed in keeping himself fit, he was one of the veteran's clients.

"He's not stale, and his game was all right," said the trainer. "But it wasn't Manning playing, just his body. When he's right he outguesses 'em right along. Something on his mind lately, I imagine. Mebbe it's some tough business deal."

"Maybe," said the other. He knew that Manning was an advisory counsel who made good fees, never appeared in court, had a fine reputation as consulting attorney. Then he dismissed the subject.

Manning left the gymnasium, walking swiftly to his office. His body swung along with his elastic strides, but there was a frown on his brow, a look of care in his eyes that had not been there three months ago.

Youngest major in the A.E.F., brilliantly distinguished in the Secret Service during the war, he had volunteered as special agent under the police commissioner to track down and destroy the fiend known as the Griffin, also, to use the criminal's own braggart term, written personally to Manning, as the Crime Master.

For months the Griffin had mocked at authority, at all social and civic order. The list of his mysterious crimes was appalling. His resources and information seemed inexhaustible. Without doubt he had added to his funds by the coups he had brought off. He was plunderer as well as murderer.

It was generally granted that the Griffin was insane, not a maniac, but a man whose brain had become tainted.

Upon each crime he set the scarlet seal of his identity, red as blood, an oval of heavy paper on which was embossed his crime crest, the rampant head of a griffin. Manning had worked under cover, but the Griffin had forced him into the open, had deliberately challenged him, had given him advance information concerning his latest atrocities with such carefully calculated margin that Manning always arrived too late for anything but the solution of the ingenious methods of murder, the arrest in two cases of tools of the Griffin, just pawns in the game. They had refused to divulge any information concerning their criminal.

On the third attempt Manning had come closer. He had actually glimpsed the Griffin. And he had killed, in a struggle, one of the Griffin's servants. But the Crime Master was still at large, his whereabouts unknown, ready to strike again, as he unquestionably would.

And now another element had entered into Manning's crusade. It was the girl he loved, Eleanor Severn. Sternly he had resolved to avoid her until the Griffin was eliminated, partly because of his own constant jeopardy, principally because he feared she might be included in that danger.

Fear did not enter into Manning's composition, but one might be afraid for another. And the feeling he held for the Griffin admitted the possibility, lurking always in the background, that he might not be able to circumvent the diabolic intrigues of so fantastic and ruthless a creature. Not a day passed he did not dread to hear the subtly jeering voice of the Crime Master, and to receive from him a missive in his characteristic writing, bold and unusual, sealed with the scarlet mark.

He was not given to hunches, but he admitted that, anxiously keyed-up as he was, he had times of anxiety that were usually justified. Manning had traveled in many lands; he had seen strange things; he did not dispute that mental waves might vibrate through to receptive brains.

Such a mood was on him now. He was not surprised to see the heavy envelope of gray paper in his waiting mail. The address in violet ink, the flap fastened with red wax—the imprint of the griffin's head, waiting for him to break.

Instead he slit the envelope, read the contents with narrowed eyes.

*Manning's aide sent
the box spinning
into the gorge.*

Dear Manning:

I am changing my tactics slightly. We were almost in contact on the last occasion. That proximity provided me with a genuine thrill that I trust you shared. I have often thought that the hunted and the hunter might sometimes have something in common. The lure and tingle of the chase.

Again you got rid of a pawn of mine. I am afraid he was not much use to you. Dead men tell no tales, but he would not have told you much if he had been alive and willing. As a matter of fact, I am rather obliged to you for ridding me of him. He was an overscrupulous fellow.

Next time there will be no pawns on hand for you to grapple with. To compensate for this I propose to give you the name of the next man selected from my list, as soon as that is decided. Also the date of his death. Then, my dear Manning, you will have a chance to prove yourself. You may prove a protective agent, even if you are not too successful as a detective one.

But do not overlook the fact that, as the ratio of your success increases, so does your own risk. Perhaps not only yours. I acknowledge my faults. I am a poor loser.

Antagonistically yours,
The Crime Master.

Beneath the signature was the drawing, cleverly enough done,

of a griffin's head, its hackles rampant, its tongue protruding from its open beak in derision.

The conceit, the colossal, mad conceit of it, was staggering. To announce the name of his proposed victim, the date of his contemplated death. It was sheer lunacy! Yet it was through that supreme impudence, that evidence of grandiose dementia, that Manning hoped eventually to trip his man, to get him in the toils. That happening, when it occurred, would be fraught with vital hazard to himself, he did not doubt. Nor care. He longed to come to grips with this modern Frankenstein.

And he believed that the Crime Master would make good his boast. And soon.

I I

THE STRANGE sanctum of the Griffin was vacant. It was a room with curving walls, without visible doors, without windows. The appointments might have belonged to any century. There was a gazing globe, suspended disks of bronze—an inkstand with a carved head of a griffin, in gold. Light came from invisible sources, the air was sweet, perfumed with amber. Music sounded faintly, muted music that was primitive.

Actually, the chamber itself was intensely modern. Back of the wall tapestries there was chilled steel, the floor was steel beneath the priceless Oriental weaves. Modern science and ingenuity had many devices connecting with that room.

A section of the wall opened. A bizarre figure stepped out of an elevator, black of skin, wearing a loin-kilt and turban of scarlet; deformed, long-armed as an ape. It squatted like a toad. The Crime Master sat back of his carved desk in a thronelike chair. The Griffin's strange eyes gleamed from a mask of plastic material like goldbeater's skin. Eyes of topaz, snake's eyes, tiger's eyes, cruel, pitiless. Now they glittered with anticipated satisfaction as he spoke to the hunchback dwarf in the latter's native Haitian.

"I do not think I shall need you again to-night, Quantro," he said. "I am only waiting for a report from the laboratory. You may—"

Suddenly the hidden music faltered, the bronze disks gave out an ominous note. The whole room seemed slightly shaken as if an earthquake had rumbled, save that the sound was sharper. It seemed to come from far below, where the Griffin, with the aid of expert employees, conducted certain malevolent experiments, deep in the rocky foundations of his house. He spoke sharply, his eyes flaming.

The dwarf rose, went through the opening that reappeared as the Griffin pressed a foot button. The lift shot down the steel tube. The Crime Master waited, immobile, as if carved. The close-fitting mask aided the illusion of his having turned to a statue, the folds of his brocaded robe were still.

The lift ascended again, the dwarf stepped out once more, behind him a man in mechanic's overalls, a plate round his arm bearing the numeral "12," a mask over his face, above which his partly bald head, like a monk's tonsure, seemed incongruous.

The Griffin came to life, nodded him to a chair. Quantro took place behind the man he deemed his god, his beady eyes avid. He fingered a long, curving knife in a shagreen scabbard, thrust through the band that sustained his loin cloth. He scented trouble; his nose was like that of a snuffing beast of prey.

The Griffin listened coldly to the explanations of Number Twelve. When he spoke, the syllables were like pellets of hail.

"It was, you say, the fault of Number Fourteen?—but for his carelessness the experiment was a success?"

"He paid for that carelessness. My God, I saw him die. It was terrible, horrible!" Number Twelve shuddered. The Griffin's mouth accentuated its ever present sneer, turned it to a devilish smile, licked his lips.

"I shall look at him presently," he said. Now his even tones held a gloating note, a hideous anticipation." There is no doubt that what I asked for is practical?"

Number Twelve shuddered.

"It is. I have not yet done all you asked. It can be done. But—I ask you to get some one else to complete the job."

"Why?" The word was icy, imperative.

"It is not human, to—"

"Have you a substitute? Am I to be disobeyed? Who are you to judge my actions, my motives? Yours, I think, have been challenged."

"There are limits. You goad me too far. I—"

"Exactly—there are limits."

Number Twelve had started up in his chair, his hands on its enfolding arms. And Quantro, the dwarf, had come forward, his knife half out. It was not needed. Number Twelve sank back, writhing, twisted, powerless under the current that, suddenly, galvanically gripped him.

"Those limits are yours," said the Crime Master. "I have none. I need you, so I spare you, for the present. Do you know where you are, who I am?"

"No." The current had diminished. The racked man could speak. "You brought me here drugged."

"From a place to which you can be readily returned—with all the consequences—in the same manner. Will you complete this task I have set you—or—"

Once more the galvanic current raced through the poor wretch's tissues, filled his veins with scalding fire. His head fell forward in abject assent.

Again the opening appeared. Number Twelve staggered toward it, his momentary mutiny quelled. A little later the Griffin descended, with the dwarf. At the bottom of the shaft he walked through stone chambers where strange lights flickered, where the hum of a dynamo prevailed, through to where the pawn who had been known as Number Fourteen lay. It was a ghastly sight, but the Griffin seemed to revel in it. The dwarf

Quantro, voodoo worshiper, steeped in bloody ritual, looked on, rubbing his clawlike hands and, for the moment, there was little to choose between the two.

III

WITH THE first tinkle of the telephone Manning knew who was calling. He was on edge. He had been for days, with the horror of experience, the hope of this time grappling with the Griffin himself. There were to be no pawns. If that was true, the Crime Master would not be far off to witness the success or failure of his coup. If Manning could cope with him it might be failure. Surely this time the Griffin would overreach himself.

He knew it was hopeless to trace the phone call. There was some principle of induction involved by which the Griffin got through to the circuit he wanted without himself using a commercial instrument. Manning's pulses beat high as he lifted the receiver in his own study, at Pelham Manor.

He knew the voice well, every inflection of it. Refined, subtly mocking. He could never mistake it.

"Manning. This is the eighteenth. Some time on the twentieth—that gives a twenty-four hours' margin, and it happens to be the birthday of a man who has lived too long"—here the voice became momentarily strident, vindictive, hinted of madness hard-curbed—"some time on the twentieth I shall kill Richard Pollard. Unless, of course, you contrive to prevent it. Good-by."

There was a strain of music—bizarre accompaniment to such a threat. The merest echo of a mocking laugh.

Richard Pollard! The thing was inconceivable. Why Richard Pollard? What could that man have done to provoke the Griffin's vengeance, if it was vengeance, and not the mad tangent of a lunatic, striking only at the best and noblest.

The sheer audacity of it chilled Manning's blood, brought

down his beating pulses to normal, set his face in grim lines. Pollard!

It might be that, in his colossal conceit, the Griffin envied him, considering himself the Lord of Destinies. The mad reactions of such a creature could not be calculated.

Pollard was the famous explorer-scientist. He was resting now from his latest trip, preparing for another, after a lecture tour, that fall. A man between fifty and sixty, still vigorous, yet in his prime.

He was studying the ocean rifts, the faults of submarine formations, with a view to solving the questions of changing climates, altered currents, the seismic disturbances prevalent in certain lands. Living on his country place on Long Island, a national hero because of his adventures, though not yet recognized, save by the few, for his scientific exploits.

He must be warned, protected.

For a while Manning sat still and silent. Then he drew the morning paper toward him. Pollard had been mentioned there, strangely enough, on the sporting page. He had made a hole in one on the golf course close to his home. That was one of his relaxations, almost a hobby. On one expedition he had made a nine-hole course on snowy wastes, played with crimson balls. He had what was jokingly known as his golf cabinet. In final decisions of associates, Pollard would lean to the man who handled a good mashie, made a long drive.

Manning could understand that. He liked the game himself. It had nothing to do with the matter in hand, save that Pollard's picture was published, the face of a fine Nordic, intelligent and forceful.

He must be warned, protected. The day after to-morrow. There should be time, plenty of time, to circumvent any schemes of the Griffin, satanically ingenious though they were. Manning roused himself to start a chain that would give him access to Pollard, no easy man to know; not because of his nature, but from the demands made on his time. He meant to be with him every minute of the twentieth, from midnight to midnight.

It was not so readily accomplished. Pollard met him when he arrived, greeted him cordially, listened to all Manning had to say—and laughed.

"It would seem this Griffin, as you style him, should be destroyed. You say you have undertaken that office. But I cannot conceive of any hate against me.

"Except that he is mad," said Manning.

"Grant that. Then, sane brains should cope with him. I have had several communications concerning you, Manning. It would seem that you have already crossed swords with this Griffin, are well equipped to cope with him. But, if you will pardon me, I am well qualified to take good care of myself. There have been times when my life has been threatened by a horde of fanatics—madmen of a type. I refuse to be coddled."

"Let me tell you a few things that have happened," said Manning. "This man has more than the cunning of a savage, more than pits and poisoned arrows. He studies his victims, and he has never failed. Whether you like it or not, Mr. Pollard," he added, with his jaws grim, his eyes like the points of steel drills, "I intend to see you well guarded to-morrow. If you will give me the privilege, I should like to be within sight of you all the time. I am sure the Griffin will strike.

"You have not only yourself to consider. There is our own prestige, the prestige of the police force, to which I am unofficially attached, but which is being undermined by these crimes. I have a feeling, a presentiment, which you may laugh at, that this time the Griffin himself will not be far away. He plans some mechanical method to take you off. He says he will use no pawns in the actual play. It is imperative that you are guarded. Your life, your work, belongs to the nation, to the world."

"I hope so," said Pollard more soberly. Manning admired his poise, his physique. The man was eminently fit, his personality compelling. "I do not laugh at your presentiment, as you call it," Pollard said. "I have had them myself. They come, I think, from the quickening of natural senses by circumstances, coupled, of course, to observation and experience.

"I have sat long nights in the jungle waiting for some rare beast to come along—and generally have had the luck to bag him. Usually I resorted to bait—a live goat, perhaps. It seems I must take you seriously. And this time I am to be the bait, the goat, though I shall not be a helpless one. You may bring your men, if you wish, search the house and grounds, patrol them. But I imagine your Griffin, who cannot be fabulous, with his grisly record, will be expecting some such move, since he has warned you.

"You and I will sleep together in the little cabin I have, outside, where I go when I want to be entirely alone. It is not actually a cabin, though the front of it is built of logs. It is actually a cave in a rocky outcrop on the grounds. We can make sure there is no undermining"—he was still quizzical, Manning noticed—"they can only come at us from the front.

"It appears to me, from what your Griffin has said and you have told me, that he is playing some sort of game with you in which he feels himself the master. As long as you are with me, he will not risk losing you as his future adversary. A kink of insanity. And I shall be pleased to have your company. But I have no idea of having my holiday spoiled. My birthday is the one occasion on which I refuse to do anything but enjoy myself. Do you play golf, by any chance?"

Manning answered in the affirmative, adding that he had no clubs nor shoes with him.

"I can outfit you, or the pro', on the Cold Brook Club Links. I had planned to play in the morning with him. He is far too good for me, but I have a reputation now. I made the seventh hole in one. A hundred and eighty-three yards, across the stream, to the green.

"Sheer luck, of course. I have got on the green before, but this time the ball went beyond the pin and trickled down the slope. The pin was in the cup, but the ball made it. I shall never make it again, but, from now on, that hole is mine in two. What is your handicap?"

Manning told him.

"Then you should give me three bisques at least. Nearer five. I'll tell you what we'll do. We'll spend the daylight on the links. Few play here in the middle of the week. It is open country. If you want me to, I'll promise to pack a gun and stand by if any one I do not know comes near us. We'll lunch on the veranda of the clubhouse. When dark comes, we'll go back to my cabin. I am doing this largely on the recommendations you have had poured in on me, Manning. I still feel the whole thing is a hoax, perhaps a draw-off to let your Griffin strike elsewhere."

Manning did not agree with him. But the prospect of staying out in the open pleased him. It looked as if the Griffin's problem would not be solved so easily, so bloodily, this time.

"You got a letter from the Police Commissioner?" he said. "It included a set of my finger-prints, my signature. I want to reproduce them."

"Nonsense. I know a man, a sane man, and a real one, when I see him."

But Manning insisted.

When they went to the cabin at eleven o'clock he was assured that the Griffin had planted no mines timed to turn Pollard's birthday into his day of death. He was inclined to subscribe to Pollard's theory that the Griffin would not include himself in the crime that would surely be attempted. Unless he got the Crime Master this time, others would follow. He had not yet cornered the man. And the Griffin enjoyed this game of cir-cumvention, of mad wits against sound ones, too much to re-linquish it. Perhaps he had not reckoned on Manning staying close to the advertised victim. Perhaps? Deep in his conscious-ness, Manning did not think the Crime Master overlooked many moves.

Manning had men posted on the grounds, two close to the

cabin. Nothing had happened, nothing suspicious had been seen or heard. Pollard rallied Manning.

"You're more nervous about this thing than I am," he said. "Shall we have breakfast in this funk-hole, or go over to the house?"

Manning tried to respond somewhat to the other's mood. He felt his responsibility, he had seen the work of the Crime Master, knew the resourcefulness of his methods.

They had breakfast in the main house, started for the Cold Brook links in Manning's own roadster.

It was a glorious morning in fall, a crisp tang in the air that was exhilarating, that roused Pollard to enthusiasm, that had some effect upon Manning's still somewhat pessimistic mood. He could not shake off the feeling of evil intended, if not actually impending. The cries of the crows in the thinning elms seemed to him to be melancholy, prophetic.

"Snap out of it," said Pollard with a laugh. "They can't do much to us while we're in the open, that's certain. We've got the day before us. We'll see how we come out this morning, and this afternoon we'll rate our handicaps to make a close thing of it. To-morrow you'll go back with the satisfaction of having baffled your Griffin, which, by the way, is a fabulous beast, I believe."

"There is nothing fabulous about the crimes he has committed," said Manning. He was feeling some relief as he surveyed the links. The country was open, with scattering trees, one or two natural hazards in the shape of brooks and gulches. Where there was considerable growth of trees or brush the leaves were no longer thick. His men, following in other cars, could trail their play, make sure that no coverts were turned into ambushes.

He was taking all precautions, but he did not actually believe that the Griffin would do anything so crude. The Crime Master might be mad, but he invariably lived up to his announcements. He would not relax vigilance for a moment. The links were the safest possible place. It was the coming night, until twelve o'clock, that Manning feared, in spite of their immunity until now.

He had slept lightly but he felt fit, always in training. He looked forward to the game with growing interest as he inspected the clubs the professional offered him, testing them for length and weight and spring. He changed with Pollard in the locker room, using some of the latter's toggery, finding shoes that fitted him, a light sweater.

Pollard was in high spirits, chuckling over the posted announcement in the clubhouse, and again in the caddy house, of his "Hole-in-One" achievement.

McKenzie, the pro', had a word with Manning.

"Mr. Pollard is a good player, sir," said the pro'. "He's a wee cranky over the etiquette o' the game, but 'twould be better if more were so. Gie' him the tee to himsel' when he drives. He should make an eighty-three or four," McKenzie went on. "Mebbe better, since he's got confidence ower this one-hole of his. He's a bit weak wi' his brassie yet. You're the first oot. You'll not be crowded. There's few on the links this time o' the week until the afternoon."

They stood in the door of the caddy house, close to the first tee. Pollard had his favorite caddie, the pro' had picked one for Manning. And Manning, watching Pollard practicing short chip shots, noticed his men taking up their work. They were unobtrusive. There was no need for them to come out into the open. For the most part they would travel the boundaries, see them clear.

"How about a little wager, Manning?" asked Pollard. "Say a ball on every nine holes. I warn you, I'm feeling in rare form. Let's go. Your honor. Three hundred and ninety-four yards. Par four."

Manning teed up with a wooden peg, looked down the fairway. Road to the right, with a low stone wall, beyond which two operatives were sauntering; to the left wide open country, boundary stakes. An old stable with two or three trees near it that threatened a sliced drive. The checkered direction post was two hundred yards ahead. He meant to watch that stable.

He smacked the ball fairly with a low, hard drive that went well past the pole, clear on the stable, rolling to a good lie.

"Looks like the green in two for you," said Pollard. "Here goes."

He hooked a trifle, but made good distance. The match was on. They kept fairly even, playing for holes, but keeping score for the afternoon's handicap. Pollard lost a ball in a quarry pit, was one down on the first nine.

Manning played well, but not his best. It was like a handball court. The sunshine seemed to lack warmth, the brisk air was depressing instead of stimulating. Once an airplane roared overhead, and he watched it intently. Pollard laughed at him. Laughed again when Manning held up a shot as the mowing-tractor crossed the fairway, taking advantage of the lack of players. Pollard waved a greeting to the driver, called him by name.

"You act as if it were a tank sent out to annihilate me," he jested.

"I'm taking no chances that I can help," said Manning. "Not even of the Griffin's lying."

"That chap has overreached himself this time. His colossal ego has made him tackle something he can't carry out. This nine I beat you."

Manning could see the flat shape of the automatic in Pollard's hip pocket that he had promised to carry. A futile weapon against the Machiavellian cunning of the Crime Master. For himself he had none. His cane was in the bag the caddy was carrying. Strips of leather—rings of it—shrunk over a rod of steel, formidable enough, if an opponent came within reach.

IV

LUNCHEON WAS served on the clubhouse veranda, as Pollard had suggested. There was no one else present. Manning's men had come in, were still vigilant, though out of sight. The meal was excellent. They compared scores, settled on the afternoon's game.

"Play till it begins to get dark, eh, Manning? Then back to the funk-hole. I'm enjoying myself, thanks to your company, but you must admit I've been most amenable. I still think your Griffin is a bugaboo so far as I am concerned. Anyway, we're safe on the links."

"It looks that way," said Manning, but he was not easy. He knew how men approaching execution had often to fight against the fear of the swinging pendulums, the inexorable tick of clocks. A man could look at a watch and go into a frenzy. He had something of the same feeling, the sense that, fair as the day was, apparently perfectly safe, something was approaching, stalking, step by step, closer and closer, not to be defrauded.

Pollard roared with laughter.

"You remind me of the cautious Senator," he said. "His friend pointed out some sheep as they drove past a field, remarking they had just been sheared. 'It would appear so, from this side,' said the Senator. Yes, what is it?"

"Somebody to see you, Mr. Pollard," said the caddy master. "He has a parcel he wants you to sign for."

Pollard and Manning exchanged glances. Pollard gently patted his hip pocket. Manning took up the cane he had brought to the clubhouse.

"Send him over," said Pollard.

They were both a trifle tense. Pollard's tone was not as light as he intended it to be when he spoke.

"If the Griffin hasn't changed his plans, this should not be the actual assassin," he said. "He don't look much like one."

The man was young, comparatively, deferential, smiling.

"I'm from the local agency at Springport," he said. "Spring-port Athletic Emporium. We carry Ski-Flites, you see. Got a wire from the manufacturers to present you with a dozen, sir; if possible to get your signature and maybe a word about Ski-Flites."

"Ah! On the theory it's the ball and not the player, eh? Perhaps you're right. Where do I sign?"

"Let's have a look at those balls," said Manning. He was not too sure of what might be in that box—and he wanted to be.

Pollard winked at him when the man took off the paper, opened the lid and displayed a dozen Ski-Flites, nested in partitions, wrapped in the transparent celluloid envelopes, sealed with the Ski-Flite seal.

"The paper said you were using a Ski-Flite when you made that hole," the man went on. "These are presentation balls. They are marked with your name and numbered. If you find you improve your play with any of them, perhaps you would let us know; a longer drive, a better pitch, or smoother putt."

"I will. It's a birthday present, though you may not know it. Set them down on the table. Manning, I'll play Ski-Flites against your favorite Dimples. And many thanks."

"You're welcome, sir. And many happy returns of the day."

Pollard took three of the new balls, two for his bag, one in his pocket for the new game. He gave the box to the caddie master, asking him to have it put in his locker.

"Ready, Manning?" he asked. "Then, let's go."

"You take the honor, this trip," said Manning, taking seat on the bench beside the sandbox and ball-washing tub on the edge of the wide tee. The two caddies stood off to the left. There were as yet no other players ready, though a car or two had driven up, their passengers presumably in the locker room.

Pollard tried his swing, whipping at late flower heads, took his stance. His form was good, left arm straight, right elbow well in, left foot lifting in a final preliminary test; following well through, a fine figure of a mature man, virile, keen on his game.

Manning heard the purr of an engine, the easy shift of gears. He glimpsed the car. The driver was the man who had brought the presentation balls, one of which, stripped of its envelope, was poised on the top of Pollard's patent tee. It was a good car—eight cylinders—it slid into high, accelerated, racing down hill, passing the two operatives, who were once more sauntering down the road. The man was in a hurry. He might have been waiting until they finished lunch—he might—

A swift and sudden certainty of something wrong, of danger close at hand, surged over Manning. Something, he fancied later, to do with the haste of the man to leave, an echo of the manner in which he had wished Pollard many happy returns of the day. At the risk of spoiling Pollard's drive for nothing he rose to his feet, starting forward.

"No pawns at hand," the Crime Master had said. What if one had just left? He barely grasped what the diabolical genius had planned. It was intuition, working like lightning, developing—but too late.

Pollard's club had gone up slowly, came down in perfect rhythm, his wrists doing their work at the last moment. Then—

A blast of pale flame, an acrid odor, fierce fulmination, an explosion that swept Manning backward, over the bench, with the violent impact that shook the ground, the trees, tore a hole in the turf of the tee.

Pollard was down, hideously wounded, unconscious, his broken body moving slightly, terribly stained, his clothes saturated with gushing blood.

Men came running up as Manning regained his feet. Players, the professional, caddie master and caddies, staring horror-stricken while Manning's own men vaulted the wall, others hurrying up. He turned to them.

"Get after that car that just passed. Stay where you are, boy," he shouted to Pollard's caddie. "Don't move. Take Mr. Pollard in. Send for a doctor."

He knew no surgeon could avail. Pollard was starting on his last adventure, exploring the unknown.

Manning ran to the caddie, took Pollard's bag. There was slight danger, he imagined. Those balls had been so constructed that the pent-up and supremely powerful explosive needed a hard blow to release it. A man might have putted with them. They were evidence, though he feared they might not furnish any clew beyond the cause of death. There were nine more in Pollard's locker—should be. Spheres of death if mishandled.

They carried Pollard in and laid him on two tables in the locker room. His clothing had been almost stripped from him. Manning had seen other terribly mutilated bodies after high explosive had struck close by, in the war; men flung into trees, left there, dismembered, naked. There had been but a small amount in the golf ball, but it had been compressed in the hollow core. Pollard's driver had utterly vanished.

The man's immense vitality still lingered. Some one came running with a car robe, spread it over him. The stains of blood came through.

"Where is his locker?" Manning demanded of the professional, whose Scotch stolidity had given place to an exhibition of rage and grief. "Quick, man," he said, "there may be life and death in it. Those other balls!"

He was determined to get hold of them. A doctor had been summoned. McKenzie stared at Manning as if he thought he were demented, but led the way down the room, between files of steel lockers, pointing out Pollard's.

"It was open, sir," he said. "I closed it when I put the balls there. It was one o' them? Guid God!"

"Get a pass key," Manning commanded. The professional vanished, while Manning waited. There was nothing he could do for Pollard now but see the body taken back, notify the authorities. He had failed—failed. He fancied he could hear the mocking laughter of the Griffin. He wondered if the Crime Master was close at hand. If he was, if he could get to grips with him. He held faint hope that the other car would be overtaken. It was too powerful.

Once he had chased the Crime Master in his own fast roadster and lost him.

There was a murmur of voices. McKenzie came back.

"There's a doctor here now, sir," he said. "A guest of the club. He's lookin' at him, but he's dead, lang syne."

Manning took the box, set back the two balls from the bag. He saw now why they had been nested, like eggs, though the risk was comparatively slight, unless the car had met with accident. Slight chance of that. The Griffin's emissary had gone swiftly, but he had probably driven up carefully enough.

The doctor had gone. The robe was again covering the dreadful sight. But one of Pollard's arms had been displaced. It hung down from the edge of the narrow table. There was something on the dangling wrist like a clot of blood.

Manning looked at it.

It was the sinister scarlet seal of the Griffin!

v

"WHERE DID that doctor go—what did he look like?" he barked at the bystanders, already stupefied by the tragedy, bewildered still more by Manning's demand, the set fury of his face.

"Out, down to the cars. He said he could do nothing. Felt his pulse. A man with a pointed beard. In brown golf clothes."

Manning brushed by them, through the door that led by an outside stair to the club's parking space, between club and caddy house.

"No pawn on hand!" But the Crime Master himself, in person, masquerading as a guest, as a doctor, with a forged card, perhaps a false beard.

He raced to his car. One of his men came at his beckon, answered him.

A man with a beard, in brown golf clothes, had just left in a big car, gone down hill, in the same direction taken by the messenger who had brought the fatal balls.

"Get in with me," ordered Manning. "You've got your gun? Here, hold these in your lap. They won't explode if you're careful. If anything goes wrong, get rid of them."

The man took seat beside him, his face pale, but steadfast, holding the box gingerly. They might get a flat. They might?

Manning switched on, let in the clutch, was in the road, in high, a master at the wheel.

Cold Brook Country Club was in the hills. The road curved. To its right there ran Cold Brook, between high banks. The fallen leaves from the trees gave Manning a glimpse of a cloud of dust, a car rolling rapidly about a curve.

He went hurtling down the grade in headlong pursuit. The car might have the speed of his, but he would make that up by more reckless driving. Reckless, with less consummate a driver. This road had taken its toll of others not so skillful. It was marked with danger signs, with boards indicating snake curves.

The man beside him sat with feet braced. Temporarily Manning had forgotten about the loaded balls, intent only upon overtaking his man. There were two figures in that car ahead, one driving, hunched over the wheel. Now it was out of sight, and Manning pressed down his accelerator. The roadster fairly leaped ahead. It was a heavy car with low clearance and should hold the road. Dust rose back of them like vapor.

His tires were new. The speedometer crept up, trembled at eighty, as they skidded round a curve, another, perilously close to the brink of the deep gulch where Cold Brook brawled along. They touched the protection fence, tore off a sliver of white painted wood.

The other car was in sight again. Manning had gained. He saw one figure turn in its seat. The so-called Death Curve was at the bottom of the hill, a twist in the highway beyond it, going up, steep.

There was sweat of fear on the face of the operative beside Manning. He had come over that road. He believed they would never make that curve, nor the car they were pursuing, unless it slowed up. It had margin enough for that. He glanced about him, resolved to toss the box into Cold Brook at any moment, stiffened at sight of Manning, driving like a demon.

The operative's gun was out, tucked under his thigh. He meant to shoot at the first chance, tires, men. He was a chosen man, one of eight on the job, a crack marksman. But he had faint hope of getting a shot.

Manning was past hopes, centered on sending the car at top speed, better than top. Time after time they veered round the curves and his strong wrists brought it under control.

On the short straights he pressed it up to ninety, changing no gears, using no brakes. Brakes at their speed meant disaster. And he was cutting down that lead.

Round a bend, on two wheels, rocking back to base, lunging on. The Griffin's car disappeared about a curve. Death Curve close now. Very close. The wind whistled over the top of the glass shield behind which Manning bent over the bucking control.

A side road on the left. A light truck coming out of it, the driver with a face of chalk, tugging at emergency brakes.

This time they crashed a protection post, they went out beyond the solid edge. The nigh wheels still held traction, clawing at the road. The operative started to hurl the box away and they were back, with a crumpled fender, a broken running board, swaying, but safe, the truck driver, a local farmer, gaping at them, too terrified to find voice.

Death Curve!

Muscles stood out along the lines of Manning's jaws. His wrists were wrenched, but his sinews were of steel, handball-hardened. The roadster was exceeding its limit. It was in danger of freezing, for all its plentiful oil supply, its daily overhauling. But it was a magnificent climber. It might yet catch the Crime Master's car on the hill.

They shot round the last curve, almost out of control, actually out at moments, the rear tires spurning the ground to regain it. They had made it. Here Cold Brook swung off in a rocky defile.

"Throw it!"

Manning's yell was not needed. His aide sent the box spinning out into the gorge. The lid opened, the balls scattering, falling in a shower.

Across the road was the car of the Crime Master, blocking the way.

Empty!

Up from the ravine there came the blast of terrific explosions. Trees rocked. Some, at least, of the explosives had hit rock hard enough to set off the fulminate, starting the rest, destroying evidence. Boughs sailed across the road. Twigs showered down.

To the right were birches, thick-set. Manning saw their white ranks, their scanty leaves, yellow as gold pieces.

He set the roadster to the left, charging up a cut bank. It plowed through the soft soil, tilting, passed the other car, lunged in sharp zigzag as he strove to hold it. It ripped into the trees.

It could not have been long before other cars came, with due caution, down the dangerous hill. Manning's scalp was slashed. A flap of flesh and an eyebrow obscured his sight as he came back to consciousness. The roadster was a wreck, the radiator smashed, one wheel gone. They had been flung over the windshield.

His aide lay with his leg badly crumpled, broken, still unconscious from a fractured skull. Manning wiped blood from his eye, sat up, aided by a sympathetic arm.

The Crime Master's car was gone!

"He Will Not Be Alive After the Thirteenth!"—
It Was the Griffin's Ugly Promise

IT MIGHT well have been a scene in some medieval torture chamber. The place had been hewn out of the rocky foundations of the Crime Master's house. From it an arched doorway led to other cavernous recesses. There was a steady hum, as of some infernal machine, which was actually the great dynamo that supplied the arch-criminal with power, light and heat. There men worked, nameless, masked, with brassards about their arms bearing their numbers as cogs in his infamous organization. Strange lights flashed in green and blue flares; there was the clank of metal.

The Crime Master, as the man known as the Griffin had boastfully styled himself, a boast not yet broken down, was clad in an Oriental robe. His face was masked by a visor of thin, plastic substance that did not mar the perfection of his features, but yet effectually disguised him. Through this visor his eyes gleamed steadily, charged with an intense cruelty that took satisfaction from the torment of his victim, a satisfaction that was sadistic.

His gaze never varied. It was the gaze of a serpent, sure of its victim, gloating. Only the mocking sneer that marred the finely shaped mouth deepened as he watched the writhings of the unfortunate man, bound to a chair. The man's almost naked body was wet with the sweat of anguish. The Griffin listened to his cries, now wails of pain, now a babble of seeming gibberish.

There were four in the room. One was in a gown with a hood. He barely moved and he was listening with more intensity than even the Griffin, catching every syllable. Now and then he raised a hand in assent to the Griffin's question as to the progress of the inquisition.

The fourth was a dwarf; an apelike creature, hideous of face, distorted of body. His hairy arms were almost as disproportionate as those of a chimpanzee. His skin was plum-black. Hair grew on his fingers to the nails, on his shoulders, matted his chest. Above his small eyes, his forehead, low and brutish, was corrugated; his cheek bones stood out like knuckled fists.

He was the Griffin's personal bodyguard. One affected by the weird scene might have said it was an evil spirit, a demon, under the control of the Crime Master, whom Quantro worshiped as supreme. A Haitian, steeped in voodoo, ineffably vicious and depraved.

He wore a turban and a loin-kilt of scarlet. In the band that was wound about his loins was a curving blade, like a machete, in a sheath of sharkskin, razor-edged. Now and then he chuckled as the man he was torturing twisted in torment, straining against his bonds.

He had been stubborn, with an endurance that was marvelous, this unfortunate. Some strong resistance of fealty, of principle, had sustained him, but his spirit had broken down at last beneath the devilish device used upon him.

A fine cord had been tied about his forehead. In it a hardwood stick had been twirled to form a tourniquet. The cord was stained with sweat and blood. It ate into his flesh and affected his brain like a ring of fire. It seemed as if it must sever his skull pan. It compressed veins and arteries; there has never been a greater, more efficient torture discovered by man. Now the slightest touch of the dwarf's fingers was supreme agony, yet so cunningly had he used it, the victim did not swoon, and could reveal the secrets they wrested from him.

*The glass fell
from his hand.*

The listening man in the hooded gown professed himself satisfied.

He told what he had learned, and the Griffin gave approval.

"See you forget nothing," he said. "Then your payment will be great. A slip might cause your death. You understand that I cannot protect you. You may go."

He pointed to a door and the man went out silently. Quantro turned to his master with the look of a hound that has brought down its quarry, and begs permission to kill. His red tongue showed its tip between teeth that had been filed to points.

The Griffin folded his arms, nodded.

"He must be destroyed," he said briefly.

When he later shot up the steel tube of the elevator shaft to his own strange, luxurious apartment, the man had been eliminated. Quantro had been dismissed, not from any revulsion at his butchery, but because the Crime Master wished to be alone. His mood had changed, none the less cruel, none the less charged with malice toward the rest of the world in the revenge that fermented always in his brain, tainted with madness; a determination for reprisal of wrongs, fancied or real, magnified through the lenses of insanity, of grandiose dementia.

The Griffin's atrocities might be fantastic in conception and execution, but they were horribly real. They shocked the world, they defied the police, they mocked the press and terrified the public.

Now he sat at his carved desk and look from a drawer a list of names through several of which a line of scarlet crayon had been drawn. Against each of these a date had been set down. He now wrote one after a name that stood seventh on his long list, dipping his pen in the violet ink of a container whose top was the golden head of a griffin, the fabulous beast of Greek mythology, half eagle and half lion.

Now music sounded faintly. The perfume of burning amber floated through the room, which was built with curving walls that showed no door, no window, only golden tapestries. Yet the air was sweet, light coming from hidden sources.

The Crime Master took sheets of heavy gray paper and wrote in bold script with the violet ink, his sneer now a smile of derision. For signature he made a clever pen sketch of a griffin's head, with its curving, rapacious beak, a fitting emblem for such a creature as the man who used it.

He read the letter over, addressed an envelope, sealed the missive with a cartouche of scarlet, an oval embossed with the griffin's head. He filled a Turkish hubble-bubble with tobacco, picked up the tube and smoked through the cooling rose water.

"I am afraid," he said softly, "that my friend Manning is achieving a little false confidence. It might be well to reduce that."

Once more he addressed an envelope, this time to a woman. He placed no scarlet seal on this, but in the center of the sheet it contained, unwritten upon, he affixed the sinister cartouche of heavy paper.

"He may not have told her about this emblem," said the Griffin, "but she will have read the papers since she returned from abroad. It may unsettle her, but it is more likely to disturb Manning when he hears of it, as I think he will."

Then he leaned back, smoking, the fumes of the tobacco mingling with the amber incense, his mask off. None could enter the room, with its walls and floor of steel, without his consent. His face was that of Lucifer, proud, beautiful, but subtly marred. With his serpent eyes veiled by half-closed lids, he listened to the music as the smoke bubbled through the cooling fluid.

II

GORDON MANNING late major of the A.E.F., youngest of his rank, brilliant member of the Army Secret Service Corps, sat in his offices where the outer door announced him as Advisory Councillor.

He was a volunteer special agent to the police under appointment by the commissioner to grapple with the Griffin. Police methods had failed. For months the Crime Master had achieved his devilish ends, leaving always his emblem, the scarlet seal.

Now, despite all attempts at secrecy, he had discovered Manning's appointment, written to him congratulating him as a worthy adversary, challenging him, forcing Manning into the open.

Manning had discovered the subtle methods of the crimes with which he had grappled. He had arrested or killed the Griffin's tools—his pawns, the Crime Master called them. He had been almost in actual contact with the Griffin himself, but the latter had eluded him. The pawns were unwilling or unable, to tell anything about their principal. No efforts could make them reveal the slightest clew.

More than that, the Crime Master's colossal egoism had led him to the announcement of the name of his intended victim, the day of the death he was to meet. He mocked Manning's efforts to prevent it.

And he had won.

Manning sat looking out over lower Manhattan, its towering buildings, listening to the sounds of the great city, and the river that swept about its southern border. He was haggard, worn, not from personal fear, but because of the bafflement with which he had met, the certainty that the Griffin was planning another coup.

A maniac, undoubtedly, but infinitely cunning and resourceful. He overlooked no details. He was like an old fox that deliberately shows itself in the open, lolling out its tongue at the pack before it starts off on the chase it actually enjoys, knowing its ultimate refuge certain.

His secretary entered, bringing the mail. It was not so much her manner or the look on her face that warned Manning. He had *known* that morning would bring a letter with the red cartouche, the abominable, boasting emblem.

Manning had traveled far since the war, largely in the Orient. He had looked into its mysteries, divided the chaff of fakery from the true effects of knowledge, knowing magic to be only the enigma of the unknown. He believed in telepathy, the affection of one mind by the emanations of another, through mental vibration. Especially he believed that evil vibrations held peculiar force. Many centuries backed his belief. He knew himself attuned to the Griffin's sending because of expectancy and a certain dread of failure; though that did not affect his resolution to persevere, despite the Crime Master's open warning that, if he came too close, he might pay the penalty.

He realized that the Griffin was subtly striving to undermine him, to destroy the quality of his spirit. Not only by his announcements of crime, with their invariable gap of two or three days in which he might make his preparations for defense yet know that the Griffin was making his offensive, but because of another element.

There was a girl he loved, as virile men like Manning love. Eleanor Severn, lately returned from Europe. He knew that she had expected him to renew his attentions, to carry them to courtship; that she was hurt because of his apparent indifference.

The Griffin had already sent her a scarlet seal. Manning dared not include her in his peril, had sought to avoid that by staying away from her, not mentioning his mission. But the Crime Master had embroiled her in the contest between him and Manning, a contest the Griffin continually referred to as a fair and open one, save for the fact that he was privileged to make the first moves.

To think that Eleanor might be involved shook Manning's sturdiness at times, at times stiffened his fibers. Now—

He opened the envelope with a steady hand that did not quiver as he read the ominous contents. Only his lips closed more tightly, little muscles bossed along the clean line of his jaw.

> DEAR MANNING:
>
> A little closer last time. But the horse named "Almost" never won a race. You are deserving of another trial. It is possible you know this gentleman who was born under an unlucky star. I do not know if you hold any credence in horoscopy, but it is certain that the horoscope of Edward Poindexter shows the House of Death in the ascendency this month.
>
> By my calculations I find he will die sometime on the thirteenth.
>
> That is an unlucky number. Many scoff at it, but you will find the reasons for such "superstitions"—shall we call them, well founded?
>
> Poindexter himself has traveled in the East. You may be able to persuade him to take extraordinary precautions, to accept your protection. Do your best, my dear antagonist. But Poindexter will not be alive after midnight of the thirteenth instant.
>
> He is one of those fools who takes it upon himself to change the ways of the world. He styles himself a Peace Maker. May he be thrice blessed, in the next world, which he will surely enter shortly. If there is one. In this one he is doomed.
>
> Remember, Manning, the nearer you come to me, the greater your peril. There may be peril to others. I like you as an adversary, but I do not accept defeat gracefully. I see no present prospect of it.

So, I leave you to plan your moves. Mine are already well arranged.

It was signed with the seal of the Griffin.

Manning set down the letter, lines in his face swiftly graved there. Death was on the wing. He could almost hear the beating, feel the chill draft of its somber pinions. He had faced it many a time. In the trenches, on perilous missions, in the jungle, with lurking bushmen creeping up unknown trails with poisoned darts for the intruder. Not death for him, this time, unless indeed he came in actual contact with the fiend; then he well believed he would be in dire peril; but death for another, for a man who had already served well and was now coming to the crux of his usefulness.

Death, hovering, ready to strike from an ambush that all Manning's wits might not uncover.

He knew Poindexter, admired him. Poindexter was a path-finder in the cause of humanity.

Manning had met him in the Far East where Poindexter had served in the diplomatic service of the United States with signal success. Those brilliant capabilities of his were now devoted to the peace movement.

It was quite feasible that the Griffin, enemy to all mankind, should have selected so prominent a man, engaged in a project that might well irritate the inflamed mind of the Crime Master.

Manning had seen Poindexter two or three times since his return, twice dining with him. He lived on higher Fifth Avenue in what is known as a roof bungalow, a place that could only be reached by elevators, or many flights of stairs. Entry could be easily guarded.

It should be an easy matter to protect him, if he permitted Manning to take charge. And Manning thought he would. Trained in Oriental ways, Poindexter was more willing to admit the possibilities of secret assassination than the Griffin's last victim, who had laughed at the idea, and been killed in the open, before the very eyes of Manning, impotent to save him, unable to avenge him, swiftly though he had acted.

He would get in touch with Poindexter at once. They had many things in common, liked to talk over affairs of the East, in which the diplomat still held keen interest. Poindexter would see him, consent to Manning taking charge of guarding him for the twenty-four hours of the thirteenth. He *must* permit it or it would be carried out despite him.

The telephone rang sharply. For a split moment he paused. This was not from the Griffin. He had used that instrument, he had worked out some method of induction that made it impossible to trace a call, but the bell always held a higher note. Yet Manning felt a dire foreboding that he conquered as he answered. There was only one way to treat danger—to face it.

"Gordon? This is Eleanor. Why have you not been to see me?"

"I have been very busy."

"Trying to find this Griffin?"

Manning's brown face twitched. He sensed that this was no ordinary call, that it might well be one the Griffin had antici-pated. He might be listening in.

"Don't mention that subject over the line," Manning said, his voice acute with apprehension. But he could not check the girl.

"I have been reading about him. It was he who sent me the seal on the card that came with the flowers brought me on landing, that I thought had come from you. I got another seal this morning, a few minutes ago. What does it mean? I must see you. Gordon, I am afraid."

Manning's lean features set into a mask of determination that many men had seen and recognized. Soldiers, tribesmen, carriers on *safari*. The look that carried on. Now, blending with it, showing in his eyes, was pain, the anguish of evil portent.

She was afraid. And she was not the kind to be afraid. He knew that. Knew her spirit was brave. He did not believe her in imminent danger, but now she was linked with his mission. If anything could have knitted his resolve, if anything was needed to stiffen it; her call did so.

"I will see you," he said.

"When?"

"I will send a message. Not now, not over the telephone."

This was the only thing to do. He must let her know. He did not think the Griffin meant to strike, only to threaten. But the threat was like the sound of sappers to beleaguered garrisons, the steady advance of tunneling from which, at any moment, death might belch with terrific force.

The Crime Master had never yet failed. He acknowledged neither God nor devil nor man, considering himself invincible. It was through this arrogance of his that Manning hoped some day—some day soon—to trap him. But here was a diabolical complication. He was using Manning's love for the girl as a factor to weaken him.

Manning hung up. For a moment his bowed head rested on his clenched hands, his shoulders heaved. Then he stood up, and in his eyes there shone something that could meet and match the Griffin's serpent gaze, a fire that glowed brightly, the flame of his soul.

It flickered, but did not die, flared with even more intensity, as the telephone bell rang once more, this time with a peculiar pitch.

It was the Griffin.

Manning listened to the cultured voice with its sardonic inflection, the voice he would never fail to recognize. Through the speech he heard the sound of music, faint, sweet, but curiously primitive. It did not interfere with those clear tones, but lent intensity to the mocking phrases.

"You may as well see her. Manning. A charming girl. It would be too bad to spoil your idyl. I am afraid I have marred it somewhat. But only in the game.

"Don't forget, my dear Manning, that in this chess tournament of ours, the queen should always be guarded. I advise you not to try and send her away, to take her off the board. That might precipitate matters."

Manning seldom cursed, save in times of stress, when men understood only strong talk. Now an oath rose to his lips as he heard the derisive laughter of the Griffin blending with the music. He checked it, replaced the receiver.

That he was shadowed by the Griffin's men he did not doubt. He had never been able to detect the "trailers," expert as he was in such matters, but many things had proved their existence. And now Eleanor was spied upon. To meet her could not increase her danger which, as yet, was only a menace. She knew enough now to be told all. She had the right to know. After all, he had unwittingly involved her.

It revealed the close study the Crime Master made of those against whom he was actively arrayed. Manning's devotion was only a matter of social rumor, yet the Griffin had unerringly set his finger upon the romance. Manning's love was danger for her, instead of the protection he had meant it to be.

III

HE MET her in the reception parlors of a select hotel, talking briefly, seemingly unobserved, unheard, in a palm-shadowed niche. For the first time in his life Manning had to battle with jumpy nerves. He imagined lurking listeners, watchers. But he showed no nervousness before her.

She was frank, as she always was, and so was Manning.

"It would seem that the Griffin, as you call him, has a fixed idea that he can strike at you through me—that he believes you entertain a feeling for me you have never told me of, Gordon. Would you have told me if I had not received a scarlet seal, if you had not undertaken to rid the world of this fiend, for he is nothing short of that?"

He met her gaze. She was modern. She did not hide her emotions. He saw more than friendship in her eyes.

"It is true," he told her. "I would have kept on avoiding you, but he has made that impossible."

"You would have let me think you did not love me, that my love for you was not what you wanted? That was not fair, Gordon. When a woman loves, as I do, she wants to know, to share the dangers of the man she loves. To help him."

Her hand went into his. A clasp was all they might indulge in there, all they needed. Through both of them there ran a thrill at the contact. It left Manning with a sense of power.

"You must not try and help me," he said. "I thought of asking you to go away, but that is too risky. This time I shall be inspired to do my more than best."

"I may help you," she said steadfastly. "If he wins this time, with his satanic ingenuity, I may act as a bait to tempt him within reach. With you to guard me, I am willing. You know I love you, Gordon."

"I do. But God forbid that you should ever be used that way! Eleanor, it seems impossible that God, Fate, what you will, should permit such a monster to carry on. The balance must be struck, but not with your aid. It is frightful to me to think that my love for you should have drawn you into this web."

"That love came to you, as it did to me. And true love is not harmful. It will help us."

He had not told her about Poindexter. He knew her gallant spirit, knew that she might try to aid him in some way she would not tell him of. She had a brilliant brain; but he was not going to let her do what she plainly desired—share his risks.

They rose to go. Between them was a new bond. The sense of power that had thrilled him at the caress of her fingers still tingled in him as he saw her to her car. Her liveried chauffeur opened the door, then checked his action, starting back.

Over the Severn monogram, her own entwined initials, some one had set a scarlet oval, vivid as a clot of blood. To the casual observer it might have seemed merely the rather blatant crest of the car owner. But Manning's blood chilled. He saw Eleanor pale and shiver slightly.

"They are trying to frighten us," she said, "to work on you through me. Your Griffin is a coward at heart. But I am not afraid any more, Gordon. You will win."

But Manning was afraid. He felt as if an icy finger, the finger of Death, had traced his spine. Sweat started on his forehead as he stood gazing at the griffin's head on the cartouche.

He met Poindexter at New York's most exclusive club, to which both of them belonged. The diplomat listened to his story gravely.

"The contemplated act of a madman, undoubtedly," he said. "But, if we can foil him once, we will shake his confidence. Once break down that colossal self-esteem of his and you will be close to capturing this wretched being, Manning. I place myself in your hands. You will be my guest from the night of the twelfth until the morning, at least, of the fourteenth. I shall take my own precautions,

"It seems incredible that he can succeed. I think he has over-estimated his resources. He has inflated ego which may be punctured. Of course, you understand that I place no responsibility on you, but surely the two of us can circumvent him.

"I am having a dinner party on the thirteenth, as it happens. All men well known to me, save one, who is well vouched for. James Fleming, the man who has lived most of his life in China. I had a letter from him two weeks ago. He mentioned others, who will be at the dinner, by the way, so there should be no doubt as to his identity. You know of him."

"I know of him," said Manning. "But he is an unknown, comparatively. If he arrives, seat me next to him. You have made no change in your domestic staff of late?"

"None. Tolu is still my major-domo. You remember him. There is no question of his fidelity."

"None," answered Manning. He knew Tolu, a Filipino, who had been with Poindexter for years. Manning had spoken with him in his own dialect. A man who could not be bribed, safe as Manning's own selected Jap who served him at his home at Pelham Manor.

They went over the other servants. Two maids, a Negro cook. All had been with Poindexter for the three years since he had retired from active diplomatic service. Manning meant to look them up. They did not sound dangerous. He could have the building guarded by detectives, on the ground floor, on the roof. The special elevator that served the upper stories would be given a special operator. There would be other operatives posted outside the bungalow.

Fleming seemed the only doubtful quantity. And Manning resolved to make sure of him, aside from being his neighbor at the dinner. That seemed the vulnerable point of attack, yet might not prove so. He determined that there would be no minute of the twenty-four hours when he was not in personal touch with Poindexter, who agreed to all his precautions.

They would occupy adjoining beds, if Manning went to bed, which he doubted. He did not expect to sleep, to relax his vigilance for a second. This time, surely, they would foil the Griffin.

IV

IT WAS seven thirty. Almost twenty hours of the day set by the Griffin had passed. All the guests had assembled, save Fleming, who had telephoned from his hotel that he was unavoidably detained, but would try to arrive later.

Manning had checked him up. It was without doubt the Fleming who had but recently returned from self-imposed exile in the cause of science. He had been called upon, returned those calls, been recognized by old acquaintances, dined, received, arranged lectures.

Yet Manning felt an indefinable relief at the fact he would not be present at the dinner.

He had not slept, but he was still alert. His men were on the premises. There had been no sign of attack, but, until the clocks chimed midnight, he was on the alert, strung up to the zero hour. If Poindexter was alive on the morning of the fourteenth, Manning believed that the Griffin would abandon his plan; acknowledge, however grudgingly, defeat.

That a setback might crush him was not beyond conjecture. His inflamed brain was nourished upon his belief in his supremacy. It might well crumble under failure.

There were six at the dinner, to which seven had been asked. Outside of the host and Manning, the rest were men of affairs and accomplishment. A celebrated physician, a brilliant writer, the editor of a modern magazine that devoted itself solely to world affairs, supported by a group of prominent people of whom one was present, America's greatest financier, far-seeing beyond material matters.

The cocktails were served in Poindexter's library, furnished with things he had brought from the Orient, many of them gifts from grateful governments. Tolu had served them. He was a short, compact and dignified Filipino of high class, son of a chief, devoted to Poindexter, scholar as well as butler, proud to serve him.

Manning greeted him in Mindanao and he bowed gravely, but did not reply. The perfect servant. Manning thought him a trifle changed in manner, almost as if he, too, sensed some special gravity in the occasion, some menace to his master. It would have been a passing fancy, save for the stress of the condition of affairs. Manning knew that these half-primitive races were quick to feel unusual conditions. And Tolu, if he felt some hidden threat, would be an efficient aide.

Poindexter showed nothing of what he might be feeling, though Manning knew he did not underestimate the situation.

The table was a masterpiece. The usual cloth had been replaced with Chinese weaves. Overhead was a lattice from which dropped wistaria blooms amid their greenery. The centerpiece was a glass circle in which fan-tailed goldfish lolled through weeds and coral.

They took their seats. Fleming's place was vacant. The setting of service plate was removed. Now the arrangement was well balanced, two on each side, Poindexter at the head, the physician facing him.

In the right-hand pocket of his dinner jacket, Manning carried a flat, snub automatic. He did not often have a gun. He relied mostly upon his favorite weapon, a cane of steel core about which were shrunken rings of leather. But this could not be brought to a table. It did not look as if he would have use for the gun, but he was prepared.

For all the seeming security, he was conscious of high tension. He knew the Griffin.

On the roof, where Poindexter had placed carved benches of stone, a fountain, shrubs and flowering plants, Manning's picked men were stationed, unobtrusive, but prepared for the slightest irregularity. The entrance was guarded, and the elevator. There was a man acting as telephone operator in the lobby. The protection seemed perfect, but Manning was uneasy.

When they went in the oysters had been placed for them. They swallowed them and sipped at the light wine that had been poured.

The floor was of marquetry, exquisitely inlaid woods, without rugs. By Poindexter's right hand there was a service button clipped to the table edge. Tolu had retired between the courses.

"I have for you," said Poindexter, "a special soup. Manning knows it. Some of you may have tasted it. All of you heard of it. Made from birds' nests. I assure you it is delicious. A rare chance that I could obtain it."

A murmur of appreciation went round. Edible birds' nests, the prized potage of the Chinese.

"I am sorry," said Poindexter, "that Fleming is not here. I had him in mind when I planned this dinner. He may have enjoyed American cooking, for a change, but I am sure he would have relished a return to the delicacies of the East. I have been accused of being a gourmet. I received a letter two days ago from the president of the Vegetarian League stating that, as a pacifist, opposed to the shedding of blood, I should not eat meat.

"Unfortunately, the chemistry of my body, not to mention the arrangement of my teeth, does not subscribe to that. But I have a Japanese seaweed salad for you later, then some red snappers from the Caribbean and a caribou steak from Canada. Then candied fruits from Se-Chuen; lychee nuts, a cordial from Kwei-Chau, made of apricots. I propose a toast to our absent guest, whom, I hope, will be with us later. Fleming, devotee of Science!"

He touched the button by his side for a change of course, half lifted his glass.

It fell from his hand, spilling the contents. The fragile crystal broke into fragments as they all started from their seats and Poindexter dropped back heavily into his chair, slid beneath the table, suddenly inert.

Manning felt the weight of his automatic pistol in his pocket as he sprang to his feet. It was useless here. The Griffin had struck. How, he knew not. The wine had been poured from the same bottle for all of them. Automatically, he had watched that, though not suspecting much danger from the pantry, none from Tolu. The latter came in answer to the signal, hurrying to his master, helping Manning and another to lift him while the physician rushed from the bottom of the table. They had all drunk some of the wine.

"He has had a stroke," said the doctor. "His motor centers were paralyzed. He seems to have choked to death."

The expert's face was grave as he felt heart and pulse, strove in vain to detect a laboring breath. Manning was beside him; he had some medical knowledge, some experience.

Poindexter's face was pallid, the hue of wax. There seemed no surface congestion, such as apoplexy might have caused. He was a florid man, but the veins were not swollen, his eyes were almost normal, save for a slight contraction of the pupils, which might, or might not, be imaginary.

"He is dead," the doctor said. "Beyond the question of a doubt."

V

THEY LOOKED at each other, perplexed, disturbed, shocked at the dramatic ending to their dinner. Manning took charge.

"And not from natural causes," he said. "Doctor, there must be an autopsy, though that may not help us capture the assassin."

"Assassin?" They all spoke the word together.

"The Griffin! He announced that he would kill Poindexter before to-day was over. He has succeeded. I was here to protect him. The place is surrounded. No suspicions can attach to you gentlemen, but I must ask none of you to leave until the police arrive—to take your depositions. I will look to the help."

They had borne Poindexter's body to a lounge. Death had left no trace of his fatal dart, to all appearances. Tolu, still stolid, though to Manning he showed sign of emotion, asked, in his clipped American, what he should do.

"Leave everything as it is," ordered Manning. "You gentlemen might go into the library, except the doctor."

He had no hope of resuscitating Poindexter. There was none. He remembered Poindexter's words, that Manning should not be held responsible. He had done his best, but the Crime Master had scored again, under his eyes, despite all precautions. For the moment the Griffin seemed more than human. His was the invisible hand that had killed.

Manning's men were all on post. That did not enter into the matter. To his brain returned the clear picture of Poindexter with his wineglass held in his hand while he spoke. He had not even sipped from it. What he had drunk before could have had nothing to do with the sudden collapse that none of them had shared.

Manning secured the bottle, followed Tolu into the kitchen, gave the bottle over to one of his men whom he summoned. But he was certain that there was no poison in it, that the wine had not been juggled. He had watched the pouring, instinctively.

The Crime Master had won once more.

The police surgeon came, but could offer no suggestion beyond the verdict of the eminent physician. It looked like a stroke. But there would be an autopsy.

Manning doubted if it would determine the cause of death. That cause was there, somewhere in the little roof-house.

He nodded to the sergeant of the crime squad as the latter asked concerning the detention of the guests. They were beyond question, should not be held, could easily be reached. They left, grave of countenance, taken down in the elevator by Manning's own operator.

The body was taken away. It was nine o'clock, three hours short of the limit set by the Griffin. Manning held a fancy that he could hear the latter's sardonic laughter. The thing that had happened seemed incredible. There was no clew.

But there *must* be one. This was murder!

Manning had examined the servants himself before the sergeant had done so. He was confident of the results of his own inquiry. The death had not been caused by food. And Tolu could be trusted.

Could he?

Manning, in the library, alone, remembered the change he had observed in the Filipino, slight, explicable enough, but—the man *was* different. He was still on the premises. He could not leave. They were held on the roof, where Manning's men were still on duty. The two maids did not sleep on the premises, but Manning had ordered all the help to stay until he was ready to let them go. He was convinced that the Griffin had made his preparations for the commission of the crime through the household arrangements, not through the unquestionable guests; though he had been suspicious of Fleming, who had not even appeared.

Manning sat brooding, seeking solution.

The vibrant ring of Poindexter's desk phone brought him to his feet. This was the Griffin. For a moment he thought of ignoring it, then realized he could not afford to overlook anything that might lead to a clew, even the taunts of the Crime Master.

"It is still the thirteenth, Manning. I have time still in hand that I shall not need. I have just seen Poindexter's body borne away for the inquest. It will reveal nothing. You will discover nothing. You might as well leave, Manning. This time I have entirely mastered you."

There was no doubt about the sardonic laughter now. It rang from the transmitter as Manning closed the switch.

The insult brought Manning to his feet, stung with his failure, spurred to action. Somewhere on the premises was the solution—perhaps the murderer—the killer—for, though it would seem that the Griffin never was the actual slayer in any of his crimes, he was responsible.

Tolu?

Manning could not reconcile his conception of the Mindanao boy, Poindexter's knowledge of him, with the fixed idea that Tolu must have done this thing, must be the Griffin's pawn. Nor could he see how the deed had been accomplished in plain sight of five of them, all men of perception and intelligence, with Manning watching for some such move.

He went again into the dining room. The table had been cleared of all but the glass container in which the languid goldfish swam leisurely, coldblooded creatures, unmindful of what had occurred beyond their limited dimension. Above them, the latticed wistaria drooped.

Tolu, cat-footed, precise in his black clothes, was taking the clip from the table edge. To it was attached the service button that Poindexter had pressed as his last act. From this the cord had trailed over the floor to the wainscoting and along that to the pantry, held in place by brass eyelets.

Tolu held the clip in his hand. He had taken out the junction plug and the cord was loose. He handled the clip and button as if it was some precious object, something to be treated with great care—or with great caution. He did not see or hear Manning. Manning stood observing him, while in his mind there rose a vision of Poindexter, glass in hand, pressing the button, stricken.

Pressing the button! Which Tolu alone set in place, removed!

An answer came to him, possible, probable.

Suddenly Tolu turned and observed Manning. His decorous mien seemed to vanish. He was, for a flaming second, a savage surprised in the bush, his eyes gleaming like crimson spangles, his black pompadour bristling. He seemed about to crouch, as if to fling a spear or discharge a poisoned dart. With this atavistic throwback Manning knew his answer was correct. And he knew how to handle such a savage.

He spoke sharply to him in Mindanao.

"What have you done with Tolu?"

The man gasped. He seized at the automatic in Manning's hand, seemed to strive for control as he answered that he did not know what the *tuan* was talking about. He answered in a strange tongue, automatically, as Manning had expected him to. And, so replying, he revealed the secret, sealed his own fate.

Tolu spoke Mindanao; this man spoke Palawan.

It is as easy to find two Filipinos that look alike—though they may come from different islands, speak varying dialects— as it is to discover two Chinese or Japanese who cannot be distinguished apart by any but their own countrymen. Easier.

And this was not Tolu. Tolu, the faithful, had been decoyed away or seized, this Palawan set in his place, instructed in Tolu's duties, an education which must have been obtained from Tolu under duress. Manning was not far from imagining exactly what had happened in the Griffin's torture chamber. He knew too that Tolu had been eliminated.

As to how this Palawan had killed?

The Filipino, all savage now, poised the clip so that the button was toward Manning and flung it straight for the latter's face. Manning ducked as he fired, felt the contrivance graze his head, knew that it carried death. It had spoiled his aim, though he winged his man. The Filipino ran, swaying, and leaped for the swinging pantry door, disappearing through it as Manning's second bullet struck the little square of glass set in the upper panel to facilitate service and avoid collisions.

Manning raced after him. The frightened cook and maids blocked his way, blocked his third shot.

The killer had snatched up a knife, flourishing it, darting out to the roof garden. Other guns from the waiting detectives stabbed red flashes through the night. The pseudo-butler staggered, badly hurt, dropped to one knee, pitched to all fours as Manning's next shot hit him between the shoulder blades. With incredible vitality he got to his feet, reached the coping and, in a last, prodigious effort, vaulted over it.

They saw him fall, hurtling down to the sidewalk, to lie there broken. Manning sent the men down and went back to the dining room, dismissing the terrified maids as he passed them.

He picked up the spring clip of nickeled metal, holding it carefully. With the blade of his penknife he pressed down the button and saw, as he expected, a fang of steel appear through the tiny orifice in the ebonized disk. The death-point was black. It was covered with poison.

It might never be defined, but Manning believed it to be at least allied to *curari,* the plant juice of *Strychnos* toxifers, or some related species, used for arrow heads and blowgun darts, causing instant paralysis of the lungs from failure of the nerve motors.

A few minutes more and the Palawan would have removed the button, replaced it with the regular one, got rid of the deadly evidence.

The house phone rang. The detective in the hall was speaking.

"A Mr. Fleming, sir. He says he was to be a guest upstairs to-night."

"You told him?"

"Yes, sir. He is sending up his card. He seemed shocked. He has just left."

The elevator that reached the roof dwelling came to rest in the vestibule. The special operator was still running it. He handed Manning an envelope.

Manning opened it. There was a card inside, but it was not engraved. On it was set the scarlet emblem, the rampant griffin's head with curving beak and open claw.

This Fleming had been the Crime Master after all. He had been in the building, but he was gone, swallowed up in the night.

The Griffin, Appearing at Last Before
Manning, Throws Down a New
Defiant Threat to the Manhunter

T HE OWNER and head trainer of the private gymnasium down town where Gordon Manning kept himself
physically fit, looked at the renowned investigator with a
critical eye as he came out of his shower.

"I'd let up on the handball for a while if I was you, Mr.
Manning," he said. "You're looking a bit drawn, a shade too
fine. It's this devilish hot weather, maybe."

To a casual eye, Manning, stepping naked to his locker, would
have looked infinitely fit with his lean, muscular body, brown
almost as a Carib Indian's; but the trainer was an expert of long
standing. Manning was one of his clients in whom he felt pride.
He did not feel that way about all of them, middle-aged business men striving to get rid of the fat and softness of easy living
and unchecked appetites, men with paunches like jelly bags.
But Manning was different. He had never been out of condition,
in peace, nor in war, where he had served with distinction in
the Secret Service. Now he was avowedly a consulting attorney,
but the trainer, though he did not mention it, had an idea that
the trouble might be mental as much as physical.

Manning's eyes were clear and keen as ever, but there were
lines between his brows that were deeper than usual. It could
not be the market. That was steady, and Manning never mentioned stocks. He had told the trainer that he did not speculate.
As for the heat, Manning had traveled far and wide, largely in

the tropics. Eighty degrees, even in Manhattan, was not going to bother him. Besides, he lived in the country suburbs.

He grinned at the trainer genially.

"I'll take your advice," he said. "I do feel a bit stale."

He did not seem like it a few moments later, striding along the street on his way to his office, swinging his especial cane and favorite weapon, a steel rod on which rings of leather were close shrunk, pliable and effective. Now and then he nodded a greeting. Some he did not return through absent-mindedness.

What some people call a hunch was beginning to manifest itself, stronger as he approached the building in which he had his suite. Manning believed by experience, particularly that of his Oriental travel, in many phenomena sometimes called occult; and he felt that he was becoming receptive, tuned in to certain vibrations. The "sending" was of evil influence. He had been expecting something of the sort for days of anxious waiting. Now he was certain that he would receive a more direct communication at his office. It might be in the shape of a letter, written in purple ink on heavy gray paper, in a distinctive, masterful hand. It might be a message over the telephone that could not be traced.

Whichever it was it would come from the Griffin.

Manning had not heard from that mysterious madman for many days. No one knew his name or where he lived, but his deeds were blazoned all over the country, and Manhattan cringed when they read of another of his ghastly, maniacal crimes.

Insane he surely was, but, as a madman has incredible strength, so this man's brain seemed to be inspired to fiendishness in such subtle form that he still roamed at large and laughed at law and order, at all civilization.

In that warped mind of his there might have been a distorted sense of injury that now made itself manifest in devilish determination to attack the best and most useful of men, to destroy them.

Centre Street had tried to cope with him in vain as the list of his crimes mounted, the toll of his victims grew. The police commissioner had persuaded Gordon Manning to take up the trail. Manning had hoped to work under cover, but, the day after his secret appointment, the Griffin had sent him his first communication, accepting the challenge, calling it a game, professing himself amused.

In the murders that followed, Manning had come close to the Griffin himself more than once. He burned for actual contact, though he knew it would be fraught with deadly danger. The Griffin laughed at his efforts. He had some means of synchronizing the telephone system so as to utilize any instrument entirely for his own purposes. Time and time again Manning had heard his haunting, taunting laugh come over the wire.

Sometimes there were strains of exotic music. Always of late there was information that was given in mockery. He had become so daring, so confident, that he announced the name of his intended victim—and even the day on which he would die.

"Stop! No bullets in this gun, Manning.
Only certain waxen poison pellets."

And always, in some fashion, he left on that victim, or in some conspicuous place, his seal, a scarlet cartouche of paper embossed with the design of the Griffin, the fabulous creature of legend, with its ravening beak and cruel eye, a crest of crime. A boast that he had been within striking distance.

It was enough to destroy sleep, to jangle a man's nerves, even one as possessed as Manning. It told on him. The silence as much as the open challenge, the statement of what he meant to do and dared Manning to prevent.

Manning had been thinking recently that it was not altogether the Griffin's demoniac desire to kill certain persons who had come under the ban of his inflamed imagination. He believed that the Griffin, devising some hideously artful means of destruction, experimenting with some new and subtle mode of murder; was obsessed with the desire to see its effect. His madness took the form of an exalted ego, a dementia not merely homicidal but grandiose. He exulted in choosing the most notable so that his deed should be noised abroad. He rejoiced to see the press describe him as a monster, demand that he should be caught.

It aroused this perverted vanity to pit himself against Manning. He held one great advantage. Although he chose to tell Manning when and where he would strike, he had the benefit of preparation. It was like a game of chess, he had told Manning once, and, while it amused him, he was content to play it.

"Cease to amuse me," he threatened. "And the game will end—for you. Don't be too clever."

Nor was that all. The woman Manning loved, whom he believed loved him, had been drawn into the fringes of the Griffin's net on one occasion. Her safety was threatened. That disaster was always hovering. It hung over Manning's head like the famous sword of Damocles. He dared not ask her to marry him because of his own constant danger, and the Griffin had seen through that, had used it as a probe with which to wear down Manning's vitality and powers. It was no wonder that he was drawn fine; that the furrows of thought between his eyebrows had deepened.

And now, he was sure, the Griffin was ready to strike again.

11

IT WAS there, on his desk in the office that looked out beyond the towers of Manhattan to the busy river and its spanning bridges. The biggest city in the world, the busiest, made the hunting ground, the web of this monster.

A square, gray envelope of handmade paper. The bold, somewhat erratic writing in purple ink. The scarlet seal.

Manning had tried to trace that paper in vain. As for the writing, it was at present a futile clew. To the expert Manning had chosen to analyze it, it had formed the basis of a remarkable report that coincided marvelously with Manning's preconception of the Griffin's character.

He opened it without hesitation. With the prospect of action his pulses quickened, his brain seemed charged with unusual vigor. The lassitude that had crept upon him lately vanished. This time, surely, he would cope with the Griffin, capture him, meet wile with wile.

> My dear Manning:
>
> I trust I have not been harrying you through my silence. I have been conducting certain most interesting experiments which, while they are not yet entirely finished, are sufficiently conclusive to permit me to advise you of my next enterprise.
>
> The man I have chosen to eliminate is Everett Payson, that smug saint, that medieval moron, who has been striving absurdly to reconcile science with religion, who has made the statement that Science can accept the idea of a future life with—mark this—individuality retained after death.
>
> It is my intention to let him prove his own theory. You may have noticed the controversy of late in the *Times*. I don't know if those matters interest you. If so it may not altogether sur-

prise you to know that the letters signed Lucifer came from me. To any sane person they would be utterly convincing, but this self ordained professor, this champion of worn-out creeds, refuses to acknowledge defeat.

There is but one way to stop it.

It will be on Tuesday, which is to-morrow, my dear Manning, to-morrow from the day you receive this.

I throw down the gage to you. Surround him with protection or let him depend upon Divine Providence, coupled of course by your own personal efforts. But he will surely solve the vexing question some time between daylight and dark on Tuesday—which happens to be the thirteenth.

Payson, of course, thinks he is not superstitious. For that jest I could almost let him off if the fool did not go spread his nauseous, noxious syrup. But there is, as you must know from your own experience, much virtue in numbers, figures. I have calculated the horoscope of Everett Payson, and his star even now enters the House of Death.

It is even possible I may see you on this occasion. I am not sure that you amuse me any longer.

Most sincerely,
THE GRIFFIN.

There was a clever sketch of a Griffin's head in lieu of actual signature.

As Manning laid the letter down his telephone rang. The vibrations of the bell were not as usual. They held a quality that was distinct, sinister. It seemed as if the Griffin had timed the reception and reading of his letter, for it was the Griffin talking.

"Lest you forget, Manning. To-morrow, Tuesday, the thirteenth. Everett Payson. And who knows what else may happen? I have decided to leave the matter of your elimination to chance and circumstance. Don't let it upset your judgment, or lose you any sleep. You are not looking too keen the last fortnight."

The deep voice ceased. Manning would know that voice anywhere. There came the echo of a derisive laugh, a faint sound of macabre music.

Everett Payson!

A man unique in this time and generation. A man of simple, steadfast faith, who sought to offset the evils of the age by its restoration. A man who went about doing good. Universally beloved and respected by all but those who jeered at righteousness.

That he should be marked for death was too hideous.

Manning did not know him, but he knew others who did, and he commenced immediately preparations to get in touch with him, to take precautions for his defense.

Some time between daylight and dark!

The Griffin never spoke falsely; until now he had never threatened idly.

III

THE GRIFFIN sat at his carved desk in the circular steel room at the top of his dwelling. Back of him squatted his West Indian dwarf, his bodyguard, fantastically arrayed as some court manikin of the middle ages, inordinately proud, devoted, chiefly through intense fear, to the Griffin. He bore a great knife, keen as a razor. He waited constantly for the word that would unleash him upon some one whom he could butcher to show his devotion.

Squat and misshapen, ugly and apelike, he was as strong as an orangutan.

The walls were covered with a golden weave. Curiously enough incense burned. There were no windows but the air was kept in circulation by mechanical means, the lighting was hidden. From somewhere came strains of music, ultra-modern, sensuous.

Deep in the cellars of this place the Griffin had his laboratories where men chosen for their genius in various arts labored like slaves, nameless, never permitted to leave the place, brought there by means that left them no inkling of their whereabouts.

All of them were outcasts from their professions, from their friends, by some act against the law. The Griffin held them in thrall with that knowledge. They were his, utterly.

Under the rich weaves that were spread upon the floor a shaft could yawn at a touch from the Griffin's hand or foot, opening with a clang like a greedy cry from its steel month, closing on secrets not to be revealed.

In front of the Griffin was a bronze disk skillfully suspended. On the desk also were writing materials in semiprecious stones, an exquisite carving of a griffin—entire—the winged beast of mythology, of heraldry and ancient Greek architecture; progeny of a lion and an eagle, winged, four-legged, armed with claws and beak. Fitting symbol for the ruthless man who sat silent, listening to the music.

He was clad in a dressing robe of somber but elaborate brocade, a skull cap of the same material covering the crown of his head. He wore a mask, yellow, pliable, thin as gold-beater's skin. It clung to his features, to his nose, hooked as the carved griffin's. It showed his broad brow. It revealed the formidable jaw. It revealed, and yet it screened, confused. It gave him a frightful, lifeless aspect, made the more fantastic and sinister by the burning eyes that looked through slits, like jewels lit by internal flames. Hard as jewels, these orbs. At times they seemed like tiny windows of dark glass through which one saw the murk and flame of hell. The eyes of a madman.

The disk vibrated, gave out a mellow boom.

A section of the curving wall slid aside and revealed an elevator that had just ascended. From it stepped a bewildered-looking man, habited like a tramp, unshaven, dirty, dusty in his rags. He stared at the room, at the image-like figure of the dwarf, at the awesome being behind the desk, still as a statue, with eyes that seared the newcomer. He listened to the music, sniffed the incense.

"Say, what's dis racket?" he asked in a professional whine. He was a typical jungle buzzard, picked up out of town by one of the few of those who served the Griffin and had liberty.

He had tried to cadge the price of a meal, a flop, or a shot of alky; and he had been told that he would be taken to a man who was a philanthropist. He knew the meaning of that word. He had grafted from many whose sympathies were as soft as he imagined their brains to be.

But this—this was different. He wanted to get away from that silent and sinister figure, but the elevator had gone down automatically, the wall had closed behind him. It showed no seam, no sign on its golden tapestries.

"What's the idea?" he faltered, his professional braggadocio leaving him, his ideas of a soft snap vanishing.

"You have no need to be afraid," said the Griffin. The mask covered his mouth, but his voice was not muffled, resonant and deep. I am a benefactor of men. I presume you are hungry?"

"Yes, guv'nor."

"You will be fed immediately. I suppose you would prefer a chopped steak and onions, but you must permit me to serve you my own ideas of a meal. I trust it will not be entirely lost on you. There will be wines, rather than crude alcohol, the palate as well as the stomach is considered."

"God bless you, guv'nor."

"Do you believe in God? Never mind. I am not really interested. That word reminded me of some one. Do you happen to know anything of Everett Payson?"

"The guy that feeds the grease-spots, the down-and-outs? Sure I know him. I've seen him, heard him talk. He don't preach at you, but he makes you believe things. Gives you good grub, slips you a piece of change once in a while, hands out clothing and shoes. He's *right*, he is."

"Ah! Well. I am something of a wizard myself. A kindly one. After you have eaten I promise you this. That you will never again know hunger or thirst, nor heat nor cold, nor want of any kind. What more can a man ask for? No worries, no distress. And here comes the food."

The disk had sounded again. Two Negroes in livery brought

a table, a serving wagon, a chair and dishes from the elevator. They placed them elaborately in front of the tramp. They gave him wine that he gulped, turtle soup, terrapin, a tender guinea hen cooked with grapes, a generous Burgundy, vegetables, all of which he devoured in a sort of wondering haze. He stopped picking the drumstick of the fowl to speak.

"Guv'nor, this is okay. They say they give you anything you ask for in the dance-hall, that's the death-house, see, for your last meal. Well, after a feed like this, I wouldn't care if I never woke up."

A slight wrinkle showed on the mask. It might have been a smile.

"You can clear, save for the salad and the dessert," the Griffin told the colored waiters. "Leave the coffee. I'll summon you later."

"That," he told the hobo, looking doubtfully at the creamy fruit in an emerald skin before him, "is an avocado pear. In Mexico they call it Montezuma's butter. Perhaps an acquired taste. I am anxious to see how it affects you."

"Whatever you say goes with me, guv'nor. You're a prince. What do I tackle it with, a fork or a spoon?"

"A spoon. There is a salad dressing goes with it. So."

When the waiters reappeared the grotesque guest was gone. They cleared and left swiftly.

Time passed, with the dwarf still like a graven image, save when he lit the hubble-bubble pipe filled with Arabian and Turkish blend, tinged with hasheesh, that the Griffin smoked through a flexible tube, the smoke passing through rose water. The music changed from time to time.

At length the disk sounded again, the elevator ascended, its door slid back. A man, gray, almost bald, clad in overalls stained with chemicals, entered the room. He set down a crystal phial on the desk.

"It is finished, so far as I can carry it," he said.

"What do you mean by that, Forty-One?"

The Griffin's even tones were menacing. The man cringed visibly. A fellow of education and refinement once, a famous chemist who had once played the charlatan for money, and run afoul of the government.

"I mean that it is an antidote, that it will restore life within a reasonable time, but I cannot guarantee that it will restore the action of the mind. The elements of the toxical potion were new to me. They need study. You called for haste.

"And not for excuses. It might embarrass you if you were to be taken from here, set down whence I had you brought. It is a pity that your antidote was not here half an hour ago. I am afraid you have a death on your soul—Forty-One—if you believe you have a soul. Do you?"

"If I had I have lost it," said the man bitterly.

"Traded it, perhaps. Well. I have another subject on hand. As for you, see that you serve me better. Now go."

IV

EVERETT PAYSON lived in a modest but comfortable apartment that occupied one whole second floor of one of a row of houses of identical architecture west of Sixth Avenue, well below the Twenties. He was a man of ample means, who devoted most of them to charity and the amelioration of conditions of the poor, as well as the propagation of religion. He was far from narrow and embraced all creeds. He claimed the world needed faith in a Supreme Being and belief in the Hereafter.

From the first moment of the thirteenth, though the Griffin had specifically named the space between dawn and dusk, Manning had the house guarded, in front, on the roof, and from the rear.

The Griffin had said nothing about his preparations. He might keep his word—or try to—concerning the actual hour limit for his crime—but he might trick them by making his preparations earlier. There were two men on the ground floor.

They had a list of all those who lived in the house. No stranger would be allowed to enter or exit without questioning, without probable detention.

Only one apartment was vacant, the front half of the third floor, with five floors in the house. It was leased, the landlady told Manning, two weeks before by a man who gave suitable references, paid a month in advance for a friend, now in Massachusetts, detained there by a throat operation. They entered this and searched it. Two men with ready weapons were by the scuttle on the roof. With everybody warned, it would go hard with any one trying to pass there.

Several of those who lived there went to daily business. To none of them was the Griffin's name mentioned, for fear of panic, of spreading talk. Such a rumor would, Manning knew, bring a curious crowd to the street all day long. Such a crowd might well be a cover for the Griffin and his emissaries.

As to whether the Griffin was serious in his somewhat covert threat on his own life, Manning did not speculate, save as it might bring the Griffin in person. That idea—that hope to come to close quarters with the arch-fiend—seemed impossible of fulfillment. Reserves were close by. There were forty operatives in the neighborhood, with cars and motor cycles for pursuit, besides the men on beat and traffic duty.

It appeared as if the Griffin were blocked, unless he could pass through solid walls. With the first light of dawn Manning had every exit watched. On the plea of certain suspicious characters having been seen in the neighborhood he had the whole house searched from roof to cellar.

At six o'clock he pressed the button to Payson's apartment. It opened promptly. Everett Payson was an early riser. He had the habits of a monk, he looked like a prior, Manning thought, his countenance serene yet strong, shining with inner fire that glowed through the shell of his flesh. Here was a good man. Goodness emanated from him. With robes and sandals he could have passed for some one straight from the cloister.

He greeted Manning cordially.

"It is good of you to share my meals and stay with me to-day, though I feel that what may or may not happen is guided only by Divine Providence. If I can be the instrument of ridding the community of this monster, of placing him where he can do no more harm, I am more than willing to surrender my own life, if that be necessary."

He smiled, to temper words that Manning could construe as melodramatic. The place was nicely furnished, though lacking any sign of luxury. Manning examined it with a serious face, lined with responsibility. He looked out to the street, the community garden at the rear, into all closets and every room. It did not seem feasible that the Griffin or any of his men could ever break through the cordon he had set, and yet—he had seen the Griffin's work before, and while he was not physically afraid, he did not underestimate the unknown resources of the Griffin. They had too often come like a bolt from the blue when protection seemed positively proof.

"My appetite is slight, my menu a little abstemious," said Payson. "I prepare my own meals, attend to all my housekeeping. I have had certain things added to my little larder that I hope will satisfy you. There can be no danger lurking in any of them, I am sure. I took your advice of yesterday.

"Grapefruit is my weakness. It abounds in vitamines. I have a box sent in every week. It came yesterday. I shall prepare them myself. Eggs are in the shell. Coffee in an unopened can. The same with our soup and meat. I have a fresh carton of flour with which to show you my domestic skill at making biscuits. Baking powder in a can. Sugar in an unbroken carton. Evaporated milk in its tin. We shall not fare sumptuously but sufficiently, and I trust you can put up with my company, I am rated something of a crank, you know," he added whimsically.

"I am interested in your work," said Manning gravely. "And you must let me help in the cooking. I am a fair hand at it."

"Then let us start breakfast. I'll prepare the grapefruit. It is so often clumsily done—not that I refer to you—but I like to do it neatly. You will have one, or share one, with me? Or do you prefer oranges? I have both."

"I'll take the oranges," Manning replied. "Domestic grapefruits are excellent, but I have tried the wild shaddocks of the tropics. Their pith is unbelievably bitter, like quinine. They gave me a permanent distaste for the fruit. I'll make the coffee and poach some eggs."

"We must not forget the biscuits. They will not take long—to make or bake."

Payson held up one of the golden globes of grapefruit, calling attention to the marketing and advertising brand stamped on the skin.

"There is a perfect product," he said. "The Greek fruiterer and grocer at the corner selects them for me."

He halved the fruit, meticulously cutting free the pulp in sections from the rest, lightly sugaring it, placing the halves on ice before he mixed his biscuits deftly and set them in the gas oven.

"This Griffin reminds me of those who were said to be possessed of devils in the old days," said Payson. "It is sad we have no one to cast them out. Faith is sadly weak these days. Of course the devils were a form of speech used by the ignorant. His glands do not function. It is hard to minister to a mind diseased, but surely his body could be treated with modern surgery. He is sick, and should be cured."

"He is a foul murderer," said Manning sternly. "He should be put out of the way. Annihilated."

Payson shook his head in deprecation. He did not seem to underestimate his danger, and Manning admired and envied the quality of his courage.

"His chief crime," said Payson, "is in destroying Faith, the hope of a future life. Taking away the consolation of the hundreds of thousands whose lives are filled with toil and care and sorrow. And, if there were no punishment, equally with reward, no belief in the power of divinity, what would restrain any man from crime, from theft, from murder, the whole decalogue of sins? This Griffin would erase all unselfishness, all decency. It is incredible that his mind can be so warped, yet he is but a sick man."

Manning said nothing. He had his own opinion of the Griffin and what his punishment should be. There was nothing adequate under the law for the horrors he had caused, the losses the community had sustained through his acts.

Here was Payson mildly qualifying his deviltries as sickness, ready enough to forgive him—and the Griffin was surely at work, unseen, unheard, mining through all protection as a mole tunnels, unseen and unheard, beneath the surface of the lawn it destroys.

Manning was sensitive, he was wrought up. Zero hour had started with daylight. It seemed to him that he was receiving evil vibrations, that the atmosphere of that quiet apartment was charged with them. He went once more all through it. He made a patrol of the house, saw all in order, all in place, and returned just as Payson was dishing up the biscuits. Still he could not shake off the sense of impending disaster. As surely as one feels the aërial symptoms of a gathering storm, he felt evil entering, feared that it had entered.

Payson set the table. Manning had his orange juice, Payson his grapefruit. A canary was singing in the sunny window. Flowers sent by friends were blooming. The setting was pleasant, but dread stood at Manning's shoulder. He was tempted to tell Payson to eat nothing, and yet it was surely all innocuous.

"A perfect fruit," Payson repeated, spooning free a section of juicy pulp. He swallowed it, gulped with suddenly staring eyes, fell forward on the little table—dead.

Manning knew it. The Griffin had struck. How, he could as yet only surmise. Struck truly and surely. There would be no reviving Payson. Some deadly poison had stilled his heart, paralyzed his veins, curdled his life blood. Already his flesh was changing color. First the pallid, putty hue of death, then an angry purple flush that crept over face and neck, that showed in hands swelling to shapelessness.

Manning whirled to call the doctor who stood ready by his telephone, to call his men. Yet he knew they had not let any one pass them.

V

A MAN STOOD in the doorway, silently closing it with one hand. A tall man in a black cloak, a curious mask over his face. It looked to Manning in that swift, nervous moment, as his hand shot to his shoulder-holstered gun like the skin of a shedding snake.

The Griffin. He had dared to appear. How, Manning did not care. He was close to his man at last.

"Stop! No bullets in this gun, Manning. Only certain waxen pellets that will be taken up with the poison in their tiny capsules, absorbed by your tissues. I think you remember them. Stop. Unless you want to die. No report. An air chamber. I shall leave as I came, despite your men. If you still want to lay me by my heels, Manning, keep still."

Manning remembered when those pellets were last used. He kept his hands away from his gun. There was no sense in following Payson into the shades if he could avenge him.

He backed up, upsetting the telephone stand. The Griffin laughed.

"Resourceful, Manning, but useless. I have seen that it is out of order. I hardly expected to find you alive. It seems you prefer oranges to the grapefruit. And it is as well. I find you still amuse me. Sit down. We are not likely to be disturbed. All went off smoothly, silently. Not very spectacular, not like the exploding golf balls—you remember those, Manning? But efficient—and simple!

"The late Everett Payson, who is now discovering whether there is a heaven or not, to use a metaphor, since he is past discovering anything, was a methodical man. It was easy to find our about his grapefruit habit and its purchase. I had a box delivered here that was substituted for the actual one. Quite simple. It was even a Greek who brought it finally. I like attention to details.

"The fruit had been carefully punctured through one of the pores of the rind, where even your perceptive powers could not find it with a hypodermic needle—you may sit if you wish, Manning, and I will relieve you of that useless, clumsy gun."

Manning perforce obeyed. The Griffin took his weapon, searched him for more, his own air pistol with its deadly pellets ever ready.

"As for the poison, I doubt if it can be analyzed. I have very carefully prepared it. There is an antidote, but, unfortunately, if used, it leaves the subject bereft of sense, an idiot. I tested it. For a while I was tempted to use it on Payson. It would have been a rare jest to see him drivelling, but I had promised myself—and you—to kill him. I could not disappoint you."

"You are mad yourself," said Manning. "That brain of yours is rotten. There are maggots in it that will some day corrupt your reason."

Through the semitransparent material of the mask Manning could see an angry flush ebb and flow. The Griffin's eyes blazed. Here was the weakness that he sometimes feared himself.

"You talk too much," he said. "I do not find it amusing, Manning. Let us return to poisons. I have made a study of them. There is the venom of those insects that sting their victim, paralyze, deposit their eggs within the living body that will feed their young. I have worked with that, modified it, produced a toxin that numbs the body, finally the brain, for a certain period.

"That is it."

With incredible swiftness, like the strike of a serpent, he darted out his hand. Manning felt a shallow prick and then the Griffin stepped back.

"A few seconds and you cannot move. A few minutes and

you will be unconscious. Even now you will find you cannot speak. So I shall leave you. In the meantime I want you to hear how I arrived, how I shall depart. I never employ the same method twice. Each special problem has to be studied. And you make it harder for me, Manning. You tax my powers of enjoyment of your actions."

The stuff was working. Its action, though far swifter, was like that of *kawa*, which leaves the brain clear and robs the body of all coördination. Manning found that he could not even move his lips, much less his fingers. Yet he saw and heard perfectly.

"On the third floor I hired the front apartment in this house. It has stayed unused. On the third floor next door I took another. Both take in the whole front with hall bedrooms. That, from time to time I have visited, entertained others. Last night my experts went through the dividing wall between the houses. They worked well and fast and silently.

"To open the door into this house was simple. Simple for one of my men to skeletonize a key for the late Everett Payson's apartment. I used it just now. Last night he was snoring. Now he sleeps more soundly. I return by the same means, Manning, avoiding observation. Later I shall leave the house next door. While you stay here until they find you with the man you meant to protect."

Manning made a supreme effort. It seemed as if his will must break the force of the drug that held him. He could not even quiver, but his attempt must have showed in his eyes for the Griffin laughed quietly but mockingly.

"I must really let you live, Manning. After all, you *are* quite amusing. I shall communicate with you again. I have a rare idea. It will be quite spectacular this next time—quite spectacular. And now there is one more formality."

He took from his vest pocket a little case of gold inlaid with lapis lazuli and opened it. There were seals inside, oblong cartouches of scarlet with a Griffin's head embossed on them.

He moistened the gum and set one of them on Manning's forehead.

He lifted Payson's head, now hideously discolored, and pressed another in the same place.

"When you come to, Manning, you might as well have the rest of those grapefruit thrown away. I am not a wholesale killer. Ah, I see the drug is working."

Manning strove to keep his lids apart. Drowsiness swept over him. The Griffin vanished from his sight and he was left there, unconscious, with Everett Parson, who had solved his controversy with the man who wrote over the *nom de plume* of Lucifer, so far as Payson was concerned.

*The Diabolical Genius of Crime Reaches Out
to Snatch a Victim from the Broad Atlantic*

THE THREE bodies lay limp on the grass in the Bronx
Park Reservation. They were all dressed alike in brown,
zip-closing overalls, stained and well worn. Many early drivers
passed them and thought them sleepers after an alky festival.
Others, imagining they might be the aftermath of some racket,
of a highjacking raid, forbore to meddle, with the cynical
wisdom of the New Yorker.

They lay there, prone and immobile, save for the almost
imperceptible lift of their chests; like three dummies rather
than men. One was bearded, another bald. All were well on in
middle life, all showed signs of high intelligence. They appeared
to be of a much higher type than their clothing indicated. The
hands of two of them were stained with chemicals, of the third
with grease, but they were all the hands of men of imagination,
likely to be specialists, experts, rather than common workmen.

A cycle cop finally investigated, reported through the telephone.

"Three guys laid out here on the Driveway," he said. "Dead
to the world. They don't smell of hooch, but they are sure out.
I can't wake 'em, can't get a rise out of 'em. No—I tried that.
Look and act like they had that sleeping sickness."

An ambulance came, the callous interne looked them over.

"They ain't drunk," he said, then, turning up their eyelids,
"and they don't seem to be doped. But they ain't got any more

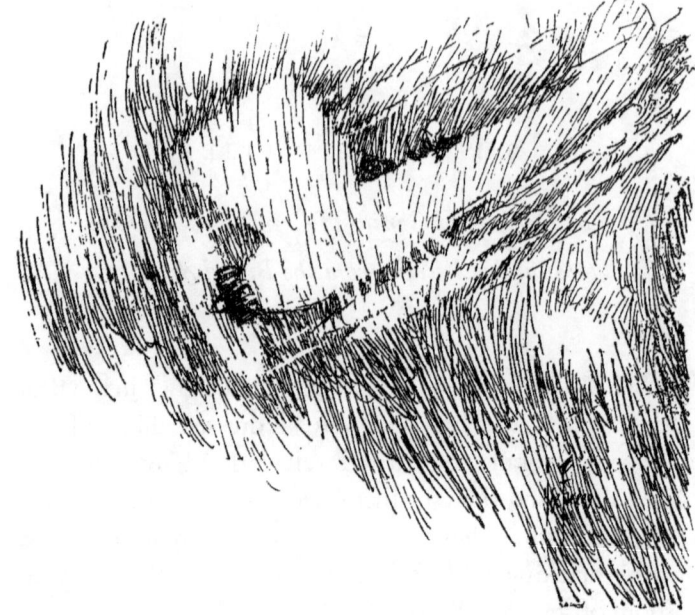

pulse between 'em than a sick humming bird. We'll take 'em in."

The tabloids made a brief of it. So did the afternoon editions. The proverbial noses for news on the part of their eager reporters were not working on that occasion. It was the morning papers that started the news, making crisp conservative comment over what the others would, and justly should, have hailed as a mystery.

Doctors on the Bellevue clinic gathered in consultation, baffled. Others came in curiosity and proved no wiser. There was absolutely nothing about any of the three to even suggest identification beyond an intimate description of their bodies. No one thought of finger-prints until later. All that was known was that they were in a stupor, that all of them were sinking, their vitality lowering hour by hour, respiration a light sigh, pulses a mere flutter. Injections, all attempts at arousing them failed. They were well nourished enough and enforced feeding was not necessary.

But second by second, minute by minute, as the hands went round the circles of the clock, their sands of life were trickling out. The physicians marked the characteristics of culture and education, the fine skull formations that did not go with the brown overalls, the coarse underwear and socks, the cheap shoes and the crude hair cutting. They noticed also that every face was lined with care, masked with a registration of dull despair.

It was a good story now. It was a better one after the commissioner of police had mentioned the matter to the special investigator he had appointed in the matter of the Griffin, the murderous madman who had terrified Manhattan and mocked at the police with his announced assassinations of the most famous and useful men of the community.

No one had been able to get any clew to the Griffin's identity or locate his whereabouts. Manning had been close to grips with him, had glimpsed him, almost foiled him, and he was ever on the alert for something that would link up with the Griffin. He had meant to work under cover, but the morning after his appointment the Griffin had written to congratulate

"My God!" cried some one. "We've only got five minutes more!"

him, to challenge him in what he termed the "game." Now Manning was in the open, so far at least as the Griffin and his emissaries were concerned. He fancied that this new, strange mystery, disconnected as it seemed on the surface, might furnish him a lead.

He entertained this idea because of the strange condition of the patients. The Griffin was ever experimenting with new drugs and poisons, or managing to gain information of them. Manning himself, once major in the Secret Service during the war, traveler in far-off places, particularly the Orient, knew of potions and infusions that could produce trances, slowly destroy life or rot the brain. These conditions resembled the deviltry of the Griffin. Therefore he investigated.

On his way to Bellevue to meet the commissioner he telephoned Von Reithmann, authority on pellagra, sleeping sickness and forms of narcotic depression.

"It looks like henbane-hyoscine," pronounced the scientist. "Not the usual variety—*Hyoscyamus niger*—probably a tropical variety, more powerful, more deadly. Ordinary henbane is a powerful poison. These men are sinking into a death coma."

He looked again at their eyes, more expertly than the interne had done, shook his head.

"Two of them are pretty far along," he pronounced. "I doubt if we can get them back. All tissues attacked. Their eyes are gone. This one is younger, he seems more vital. We can try stimulants on him. We'll start with adrenalin. It is possible he may talk," he added. "His tongue and palate are in better condition than the others. Ah!"

He had been feeling the pulses of the two others simultaneously. Now he bent down, set his head against the chest of one, called for a stethoscope. To both they gave deep injections of adrenalin, but they were gone to the Land of Shadows. He worked with the doctors in attendance on the younger subject.

Manning, forewarned, hoping for some such thing to take place, had brought a microphonic attachment by which he could hear the merest whispers. A nurse volunteered to take down the notes he gave, just as they might come from the patient, to be interpreted later.

It was hard to piece together those vague and disconnected mutterings that followed the administration of the stimulants. The man's will strove to make communication. His shattered nervous system failed to plug in on his cerebral connections, his glands could no longer supply the galvanic fluids, save weakly and spasmodically; but a gleam came into Manning's eyes as he listened.

To the rest they sounded like ravings. Talk of a subterranean place where men worked as prisoners under the will of a fiend. Men who had no longer names, but only numbers, who were under the thrall of Him who ordered their tasks. Talk of a circular room of steel, draped with golden tapestries, of mysterious music, of a Being who wore a strange mask over his hawklike features, who laughed mockingly as Satan.

The Griffin!

Manning had heard that jeering laughter, the mysterious music, over the telephone that transmitted the Griffin's menacing messages, instruments synchronized by him so that they were, for the time, private lines. He would well imagine the underground laboratory, the men enslaved there, the circular chamber of steel. He had seen the man in the strange mask.

But he could not prompt the man, could not get questions through to his failing brain. The mutterings ceased. Von Reithmann and the rest tried to restore him, but it was useless. The narcotic had done its work too thoroughly. One of the Griffin's men had been in their hands. Others, when captured, had refused to talk. This one had slipped through. They were no nearer the Griffin's real name—if indeed the man had known it—or the place where he made his lair.

"An autopsy may determine the poison," Von Reithmann was saying. Manning paid scant attention. Analysis would not mean anything to him. The stuff had not been bought where it could be traced. It had been infused perhaps by one of these men, one of the two who had chemical stains on their fingers, it might be the one who had babbled and then died.

Manning was thinking, following up the thought. For some reason these men had been deliberately discarded by the Griffin. In some way they had displeased him—failed him. Only one with a hidden well of vitality had to some extent survived his intentions. To leave them dying, but not dead, to mock at the efforts of doctors to restore them while they guessed at police headquarters as to motives; was the sort of jest that pleased the Griffin and tickled his grim sense of humor.

But—why should he have such supreme control over men whose mental capacity seemed so superior?

Because he had something on them. There were plenty of chemists, doctors, scientists, men high in engineering and all the professions who had fallen, been expunged from the society of their fellows and the practice of their callings by some lapse, some error that had, in all likelihood, branded them as felons.

They would have records.

He handed on his deduction to the commissioner of police, recommending finger-prints to be taken, the Identification Bureau put to work, requests broadcast for reports.

The prints were sent out by radio-print, but the answers were found at Centre Street.

They had their names, their records, up to the time that they had disappeared below the surface. One a chemist, one an ex-surgeon and general practitioner, the other a well-known consulting engineer. No need now to publish them. They threw light on the Griffin's methods, explained something of his seemingly infernal genius. The man was not omniscient. He had the cunning brain of one inflicted with grandiose dementia, he could plan evil, and these castaways of civilizations worked out his problems. Now their lips—and the lips of headquarters, were sealed by their death.

"There might have been some sort of minor mutiny,"

Manning said to the commissioner. "They may have rebelled against something that the Griffin contemplated as too horrible to even barter their lives against. So he made examples of them, had them conveyed unconscious to the Driveway. I wouldn't give out anything to the press about the Griffin."

The commissioner shook his head.

"The less the public hear of that scoundrel the better," he said. "Sends a wave of hysteria out that is like the circles from a rock in a millpond, extending to the outer edges of the community. It even affects the stock market. And, above all, it pleases the Griffin. Notoriety is his favorite nutriment. I shall not even give out the identity of the poor devils who have paid their penalties. No sense in making their families suffer. The Griffin is like a ghost, Manning. We seem to clutch him and our fingers close on thin air."

"I'll grip him yet," said Manning slowly. "And, when I do, I'm not going to let go—alive or dead."

11

THE TELEPHONE in Manning's suite of offices, on the outer door of which he was announced as a consulting attorney, rang with that peculiar vibration he had grown to know so well and, not so much to dread as to listen to with nerves suddenly taut, his spirit arming itself for sinister adventure.

It never rang in that fashion but when he was in his private room. He knew that the Griffin had means of watching his ordinary comings and goings—no especially difficult matter. It never rang, so far, but what it presaged death and disaster. It took a sturdy man with a strong will to not lose heart in these encounters, always fatal to some worthy and notable person.

The audacity of the Griffin had grown to the point where he deliberately announced to Gordon Manning, as his adversary, the name of his next victim and the day on which he would surely die, despite all of Manning's precautions, backed by the police force of New York. The methods of these tragedies, that left millions of people aghast as they read of them, were subtle and unique.

It was a challenge that the Griffin sought to liken to a game of chess. He would play it in this way, announcing his first moves to Manning, so long as it amused him, he announced. If Gordon Manning pressed him too far, too close, he threatened to eliminate him, to wreak his anger on the woman Manning loved, but had foresworn while engaged on the perilous mission he had accepted.

So long as the Griffin lived, love was out of the question for Manning. The girl had once been within those swift and far flung coils of the Griffin, like the tentacles of an octopus. Now she was free, yet she was threatened. Manning stood between love and duty, and relinquished the former for the girl's own sake, even though he might lose her to another.

He took up the telephone unhesitatingly and immediately the deep tones of the Griffin came to him. And, as always, there was an undertone of music, mysterious, exotic.

"Ah, there you are, Manning. A busy day for you. It was clever of you to imagine that those three disobedient fools might be men of mine, I did not set the scarlet seal on their foreheads, for that is reserved for those I choose to annihilate for other reasons than that they refuse to carry out my own wishes. These three were squeamish. Now they are dead. One, it seems, babbled a bit, but what he could tell was negligible. And the drug I gave him instantly destroys full coördination of brain as well as body.

"A useful drug, very. It comes from the Caribbean. They use it in voodoo. An active alkaloid, not unlike scopolamine, but virulent in its breakdown of the tissues and leucocytes. Most interesting.

"You continue to amuse me, Manning. I trust you have sense of humor enough to appreciate that. My next selection for elimination is...."

Manning's eyes narrowed during the deliberate pause. He refused to be annoyed at the Griffin's derision of himself, but here was another victim marked down. It was his own special mission to prevent the crime—and to capture the Griffin.

"Edward Brooks, that meddler in international affairs," went on the sonorous voice, "that self-advertising politician who has ambitions that will never be realized! That would-be diplomat! He would have been wiser to have kept to the manufacture of washing machines that made his fortune. He is a colossal egoist who shall be destroyed, inevitably, despite all your efforts, Manning, some time between midnight of the ninth of the month and midnight of the tenth. Now go to work, perfect your arrangements—and find yourself once more checkmated on the board. I shall be close by when it happens, Manning, depend on that. And it will furnish front page news."

The voice ceased with a rumble of mocking laughter, the strains of mystic melody.

In that last sentence Manning read, as he had read before, much that was the key to the Griffin's character. He was a dangerous madman. His own supreme conceit would be fed by those front page stories, while he charged the man he meant to kill with his own disease.

He claimed to give Manning every advantage in proclaiming his opening moves, but Manning knew that each crime was long thought out, perfected after an intimate study of the prospective victim's habits.

There was a kink to the Griffin's mind that may have been aggravated by the contemplation of some real or fancied injury that had set him against law and order, progress and enlightenment, made him a pseudo-iconoclast of all that was decent and honorable, a foe to justice and religion. Jealousy perhaps entered into it.

Here was Edward Brooks, millionaire manufacturer, it was true, and a man of sound sense and judgment, who had forged ahead by sheer merit. He had been ambassador abroad and served with distinction in various crises. He had aided materially the peace commissions and arms reduction boards. He was prominent in the Russian problem and the recognition question of the Soviet, the problems of Poland and the Balkans. He was the dark horse of one party for the presidency.

And the Griffin consigned him to oblivion as carelessly as a man might plan to remove some noxious vermin.

Manning sat staring out of his window, hardly seeing the towers of Manhattan, the bridges, the busy shipping of the great city he loved, infested by this monster. His face was lined and looked old in its leanness. He was in the prime of life and physical condition, but the strain of fighting the Griffin, or tracking him to his lair, of destroying this dragon against whom he was a modern St. George, had told upon him.

Always spare, he was worn to the quick in body and spirit. The burning resolve to rid the world of this perverted but powerful wretch burned high, like a consuming fever, devoured his sleep. His eyes shone with the light that also illumined the working of his brain. His hands were clenched until the knuckles showed white, little knots of muscles tossed along the lines of his jaw, veins stood out. The will of the man, defeated and enduring, gave a curious transparency and radiance to his well cut, determined features.

Manning did not meddle in politics, but he used them on occasion. Through the police commissioner he got in touch with a man powerful enough to secure for him a practically immediate interview with Brooks.

"He is laying a corner stone for the new Memorial Hospital in the Bronx," said the man. "I'll get in touch with him. If you can go directly you will be in time to see him before the ceremonies are over and you will find him ready to talk. I understand that this matter is imperative, Mr. Manning?"

"It is." Manning took no public credit for his work against the Griffin. His failure and his ultimate success—of which he was steadfastly assured—reflected on the police commissioner.

The man to whom he was speaking did not suspect the gravity of the occasion, and Manning did not enlighten him. Such matters were not to be talked of over the telephone.

He went down, got his powerful roadster from the garage and started north. He had plates, a card, a badge, and other matters that secured him right of way if he wanted them, and he used them to get through the heart of New York, to make sure of finding his man.

III

BROOKS WAS a big man in more ways than one. An astute one. He knew of Manning, he guessed on what errand he might have come, but he showed no tremor in his greeting, in his conducting of the ceremony.

"We will go back together to my hotel, Manning," he suggested with cordiality. "I suppose there is nothing likely to interfere with that?"

His words showed Manning that Brooks knew. He admired the high courage of the man. It could hardly stiffen his resolve to save him, but it did enhance the diabolical nature of the Griffin's plot. Here was the highest type of truly patriotic American, imperiled by the fantasy of a lunatic.

Brooks lived in Westchester County, but he reserved a suite of rooms high up in the tower of one of New York's newest and most select hostelries, the last word in convenience and luxury—and expense.

He invited Manning to dinner, dismissing other engagements for the evening on Manning's estimate that their talk would be lengthy. The investigator wanted to acquire at least an equal knowledge with the Griffin of Brooks's mode of living. Appraising his man, he made no restriction as to the gravity of the situation.

Brooks entered into it gravely, listened to Manning's brief recital or recapitulation of the Griffin's crimes, more particularly since he had been working on them.

"You wish, I assume," he said, "to afford me protection, to be with me yourself during the threatened period. You state that the Griffin, who is undoubtedly insane, may be depended upon, if one may use that word in such a grisly business, to make his attempt during that stated time. Not to, would, I imagine, be a blow at his own conceit."

Manning nodded.

"Without prejudice, it would seem my predecessors in his plots have been unfortunate." Brooks went on, "through no fault of yours or the police department. This Griffin is a resourceful villain with a brain inflamed to weird and bizarre ideas that, so far, have baffled protection. However, this time I think the Griffin will be foiled."

Manning listened attentively.

He had heard almost precisely such statements of assurance on each occasion of his conferences with the men the Griffin had marked for death. All had been men of brains, some of great resources, yet this confidence, backed by his own efforts, had failed.

"It happens," Brooks went on, "and this is a matter known only to the President, certain members of the Cabinet and the head of the Secret Service, that I am about to depart on a strictly secret mission. You are the only other person to know this. I may not tell even you what this mission is, save that it is important to world progress.

"The point is that I sail on the France at midnight on the eighth. My incognito may be discovered after we sail, hardly before. The suite has been retained in the name of the man, a high official at Washington, who, ostensibly, I shall be seeing off. I should have done so in any case. He will take another suite reserved in still another name. I shall simply not go ashore with the rest when the steamer sails. You know the confusion of those midnight sailings. It is impossible to tell who leaves. I shall go into the suite quite naturally. I shall have my own man along, who is absolutely to be trusted. Moreover, as I have the misfortune to be a very bad sailor I shall certainly keep to the suite for two or three days in any event, beyond the limit set by the Griffin."

Manning nodded again. This bettered matters if the secret could be kept. It looked as if it could. It would not be difficult to have a special guard.

"The captain will have to be taken into our confidence," he said. "There will be no danger there. I shall sail also, but that must not be known. I am tailed by the Griffin's men, without question. If it was known I was sailing, the inference to the Griffin would be plain that you were going to be on the boat, all evidence to the contrary.

"It can be managed. You will have to endure me whether you are seasick or not for that twenty-four hours. It is my responsibility, it is the only way by which we can hope to thwart this maniac. I shall have to see the officials of the line, but I shall not explain to them that it is you I expect to protect. The captain will not know it until we are at sea. But I must have men aboard to form a cordon round your suite unostentatiously on the tenth. They will appear as deck and other stewards. You have relieved me immensely. This trip is something that the Griffin cannot have taken into consideration."

It was Brooks's turn to nod.

"Still, if they are tailing you—as you term it?..." he ventured.

"Their skill is not so great but that I can break it when I take the trouble. I shall go aboard in efficient disguise. Mr. Brooks, you give me heart, fresh courage. The burden has been a heavy one; will be until this monster is destroyed—and this has been the best chance to show him that his game—as he terms it—has its flaws. We can hardly hope to take him in the attempt, as it looks as if he will be left in the dark. Still, I shall omit no precautions. He has extraordinary resources. Without doubt you have been on his list for weeks, perhaps months. He casts horoscopes and selects his men as they seem to be most vulnerable according to his astral reckonings. But, if he fails, I am inclined to think that it will unnerve him, or even totally destroy the uncertain balance of his already deranged mentality.

"I am sorry that you put off your engagements for this evening. If I had known at the start you were sailing I could have told you the interview would not be long."

"I am glad to have a free evening," said Brooks. "Let us spend it together. I should like to hear something of your travels. That is something denied to me as my ambitions run and my duties seem to point. It is a very great happiness to me, Major Manning, that I have been able to serve this country, *my* country in my peculiar capacities."

It was late when Manning left. He had not been the only talker. He bore with him the mental portrait of a fine American. A man the country needed, could not afford to lose.

The thought that a maniac like the Griffin should dare to even contemplate his destruction was infuriating, but Manning controlled himself in the hope that this time the tables would be turned.

He did not doubt that he was being shadowed, and he did not bother to verify it, to shake off the tailers. The Griffin would expect him to get in touch with Brooks. This merely verified it, and the long time they had spent together would suggest that they were planning elaborate defense against the machinations of the Griffin's carefully thought out scheme.

He even grinned a little, and he had not been smiling much of late, when he found, attached to the horn button, an oval cartouche of heavy paper embossed with the griffin, the symbol of the man who used the name of that mythical, rapacious creature, half lion, half eagle, to represent him and his cruel, ruthless deeds.

The burden seemed lifting. He had been chosen after the police had utterly failed. He had not, he told himself, done much better, and the responsibilities of not having saved the lives he had tried to protect had at times weighed heavily upon him. To-night, for once, he got five hours of sound, refreshing sleep.

IV

THE LINER was on her second day at sea, logging her twenty-five knots an hour. Everything was in full swing aboard that palatial steamship with its spacious salons, its elegant suites, its shops, its lounges, its big swimming pool and gymnasium.

Every one but those who, like Brooks—his presence unknown aboard—were confined to their cabins by seasickness, was making the most of the voyage, exhilarated by the sea air, enlivened by new acquaintanceships, the informality of shipboard.

It was fine weather. A good sea was running, but the liner sheared through the long, frothing hills of brine on a nearly level keel. It was the idea, rather than the fact, that made people suffer from *mal-de-mar*. Her wake was like a silver ribbon from the churning of her powerful propellers. Her graceful hull trembled ever so slightly as if with eagerness to beat the record. The sky was deep blue, mottled with shreds of white vapor to a semblance of marble. There was no haze, the horizon was sharply defined as if drawn by a firm hand and a fine brush dipped in deep purple.

This was the Atlantic, with the United States over eight hundred miles astern as seven bells struck in mid-morning, and the bibulous ones announced jocularly that the sun was over the yard arm and it was time to patronize the bar.

Brooks was wretched. Psychological or physical, as the source might be, he was a seasick man. He ate nothing. He lay like a bundle of wet rags and his face was the hue of verdigris.

His man waited on him absolutely, allowing no one else in the suite, save Manning, who did his best to cheer the patient and, every little while, quietly inspect the suite and see that the unostentatious guards kept their cordon. Seven hours were gone of the fatal twenty-four but he showed no exultation, felt none and would not until eight bells sounded at midnight. As for Brooks, he was too sick to bother much about anything. He was confident that the Griffin had been thrown off the track and that he was quite safe, aside from Manning and his men.

Manning had come aboard in disguise that was slight but effective. He used a cane and walked with a limp. He wore pads under a suit too large for his actual trim figure. He affected sideburns that were artificial but looked real enough, as a mustache or beard would not have deceived sharp eyes. In public he used cheek plumpers that altered his whole face, his skin was darkened and hollows stained under his eyes. He looked—acted—the semi-invalid, not appearing at meals or on deck save for short, rare intervals. None at all to-day. The captain was in the secret.

Eight bells struck. Luncheon was served. By two it was well over. At six bells, three o'clock, the radio operator received a message asking them to stand by for the plane.

It was a somewhat cryptic message, but in these days one never knew what new stunt might be trying out, or what flyer in distress might be sending out an S O S, sighting them far up, perhaps, making for them on long volplanes with his gasoline clogged.

The word got out, passed round. Passengers and officers began to look for the airplane that was still invisible. At length they heard its motors, sounding clear and sweet and plain, but there was nothing to be seen in the azure. Those who knew anything about flying confessed themselves puzzled. A man jocularly suggested it was a ghost plane.

The rhythmic purr sounded ever louder, nearer. The sky was without blemish, but it was empty.

At last one of the officers pointed, using his binoculars. The captain followed suit, his glasses glued to his eyes. All those who owned them, sent for them or fetched them.

The idle term ghost plane seemed not inadequate. An apter description came from a girl who said it was like an X-ray plate.

They could see suspended in apparent space an engine, certain parts of control and dials, a pilot and a passenger. The latter's face was indistinct. He seemed wearing a queer sort of mask that fitted closely enough to suggest hooked nose and harsh cheekbones yet concealed any individuality. These two sat in air, to all seeming. There were no pipes, no struts, no wings outside of a slight blur, like the flawing of a mirror, that disturbed the air behind the propeller that brought it on, to pass them at four times their speed, six times, perhaps.

This mysterious object, or phenomenon, banked and returned. They could see the men tilt, but nothing else save the bulk of the engine, the line of dials. It circled the steamer, descending until they could see the whites of the pilot's eyes, the yellow, shining mask, that screened his passenger, shining like goldbeater's skin.

Something shot down, struck the upper deck, stayed there, quivering. It was a dart and it was made apparently of toughened glass. Attached to it was a sheet of gray paper, closely clipped to the shaft.

A quartermaster handed it to the first officer who gave it in turn to the captain. He read it with frowning brows.

"This is preposterous," he said and concealed his true feelings.

An official of the line pressed through to him, accompanied by friends, all men of big interests. The captain showed the note.

Edward Brooks is aboard, in Suite B, under an assumed name. He is seasick, but unless he is placed in a boat, set afloat and left to me within fifteen minutes I shall drop something down your funnels that will scrap your engines and blow the bottom out of you.

THE GRIFFIN.

Tell Gordon Manning that, unless Brooks considers his life more valuable than that of the ship's passengers and crew, he will immediately place himself at my disposal.

It was written with purple ink on the gray, heavy paper, it

was signed with the seal of the Griffin, the blood red cartouche of the fabled beast that could fly as well as leap, rend with claws as well as beak.

Those who read first, blanched. *The Griffin!* After Brooks! Was Brooks aboard they demanded of the commander and he told them that he was, on a secret mission.

Swiftly the dread news passed. It was staggering. It was incredible. All to be killed, sent to the bottom after a frightful explosion! The Griffin could not mean that. Yet in their hearts they felt that he did. They cringed and cowered—the stoutest of them, while women clung to men as the cry rose—"He's coming back!"—and the hum of the propeller rose to a roar while that ghostly, ghastly plane, almost invisible, even close at hand, came fleeting back.

It was not to annihilate them. Only four minutes had passed but it seemed like hours of suspense and fear as a consultation was hurriedly held, interfered with by men who were beginning under the stress of their own terror and the appeal of their wives, to lose control.

Another arrow clicked to the deck, and a larger object landed fairly in the throat of the forward funnel while groans and shrieks went up and, for an instant, pandemonium reigned.

Nothing happened. The commander bellowed for silence, read the note aloud at their insistence.

"Just a sighting shot. You have ten minutes more in which to deliver Brooks or drown—those of you who survive the explosion. I shall give you a little demonstration of what that may be."

The plane was away, spiraling swiftly aloft. They saw something shoot down to the sea and then a geyser leaped aloft and the big ship rocked to the concussion of the frightful blast and the sudden onslaught of great billows.

The deck was crowded. The alarm had not yet spread to the engine room. Some sick ones might be still below, unconscious or beyond caring for anything, not dreaming of what was happening. The commander had promptly taken means to keep the news from the stokehold and the liner still made her twenty-five knots while the plane hovered overhead at will, like a kingbird over a clumsy crow.

"Ask Mr. Manning to see me at once," said the captain.

"What are you going to do? Do you expect us to stand still and be blown up—sunk?"

The passengers were approaching hysteria, the deck hands and stewards muttered, panic beginning to spread. The situation was inconceivable yet it had happened. It was true. They were called upon to sacrifice one man instead of a thousand, and many there deemed themselves of far more importance than Edward Brooks, aside from the natural instinct of self preservation, of protectiveness for their families.

Manning came on deck, not limping now, ready for action. He did not know what had happened, but he knew that the Griffin was some how in it, was striking or about to strike.

He read the letters, listened. The enormity of it was staggering. Had the Griffin gone raving, stark mad beyond control? It looked like it.

"My God," cried some one, "we've only got five minutes more!"

V

MANNING GLANCED about him, at the excited groups of people who were helpless under this menace. Some thronged, dumb with terror, whispering, white-lipped; others were wildly articulate, calling for the boats to be launched, the steamer set on a zigzag course. The name of the Griffin was known to all of them, with his frightful deeds.

And Manning knew that, sick as he was, Brooks would sacrifice himself for these others. Knew also that any moment the frenzied passengers might drag him from his bed and have the sailors launch a boat or throw him into the sea.

The plane was returning. The moments flying.

He saw the faces of some of his guards, of Brooks's own servant, the latter perhaps sent up to see what the racket was. Brooks's window to his bedroom was open to give him air, he would have heard the racket—he might....

Suddenly Manning broke away with a shout. He clubbed his way through those who tried to detain him, drawing his gun as he fought to where he could swing down to the next deck, close to Brooks's suite.

He saw a man there, by the open window, closing it. The other saw Manning's descending, rushing figure and slammed the window down, thrusting his hand under his coat.

Manning fired first. The man went down, shot through the throat, bright blood spurting to the deck, his weapon fallen from his nerveless hand. Manning smashed the window with the barrel of his own automatic. Through the glass he had seen Brooks, after one wild, convulsive leap, lie prone on the bed, his face horribly contorted. Through the broken pane he caught a whiff of some sort of gas, frightfully pungent, virulent that seared his nostrils and his eyes. He ducked, running for the door that led to the corridor off which Brooks's suite opened. He had not breathed in the vapor that he knew had killed Brooks, but he was dizzy with its fumes.

The Griffin might have carried out his threat, but the action had been a clever ruse to draw all on deck while his man killed Brooks. Undoubtedly the Griffin had learned that Brooks was invariably seasick. It was the knowledge of such details of his victims' habits that had made him succeed with his crimes. How he had learned Brooks was on board was another matter.

Manning saw Brooks's own man, faithful, returning to report, opening the door to the suite. He saw his own guards coming and he shouted to the valet not to open the door, to his own men to attend to the assassin he had shot. He held no doubt that Brooks was dead, the suite charged with deadly gas.

The valet was either willful in his eagerness to reach his

master—defend him—or did not hear. He opened the door, started to enter and immediately fell, like a moth in a cyanide jar. Manning yelled hoarsely:

"Keep away from that door. Keep the passage clear. Gas."

A cheer came from the deck. The plane was leaving, circling high. It had sent down one more dart with a message, but it was going. They did not know yet what had happened, guess that the Griffin, from his height, had watched through lenses what had occurred on the lower deck. That a servant of his was dead was immaterial to him, so long as he had scored once more, so long as his boast had been made good—and Brooks was dead.

A draught was blowing through from broken window to door, dissipating the fatal fumes. Inside Brooks and his valet lay contorted, their lungs shriveled. The actual killer sprawled in his own blood. He was free of the gas which had blown inward by the ocean breeze.

Manning, gray and grim of face, went up on deck. Men questioned him but he did not answer. They would learn soon enough. He got through to the captain who handed him the last letter that had been flung.

"It is addressed to you," said the commander of the liner.

It was clear to Manning that this letter, that the other notes, had been prepared beforehand in the Griffin's certainty that his plans would not go awry.

He read the letter that was his own humiliation—for it was scant comfort to him that he had shot the instrument of the Griffin. There, too, he had failed. It had been man to man in a death duel, but luck had forced him to shoot the other in the throat, to render him silent when he might have spoken, might have given a real clew to the Griffin's identity or whereabouts. By the way his head hung Manning knew the man's spine was broken, that he could not live long.

DEAR MANNING:
I do not know if you are alive or not. If not I trust the cap-

tain will give this letter to the press. It is too much to hope that you will.

It was all very simple, Manning. You have amused me greatly. Brooks's man, if he is living, will remember the hotel employee who entered his rooms at the hotel recently to make the usual inspection of electric lights. In Brooks's suite he never used the overhead, indirect lighting. It was a simple matter to install a dictaphone in each one, to connect it with the suite above—which was rented by me. Amusing to hear you play into our hands.

Then there was the matter of Brooks's *mal-de-mar*. It all helped.

As for the phantom plane, it is modeled after the one recently tried out by the British Government at Nottingham, England, made of the new material, *plass*, transparent and tough. It has demonstrated itself. There is no danger of our being overhauled, even if a fighting plane had been launched from the steamer. At a very short distance we are completely invisible.

And the gas, tossed into Brooks's suite by my agent while the deck was crowded to watch my performance, paralyzed at my threat—it was in a small, brittle globe of glass that breaks readily, but there was enough of it to kill a hundred. Super-gas—instant death to any one inhaling it. As much more deadly than phosgene as that was than lewisite. It is said that, though its secret is in the possession of all the great nations of the world, they would hesitate to use it because of its horrible, awful effects.

I have no such silly scruples. Manning. You must have heard of it, you who were in the Secret Service of the war. It's name is cacodyl isocyanide.

Those three fools who were found stupefied refused to manufacture it for me, but their fate proved an object lesson to others, and the experiment was successfully completed.

I rather hope you are alive, Manning, seeing you still furnish me amusement, so that you can see how readily I can carry out my threats and how childish are your endeavors to prevent the will of

THE GRIFFIN.

THE PERFECT POISON

With a New Kind of Death the Griffin Strikes at
a Man in the Top of a Closely Guarded Skyscraper

THE GRIFFIN sat alone in the circular room at the
top of his house, a room with steel walls covered with
golden brocade, walls that showed no signs of openings. There
were no windows, but the air was pure, slightly scented with
the fragrance of the incense that smoldered on the desk at which
he sat, its smoke wafting in slight spirals to the ceiling.

There was a sound of exotic music that seemed to give him
some pleasure, though his air of satisfaction only enhanced the
subtle malignancy of his finely featured face with its outbridg-
ing nose and the eyes, now narrowed, that held a cold gleam,
incredibly cruel, lacking humanity, containing a well restrained
madness.

There was no question that the Griffin, whose name and
murderous deeds held the greatest city in the world spellbound
in fear, was insane. That crafty, ingenious brain of his was warped
with the belief that he held a justified grudge against all the
world, especially against its more illustrious citizens of his own
country. It was the dementia of grandeur. Once it would have
been held that he was possessed by a devil. Certainly at times
it seemed as if twin evil spirits peered from those strange orbs
of his and jeered mockingly at his successful wickedness.

In front of him there was suspended a bronze disk. Some
papers were held down by the paperweight that was a golden
griffin, the mythical beast, half-bird, half-brute, a winged lion
with an eagle's head that was his chosen crest, that represented

159

"Don't use those pipes," said Manning. "They may have been tampered with."

his feral rapacity, his lust for the destruction of worthy deeds and the annihilation of their performers.

Under his well kept hand lay a horoscopic chart which he had been consulting, by which in his twisted methods, he chose his next victim. He had arrived at his decision, he had checked off on a list of names the next man to be eliminated, settled on the date of his taking off, the date that he would mockingly announce to the man who had been chosen by the baffled commissioner of police to mark down the Griffin, to balk his crimes, to compass his downfall and his punishment.

Gordon Manning, once of the Secret Service of the Army, during the Great War, was this person, none better qualified for his task and yet a man who so far had failed in it, though he had come close to handgrips with the Griffin, so close that he had begun to upset the Griffin's demoniacal self satisfaction.

The Griffin chose to call the contest between himself and Manning a game, a sort of sublimated chess match in which, though he reserved the right of first move, he announced his openings. Now he chuckled slightly as he reviewed his almost perfected plans for the taking off of the man whose name he had checked, surveyed others that were marked with red, names of those he had sent into the shadows of the tomb. Then, for a moment, the fierce light in his eyes became a red flame. He spoke aloud in a low, deep voice, sure of his solitude and security.

"There are times when you come close to not amusing me, Manning," he said. "When you bore me, my friend, beware! I shall strike twice and you will wish that you were not reserved for the second stroke. There are things to a man like you, with foolish, human sentiment as the weak spot in your armor, that are worse than your own death, and I shall see to it, that that is not an easy nor a swift one."

His allusion referred to the woman Gordon Manning loved, yet whose love he dared not seek lest she be marked down by the Griffin. Once already he had threatened her. It was an advantage he held over his relentless adversary. Lacking all emotion himself, serene as Satan, the Griffin guessed how this anxiety would corrode Manning's steady nerve, already at high tension with his inability to rid the world of this monster.

The red light died down to the cold gleam again. The bronze disk gave out a sonorous note. Swiftly the Griffin set away his papers in the deep drawers of the deeply carven desk, locked the receptacles by the touch of a hidden spring and adjusted the mask he always wore before those who served him. He had no confederates, only slaves, whose freedom, often whose lives, he held in the hollow of his hand.

The mask was yellow, glistening. It clung to, yet concealed his features. It seemed as another skin, repulsive, horrible, but fascinating with the sheen of his sinister eyes looking out through that domino of death.

II

THE WALL opened. An elevator had come noise-lessly up from the cellars that the Griffin had made for his laboratory. Out of the lift stepped a curious figure, a dwarf whose misshapen body was clad fantastically in turban and robes that made him look as if he might have come straight from a medieval court. His long arms swung low, his hands reached his knees. His eyes shifted like an ape's, his expression was that of a mischievous baboon, save when it rested upon his master, the Griffin.

This was Quantro, native of the Caribbean, the land of voodoo and obeah; faithful and devoted bodyguard of the Griffin though he looked more like the familiar to a wizard. The Griffin himself wore a robe of black brocade which, with his weird mask, made him resemble some Old World necromancer, some conjurer of demons, a caster of unhallowed spells.

One of Quantro's hands rested upon the hilt of the long knife he was always keen to use in the service of the man who, to him, was God. He ushered in a figure in stained overalls that, like the man's fingers, proclaimed him a worker in acids and chemicals. The man stooped, his scanty hair was white, he coughed apologetically as the elevator door disappeared and once more the walls looked seamless. He showed no curiosity, he had been summoned there before. There was dejection, hopelessness in his attitude, though he had a plea to put forth.

"Twenty-Nine," said the Griffin in his deep voice. "Sit there. Quantro, bring me that cage."

The dwarf brought forward a gilded cage on a pedestal. Inside the bars, which had been covered with a silken cloth, was a canary that now hopped on its perch, gave a chirp or two and tried to find seed in an empty receptacle.

The Griffin released his drawers, took out a wide-mouthed vial that held about an ounce of powder, extremely fine crystals that, in the mass, showed gray, but separated, scattered on to a square of paper, were almost invisible.

"You say that this needs only moisture to combine all its virulence, its toxic force?"

"With the moisture it becomes a powerful poison," said the man.

"Causing instant death? Leaving no traces for analysis?"

"No present analysis could discover it."

"In fact," said the Griffin gloatingly, "a perfect poison! A new discovery. An alkaloid that holds all the venom of a king cobra."

"It is allied to such a venom," said Twenty-Nine, shifting a little uneasily on his chair. "A new method of assembly, as you desired. And, now, now that I have done your bidding, may I have my release?"

"Your release?" The Griffin's ophidian eyes regarded the man who had no name in that establishment, was merely a number, as were all his associates, experts in many professions. "You are out on bail on a homicide charge, or rather you *were*, since that bail has long been forfeited. I brought you here and I have given you a refuge. You killed a man...."

"He was my wife's lover."

The Griffin's eyes flashed angrily.

"I want no interruptions. I dislike emotions. Your wife and her lover are nothing to me. Of what use is your release to you? You will be discovered, charged with the crime, convicted."

"I might escape, get out of the country, get away from...."

He checked himself.

"You do not like this work. You fear that this perfect poison of yours may be used for purposes of which the law would not approve, that you may become the accessory of a crime?"

Twenty-Nine kept silent.

"We will see," the Griffin went on with a sudden chuckle that was hellish in its suggestion of innate deviltry. "First we will test the crystals."

He ordered Quantro to fill the seed receptacle in the cage with some hemp and rope he shook from a package and carefully dusted with the poison powder. He stirred it all before the dwarf returned the cup to the cage. No sign of the fine crystals showed. The bird started eagerly to eat while Quantro took the drinking cup, which had also been empty, and filled it to its brim from the silver decanter.

The Griffin and Twenty-Nine watched intently. At first nothing happened. The canary cracked the seed and the hulls fell to the sanded bottom of the cage. Then it hopped across and drank, taking the water in its beak, tilting its head upward.

It fell to the sand limp, without a twitch, dead as if shocked by electricity.

"Good," proclaimed the Griffin and his voice held an indescribable note of triumph. "You have done well, Twenty-Nine. It is a valuable secret."

"And a dangerous one."

"True. But, if I give you your release, I can depend upon you not to divulge it."

Twenty-Nine took it as a question. There was a light in his faded eyes, hope in his voice.

"Absolutely."

"Ah! You will smoke a cigarette while we go into it a little further?"

He brought out a gold case, damascened with the design of a griffin on each side. Twenty-Nine eagerly accepted the favor. The Griffin took one himself, lit it, passed the lighter to the other, watched as Twenty-Nine inhaled, sent out the vapor.

"You did not know," said the Griffin, "where you were coming when you were brought here? You know nothing of this place outside the laboratory cellars?"

"No—I—"

The man without a name suddenly pitched forward to the floor. His tongue tip had moistened the tobacco of the cigarette which the Griffin had treated with the perfect poison. The combination he had himself discovered and perfected had resolved itself into its death-dealing venom. The Griffin, calmly finishing the cigarette he had taken from the same case, sent out a smoke-ring.

"And," he said, "you do not know where you are going. You have your release, my friend. And I have your secret. It will come in very useful, shortly. Quantro!"

The dwarf knew what was wanted. He dragged the dead body easily off the magnificent rug it had crumpled, pulled back the chair. The Griffin released a lever. A circular mouth to a steel chute yawned instantly in the floor. The Griffin made other smoke rings as Quantro, with his prodigious strength, sent the corpse hurtling down and, with a slight clang, the opening closed, its source invisible.

III

GORDON MANNING was in his own library at Pelham Manor. His deft Japanese butler had brought in coffee, placed his tobacco humidor handy, with two favorite pipes that he had carefully cleaned for Manning that day.

Manning, tall, lean, bronzed and athletic, sank into his big armchair a trifle wearily. The combat with the Griffin was telling on him. In their last encounter he had himself escaped destruction by a narrow margin. He had grappled with the Griffin's actual agent of death and the man would act no more. Manning had shot him, sealed unintentionally lips that might have revealed some clew by which the Griffin might have been traced to his lair.

And the Griffin had mocked him with a message, had hinted that he was getting tired of Manning's insistency, had insolently stated that, if Manning ceased to entertain him, he would make an end of him as he had made an end of all the rest. And, direst of all, had threatened the life of the girl Manning loved.

There would be a next time. When, Manning could not guess. The Griffin, for all his daring, made careful preparations before he struck and, so far, his madman's cunning had bested Manning. There were lines beginning to be etched deep in the special agent's strong, rugged face. He filled his pipe and the good tobacco solaced him, steadied nerves he was getting conscious of for the first time, nerves that had withstood scores of deadly perils in war and peace, on wild trails in strange lands.

It was the uncertainty of when and where the Griffin would

next attack that dissolved the mock-sportsmanship of the Griffin's game. The Griffin openly announced to Manning the name of his next victim, the very day of his doom. To fail again seemed insupportable. Manning would not, could not quit. Either he or the Griffin must perish.

These frightful crimes not only stirred New York, but sent their baleful influence from coast to coast. They affected the safety of social and civic stamina, they undermined public confidence in the police, they had begun to demoralize the very bases of existence, to upset trade conditions, to encourage all sorts of viciousness. And it was up to him to restore these things, to destroy this frightful being that, like the creation of a Frankenstein, stalked like a grinning, mocking, elusive specter about its grisly occupation.

Even before his telephone rang he felt the malefic influence, the vibrations to which, because he was expecting them, he was tuned in. The Griffin had some method of synchronization by which he could segregate a telephone for his own use, creating an untraceable connection. The sound of the bell was subtly different. Manning obeyed the summons with a growing heat that filled his veins, a resentment of his inability to cope in some way with this crafty master maniac.

He would know that voice of the Griffin's anywhere, deep as a bell, infinitely mocking in its inflection.

"Manning? The board is set for the next game. I give you greetings, adversary. I fear of late you lack a certain humor, a lightness, a finesse in our encounters. Do not take yourself too seriously, Manning. I warn you now that, this time, as last, your own existence may be in jeopardy. I say may, because I am not yet deliberate about getting rid of you, but it is likely you may fall into the same trap that will inevitably close on Gilman Grant."

Gilman Grant! Manning could almost see the look on the Griffin's face that accompanied the chuckle which came through the receiver, together with the faint sound of strange music, haunting, modern, yet primitive as the devil drums of cannibals.

Gilman Grant. Civic engineer and architect. The man who was the city-builder of the future, who was solving traffic and airway problems, improving old cities and laying out new ones that would meet the modern and the future requirements. Master of the problems of light and fresh air and pure water, and creator of inspiring beauty. A man who would inspire citizens by the places he made for them to live in. The genius of the century.

Manning set his jaw. The strains of music, the chuckle of the Griffin, were obscene. He fought down his fury.

"Gilman Grant," repeated the Griffin. "That projector of dreams, that waster of energies, an effete esthete who does not realize that soon men will again be at each other's throats. A believer in a false millennium he hopes to hasten. Gilman Grant, who will be dead as his own idle theories before the week is out.

"Next Thursday, Manning. I will even make the hour more specific this time. I do not ask the whole twenty-four hours. I will let the visionary live until noon. Between then and midnight I shall make an end of him. The presumptuous paragon! That is all, Manning. I promise you no immunity. I shall not be far away, in case your own luck fails to hold."

The voice ceased with a trace of laughter, like a flung-back echo. The contemptuous arrogance of the message, the murderous plan, stung Manning.

Gilman Grant must not be killed. America, the world, could not spare him. One thing stood out. Why had the Griffin limited his time, cut it in half? There was some reason. Something connected with Gilman Grant's habits which, without question, the Griffin had studied.

This was Saturday. Manning had four full days to warn Grant, to make his preparations. This time, surely, he must win. Fate *could* not grant another sacrifice like Grant. Yet… recollection of other failures swamped his energies, but he fought it off.

He tapped out his pipe, recharged it, lit it and sat in the deep chair marshaling his wits. There was so little to work on—only this declaration of the Griffin's that Grant was secure until noon. It meant *something*. It was a part of the boasting that some day would trip the arch-fiend who styled himself the Griffin, sealed his triumphs by the display of an oblong of heavy scarlet paper, embossed with the head of the bird-beast that announced his *nom-de-mort*.

IV

GILMAN GRANT was out of town, summoned to Washington as an expert on a Civic Amendment Committee. He was expected back Tuesday evening and would be at his office on Wednesday morning. His home was on Long Island. When in New York overnight, as often happened, he slept at his club.

Manning had no difficulty finding out these things and he was sure that the Griffin knew them also. The Griffin was never ill advised, likely to be prepared for all emergencies, whether Grant stayed on Long Island, in New York or was detained even in Washington. It was a prime factor in the Griffin's grandiose dementia, in his successes, that he was not misinformed and never had slipped up on one of his announced crimes, amazing as had been the precautions taken.

It was for this reason that Manning puzzled over the condition that left Grant safe until noon of the day that was set for his death. Not from any sense of honor, but merely for the satisfaction of his own pronouncement, the Griffin invariably kept his word, however much it might appear to handicap him.

Murderer though the man was, crazed and devilish, Manning believed implicitly that Grant would be immune until noon on Thursday. Almost as much he feared that something untoward would happen afterward. The Griffin's ingenuity was appalling.

He had the advantage of knowing what he would do. Manning was relegated to the post of protecting a man already doomed, of trying to not merely frustrate but anticipate the Griffin's methods.

He got through to Gilman Grant on Wednesday in his offices, occupying a section of one of New York's latest vertically designed, sky-soaring buildings. It was a busy place. Men, many of them beyond question important, talked with the outer protectors of Grant's private quarters and spare time, passed in and came out again. Cranks and committee chairmen clamored to get through without appointment. There were two special secretaries, both girls, one red-headed, the other blond, who knew their duty.

"Mr. Grant will be glad to see anybody if there is time," they said repeatedly. "He has appointments that must take first place."

"I have no appointment," said Manning to the blonde. "However, if you will take in this card, I hope that he will see me. The matter is very vital to Mr. Grant."

The girl looked at him gravely, with close attention. His voice, his manner, his face, his utter concentration, impressed her. She was pretty, but she had brains. She glanced at his card and her eyes widened.

In the affairs of the Griffin, Manning had been at first under cover. The Griffin himself had been the first to find out about his appointment, to daringly write and congratulate Manning, while flinging him a challenge. Since then, in the catastrophes the Griffin had launched and Manning had striven to prevent, Manning's name had unavoidably been linked with the investigations.

She looked again, straight at him, and there was terror in her blue eyes. She had sentiments deeper toward Gilman Grant than just those of an employee, Manning fancied.

"Can you identify yourself, Mr. Manning?" she asked.

Manning smiled at her.

"Good girl," he said in a low voice. "Any place we can do it? In private?"

He saw and interpreted the fleeting doubt of him she dismissed. Then she ushered him into a small room where blue prints lay on draughting tables and Manning showed her a special badge, his passport, with its pictures, various driving licenses that bore his signature, which he there and then duplicated.

"You can call up the commissioner at Centre Street if you wish," he said. "You or I can speak to him. He can send up a discreet person to complete the identification. But don't fail to get me through to Mr. Grant before he leaves."

"If you don't mind I *will* call up headquarters," she said. "It is not just my own judgment, Mr. Manning, but I gather that this is a very grave affair."

Manning bowed.

"It is," he said. "I applaud your caution."

Within fifteen minutes a discreet plain-clothes man, close to the commissioner, okayed Manning as genuine, greeting him with evident respect and he got through to the great architect.

"I can't give you long," said Grant genially. "Been out of town, you see, and these new ideas of ours about civic changes are so much in the public eye at present that I am literally besieged. People want to know the things I want to tell them and it's hard to deny them. What can I do for you, Mr. Manning?"

It did not take long to tell him. Manning cited the names of those who had been the Griffin's victims. Grant nodded.

"I've heard of all this, of course," he said. "Yet I've been so immersed in my work that I've almost treated this man as a sort of myth. There is no conceivable reason why he should take dislike to me save that he is a crank to whom progress is abhorrent, unless he himself conceives it. I realize you are not here to waste time, Manning. What do you want me to do?"

"Are you going to Long Island to-night? I want to be with you throughout to-morrow. I do not believe there is the slightest danger before noon, for some strange cause that has arisen in the diseased mind of the man. I do believe that once his plans do not turn out according to his schedule, his colossal conceit will collapse. To-morrow, of course is a holiday...."

"This office will be closed," said Grant, gravely. "I expected to come back here to-night and work late. I have often slept on that couch," he went on, indicating the leather covered davenport. "I have rugs to cover me. I can get breakfast here with electric gadgets and intended to do so to-morrow. This is my workshop and I shall be alone and catch up on several things. I have certain questions I want to decide and submit to Washington, for one thing. I hardly think," he concluded, "that there could be a safer place than this. If you want to be here with me, I shall be glad of your company though I cannot promise to be an entertaining host."

They both went to the window and looked out. The lofty building was a stack of cubes, as were its neighbors. The contrasting shades of the time of day brought out their modern lines in high relief. Here and there were setbacks as the high edifices tapered off to their summits, a thousand feet and more above the sidewalks.

Grant's offices were at least seven hundred feet above the busy street where people passed like ants. The suite was in the central part of the building. It did appear almost impregnable, this aerie set in a cliff dwelling of steel and stone. Safe enough, to all seeming, Manning acknowledged, if, indeed, any place was safe from the devilish ingenuity of the Griffin.

"I suppose several people know of your intention to be here to-morrow, alone?" Manning asked. "Some of them strangers, perhaps?"

"Undoubtedly. But, with you as bodyguard, if we stay in here, and keep the outer doors locked, it seems to me we shouldn't have to bother much."

Manning nodded. He did not entirely agree. Locks would not keep out the experts the Griffin employed. He did not doubt that one or more of them had been here, had inspected the locks, prepared to pass them at will, even as they had studied the habits of Gilman Grant. His best reliance was on his own success as a guard, his ability with his gun. Whatever method the Griffin employed would be subtle. There would be no tossed bombs and there was the implication that he himself *might* perish—not that he would. It was to be a question of luck.

It seemed almost ridiculous to weigh the Griffin's words so closely, yet Manning knew this should be done, that the Griffin was himself meticulous about his meanings and expressions. Whatever happened, Manning might or might not share the fate destined for Grant, which Manning hoped to offset.

"I saw a lounge in the outer room," he said. "If you don't mind I'll bring that in here to-night and use it myself. I will try not to disturb you. I need not come up until midnight, if that suits you."

"It suits me excellently," said Grant. "I shall be working and I will let you in. I have no intention of allowing any threat to interfere with my plans. They are important, not only to me but to the nation. We are beginning to work out some notable and practicable solutions as applied to modern living conditions. We are going to have cities that are at once spacious and beautiful and healthy. I'll see you later then, Manning," he added, as the secretary appeared with the name of a visitor who had an appointment.

Manning left the suite, striving to throw off a certain nervous apprehension, a premonition of evil. It was a shadow from previous failures, he knew, and must not be permitted to in the slightest sense demoralize the present occasion. But it persisted. It was with him when the express elevators hurled him up the shaft fifteen minutes before midnight and he found Grant well and cheerful. It remained as he took up his vigil.

The Griffin had granted them twelve hours.

The hours passed with Gilman Grant working in intense concentration over his problems, Manning by the window, gazing out across the City that Never Sleeps, his senses alert for any sign of danger. Apparently, aside from a few night employees, he and Grant were the only ones awake in that vast building.

V

I T W A S within a few minutes of noon, the hour that the Griffin had set as deadline. Manning had not slept, had not felt drowsy, and now he was more tense than ever, like a bow drawn back to its limit, ready to discharge the shaft.

Grant had slept for four hours, between three and seven. He was not tired and told Manning that he often got along with only a few hours of sleep when his brain was actively engaged. He made a simple breakfast which they ate together, Grant talking interestingly of the city of the future. Present ones would be remodeled as much as possible, solving traffic problems of wheel and wing and foot, permitting parks and boulevards between towering buildings; but the vast improvements would come with the proposed concentration of several small towns into one model city.

He showed Manning some drawings, descanted on the fact that, in this, America would lead the world.

"We have done it already in building," he said, "but our streets have been dirty and crowded, our air foul, our waters polluted. We shall change all that."

The great city was making holiday, millions out in the country, thronging the beaches.

Suddenly the telephone rang. Grant turned toward it, but Manning was first.

"You had better let me answer that," he said. He felt the strange vibrancy to which he was supersensitive. This was from the Griffin. The deep, mocking tones came plainly.

"One minute of noon, by my time, Manning. One minute more leeway and then, look out. As I said before, you may be included this time. It is on the knees of the gods. In that case

I may make a personal visit. I shall regret our lost encounters and I shall pay fitting tribute to your memory. Fate throws the dice, Manning. My compliments to Gilman Grant. He will be exercising his ingenuity, perhaps, in laying out a new heaven— if there is one."

Again there came the faint sound of music blending with the jeering laughter. Manning looked at Grant. The architectural genius was grave but serene.

"These things are ordered, I imagine," he said. "At any rate we won't let them upset our morale. How about a light lunch, Manning? I had some things sent in last night. Chilled soup and cold meats. All in closed cans. This Griffin person cannot possibly have interfered with them."

"All right," said Manning. "I'll take a little prowl outside in the corridor."

The passages were empty. The indicators showed that no elevators were in service for the moment. Manning's gun was ready, loose in its holster. He had traveled jungle trails before when he knew that there were lurking brutes in the bush, that the trails were trapped, that bushmen had drum-signaled his approach and were watching him with poisoned arrows and blow tube darts they might at any moment discharge. Enemies hidden but felt.

It was the same now, though emphasized by the empty passage, the locked doors of office suites, the windows through which the daylight streamed. Nothing in sight, nowhere a man might hide. If one came it must be in plain view. Yet that obsession of imminent danger came upon Manning with something like actual pressure, as if he had been suddenly transported to an atmosphere hard to breathe. The feeling of evil.

But it was not tangible. He shrugged his shoulders, returned to the suite where Grant, acting as host, had already set out the luncheon. Manning locked the outer door. As they sat down to the simple meal he took a chair facing the outer rooms and laid his gun close to his hand. Grant surveyed the grim move without comment.

"Now," he said at last. "Will you have a cigar, Manning, or do you prefer that pipe of yours? As for me, I choose a pipe. I can't keep one alight while I am working, but I enjoy it all the more when I do get at it. You must try my tobacco. I always hold off smoking myself until noon. That, by the way, is a doctor's prescription. Never smoke before noon and tobacco will never hurt you. The blood is in full circulation by then, your stomach content."

He opened a deep drawer in his desk, took out a tobacco jar of lava, brought forth a brass-bound mahogany case that looked as if it might have held duelling pistols, but proved to contain half a dozen pipes, with various instruments for scraping and cleaning bowls.

Grant took off the lid from the jar, chose a pipe, commenced to fill it, telling Manning to help himself.

Light broke in on Manning. He saw the devilish ingenuity of the Griffin, the meaning of the respite until noon.

Because of Gilman Grant's regular habit, known beyond question to many, of never smoking until noon.

"Don't use any of those pipes, or that tobacco," he said sharply as Grant stared at him. "They may have been tampered with."

"Pretty impossible, I think," said Grant. "No one comes in here when I am out of the room except an occasional trusted employee. Hang it all. Manning, I want my smoke."

"Also an occasional janitor, room and window cleaners," said Manning seriously. "We'll take no chances, please. I'll not do you out of your smoke. Take my pipe and my tobacco. I've been using them, but you won't mind that, perhaps. I see you have pipe cleaners."

"Always have a supply of those handy," said Grant. "Miss Allen sees to that. I'll humor you, Manning."

Manning watched him as he closed the case and put it and the jar away. The pipe cleaners in a sealed, unbroken package were in a brass tray on the desk, matches in a safe beside them. He felt relief as Grant took his pipe with a grin, swabbed out the stem with the cleaners of twisted wire and cotton tufts, tossed the stained ones into a wire basket and filled up from Manning's pouch.

"Sorry to deprive you of your pipe," Grant said. "It smokes sweetly. A nice piece of brier. Your tobacco is a mite stronger for me, but…."

Manning, horror struck, saw the pipe fall from his mouth, his jaws open, stiffen, while his eyeballs became rigid, bulging as if they might burst from their sockets. His flesh took on a leaden hue and Manning saw the veins swell on his forehead until they stood out like cords under some sudden strain of agony, of effort to articulate.

With a muffled groan Gilman Grant slid to the floor, dead.

The Griffin had swooped, invisibly, had struck once more. Manning knew there was no hope before he tested pulse and heart and held the inside of his watchcase to the purple lips to find no breath filmed it.

Not yet could he solve the riddle. The deed was done and once more he had failed. Yet he had smoked that pipe and used that tobacco. Grant had even cleaned it. Could there have been some other agency? He glanced round, his hand on the butt of his gun. It seemed a sorry weapon to employ against enemies so intangible. He himself was still alive. How had he escaped?

If it was the pipe, the knowledge of Grant's indulgence in the solace of tobacco at a certain hour—then the Griffin would deduce, if he held no surer knowledge, that Grant would lose no time. The Griffin had said just a few minutes since that, if Manning also died, he might make a personal visit.

Manning knew why. The Griffin loved to set on his victims the seal he used with his letters, oblong cartouches of scarlet paper, embossed with his device. Especially would he like to place this flaunting defiance on Manning.

No doubt he had some plan to find out when and how his

diabolical device had worked, whatever it was. It could not be Manning's pipe nor his pouch. The Griffin could not have calculated, with all his cunning, that Manning would offer them to Grant. He could not believe it was the food, for he himself was unharmed. Yet it was something he might have well shared with the dead architect.

If now he played dead, ranged himself on the floor so as to deceive any one coming to see what had happened, but also so that he could get at his gun—he might, after all, get one of the murdering outfit, might even get the Griffin himself.

It was a lone, long chance but he took it. He even simulated Grant's fall though he knew no one could look through the walls or the windows, seven hundred feet up.

V I

IT SEEMED hours that he lay there, each second infinitely multiplied by the strain, the hope of getting to grips with the cowardly assassin. His gun was handy though hidden by his body. The sunlight shifted on the floor, touched the rich rug on which Grant lay, moved like the finger of Fate.

Then Manning heard the faintest of clicks. Some one was entering the outer door. Faint footfalls that his tenseness magnified. His fingers closed about the butt of his gun. The intruder was close to the final partition, the door of Grant's private room. Manning fancied he could hear his breathing. He watched the handle of the door. It was turning, stealthily. The door was opening. He must let the other get a good look at him, enter— and then....

There was the sound of expelled breath, a puff of something like dust projected into the room, a tickling, irritating substance that provoked the membranes of the nose and throat. So powerful that all Manning's will power could not prevent a sneeze.

Instantly the door closed. There was the sound, plain enough now, of swift footsteps hastening away, knowing, going to report, that one, at least, of the two was alive.

Manning was up, unable to entirely prevent the convulsions, water streaming from his eyes, checked by the ingenuity of the Griffin's fantastic mind. He flung open the door, leaped across the next room, which was vacant, through that door, flung wide by the fugitive and caught a glance of a short, active figure that hurled itself through the entrance into the corridor, flinging over its shoulder a handful of the irritant just as Manning pulled trigger and, for once, missed pointblank.

His face streamed with the fluid from his tear ducts, nostrils seemed afflicted with intense coryza, as did his mouth and throat. He had bounded into the fresh cloud of the stinging dust and he was half blind as he broke out into the corridor.

The man was by the elevators, but he did not dare to summon one of them. The stairs were to the left, hidden, sixty flights before he reached the bottom. And Manning after him.

Manning saw him through a haze, but his next bullet went to its mark. The other staggered, wheeled, crouched, snatched a gun from a shoulder holster and started to shoot it out. There was none to watch the duel, slight chance of interference.

Manning felt a shock as if some one had struck him with a steel rod. There was a slug through his left forearm, but his man was down, he had lost his gun, his right wrist bored through. He tried to get it left-handed as he squirmed, but Manning was on him, kicking the weapon that went sliding down the floor of the corridor.

The effects of the irritant powder were dying. He had one of the Griffin's emissaries and the man was alive, not dangerously wounded.

There would be a notable third degree when the commissioner got hold of him. This was not the first of the Griffin's agents they had landed, but the others had refused to speak, more fearful of their mad employer than of the law. They would have to be more ingenious in their examination of this one.

He was a swarthy man who was probably a foreigner though he spoke good enough American, mostly profanity, as Manning yanked him to his feet, none too gently and frog-marched him back to Grant's offices, through to where the dead man lay.

"That's murder, my man," he said. "You're in it. You planted it after the Griffin planned it. Sit there. Never mind where you're plugged. I'm plugged myself. That can wait. The police will fix us up better than we can. They'll be here, with a surgeon, in a few minutes."

"You can't pin anything on me," said the man. He was not so much defiant, as sure of himself. The Griffin chose his active agents well, Manning told himself. "What killed him? Nothing you'll trace to me. Or trace at all."

"Perhaps not," said Manning. "But I'll promise you this. You'll be behind bars for the rest of your life, without privileges. It wouldn't surprise me a lot if they tried to lynch you, right here in New York. But, if you talk, if you tell us where we can find the Griffin; I'll also promise you some leniency."

"Yeah? Well, call your cops. I don't mind talking—some. I don't want to be cooped up in stir for the rest of my natural and that lynching idea don't sound at all good to me. Want to know how he got bumped off? I didn't do it. I didn't even plant the pipe cleaners. That was done yesterday by another man. I just came up here to see if you had croaked as well as him."

Manning ignored the utter callousness of the man, drug-hardened, in the statement he made. He looked at the package of pipe cleaners.

The other grinned in his cocaine-inspired bravado, braced also by his dread of the Griffin, chuckled.

"Sure. It was easy. We find out all about this guy. We know he don't smoke till noon, ever, and then he goes to the pipe like a Chink hitting the *chandu*. Know he's always got cleaners and matches on the desk, handy. So the Griffin gets a pack, opens 'em, dopes 'em up, see. Another guy plants 'em, switches packs."

He had picked up the package and taken out a cleaner, twisting it nervously in his fingers, rapidly.

"Drop that," said Manning. "Drop it or I'll...."

"You'll what, governor?" asked the man wearily. "Plug me? Aw, this is quicker!"

Manning was almost swift enough. His wound hindered him, but he caught the other's wrist. Then the man thrust out his moist tongue, desperate, deliberate.

The telephone had gone dead. The Griffin's efficiency had destroyed its synchronization. Manning was forced to ring up an elevator with the operator staring at him as he stood there dripping blood. He showed his badge, was taken down to a building telephone.

He rang headquarters, got through to the commissioner. His tone was flat and infinitely weary when he got the connection. The official had been waiting.

"I've got two dead men up here," said Manning. "One of them is Gilman Grant, the other the Griffin's man. When you send up have the surgeon along with his kit, will you?"

He returned to the offices, temporarily binding his hurt. The body of Grant, which had lain face down, had been turned over. On the cold forehead was the crimson seal of the Griffin.

In a Silent, Barricaded House, Manning Waits
for the Arch-Fiend, the Griffin, to Stride

T HE CIRCULAR chamber of the Griffin was empty. There was the low, sweet sound of exotic music, a strange fragrance that suggested burning amber in the motionless air, kept fresh by some ingenious method of ventilation in that windowless, secret spot where the being known only as the Griffin, almost as fabulous as that mythical beast—half lion, half eagle—hatched and perfected his diabolical plots against society in general and famous men in particular.

So far, the Griffin had never included a woman in his machinations, save once to threaten the girl beloved by Gordon Manning, the man selected by the Commissioner of Police of New York to uncover the fiend whose murders were at once the horror and terror of Manhattan; Manning self-sworn to destroy this mysterious menace, this fiend in human shape, this man cursed with the cunning of madness and the ingenuity of Satan.

There was a weak point in Manning's armor that gave delight to the warped mentality of the Griffin. Manning dared not court the girl, dared not even see her, for fear the Griffin would carry out some hideous device, some means to torture Manning by getting possession of his sweetheart.

It pleased the Griffin to consider Manning his opponent in the grisly diversion that the former called a Game. In it he made the first move, planned his campaign, and then declared his intentions, mocking Manning, who had once been the mainstay of Army Secret Service, with the announcement of the name of the victim to be and the actual day of his taking off.

This amused the Griffin and would continue to do so until Manning came too close to circumventing him. This had happened more than once. "And," he had told Manning over the telephone, "when you cease to amuse me, I shall remove you."

It was a Game that, with the increasing toll of frightful murder, the removal of the finest of men, was bound to tell on even Manning's superlative nerves, his physical perfection. On the other hand, there was Manning's profound belief, backed by the opinion of the greatest psychiatrists, that, once the Griffin failed in the horrific programs he announced, in any major detail, his colossal conceit, his grandiose dementia, would collapse, and the man would become a creature without reason, without power to plan; a mere maniac; dangerous to cope with personally, but unable to devise any more major crimes. It began to look to Manning, in his more despondent moods, as if only in such fashion would the Griffin be conquered.

II

THE CURVING walls of the Griffin's chamber were of steel. So were the floor and the ceiling. It was soundproof, fireproof, bulletproof. The walls were covered with golden tapestries; the floor with rare rugs. The great desk where the Griffin sat in contemplation and in judgment, where he cast the horoscopes that his weird fantasy connected with his selection of victims, was elaborately carved.

On it stood a brazen disk, suspended between two standards of bronze, each tipped with a small statuette of a griffin. The lid of his inkstand was of the same design. A paperweight was a griffin cast in gold upon black onyx that held crimson streaks, like blood. A creature that could fly and swoop, run and leap, rend and tear with beak and talons, ruthless, infinitely malicious. That was the symbol of the Griffin.

It was seven minutes beyond the hour appointed.

Noiselessly, an arc of the wall slid aside and a grotesque figure, bizarre, like some dwarfed, distorted butt of a medieval court, stepped into the empty room from an elevator that immediately descended again as the door vanished.

This was Quantro, the bodyguard of the Griffin, looking like a fiend's familiar. He came from Haiti, the land of voodoo, and it seemed as if its bestial customs surged through his veins. A high turban surmounted his grotesque head, too long, too narrow, too close between the mischievous eyes, red-rimmed, that looked like the eyes of a chimpanzee, furtive, not quite human. His hands could scratch his knees without his stooping his enormous shoulders. His costume was fantastic, vivid in its velvet and brocade contrasts.

There was a long knife thrust into his sash. His fingers itched constantly for the feel of its hilt; he ached for the sensation of the sharp steel sinking home. He was a deaf mute and his perceptions were limited. He was the Griffin's dog, but at times he was a moody one, sulky or merely curious. His strength was prodigious.

Now, with a duster of ostrich plumes he removed imaginary dust from the furnishings. The chamber was dustless in its own construction, but the Griffin sometimes gave audiences to strange and not altogether spotless characters; therefore the dwarf performed his perfunctory and meticulous task, his eyes rolling in their yellowish, blood-flecked whites.

He tested, as he had scores of times, the locked drawers, fruitlessly. Then, swayed by an irresistible impulse that, for once, broke down his fear, he pointed his finger at the brazen disk, his red tongue thrust between his blubbery lips. He was like an overgrown child stealing jam as his finger gradually approached the object he had been strictly forbidden to touch.

Suddenly it gave out a low, deep sound, infinitely musical, penetrating, like the soft vibrations of a distant temple gong.

Quantro shrank back, his dark skin turning the hue of cigar ashes, his eyeballs projecting. He looked like nothing so much as some masquerading ape that had inadvertently, ignorantly, touched a red hot stove. Yet he had not touched the disk. His soul, if he had one, shriveled within him.

Again the elevator door showed, and the Griffin stepped into the chamber. His tall figure was clad in a voluminous robe of dull black velvet, the loose sleeves lined with vivid scarlet His face was masked with a close clinging domino of yellow, shining fabric, like goldbeater's skin. Through it his beaklike nose projected, his cheekbones and outstanding jaw showed as if through some outer, leprous skin. His eyes glittered like balls of jet, reflecting lurid flame.

He did not speak, since Quantro could not hear, knew no language beyond that of a limited system of signs. The Griffin had no mind to lessen his ignorance. He stood there until the wretched dwarf slowly turned his head on his neck, owlishly, like an automaton.

The Griffin pointed, inexorably. His eyes flashed fire. The eyes of a madman, beyond question, but a madman whose brain tissues were inflamed, but functioned. He exuded evil. He entertained the persistent idea of some real or imaginary wrong that had set him against all that was worthy, all that was beneficial. His was the mind of Lucifer, cast out of heaven, powerful for sin.

Quantro understood. He gibbered, and then, in hypnosis, he moved forward with extended, faltering finger that at last touched the disk. It gave out a hideous clamor that might have been the barking of Cerberus, that blended with the brutish howl of Quantro as he rolled in anguish on the floor, half numb, his coördination severed, while the agony of the shock he had sustained seemed to flood his veins and arteries with searing acid.

He rolled into a corner while the Griffin took seat in the thronelike chair behind the desk, touched a secret button that opened a drawer and took out a scroll on which were written names. Some had been marked with a scarlet pencil. Now he checked off another with a low, indescribably malicious chuckle.

The music swelled, died away. The brazen disk gave off more vibrations, melodious again. Quantro crept on all fours to his post behind the chair, submissive, whimpering.

For the third time the lift ascended. A man stepped out of it who was dressed in an overall stained with smears of oil, with metallic filings that grimed his artistic hands. He looked with apathy at the strange surroundings, his face devoid of expression, unless it was that of utter hopelessness.

He was a man without a name, a number, one of the Griffin's clever slaves, bound by the Griffin's knowledge of the other's indebtedness to the law. With others who had been carefully selected for their skill, this one had thought to find a refuge and had realized only a stern and unrelenting drudgery, known by their tasks that they were participants in crimes far worse than they had committed, fettered faster than any links of steel could hold them.

In his hand he carried a mechanical contrivance which he set down on the desk at the Griffin's gesture and exhibited in action. The Griffin watched, nodded.

"You have done well, Number Twenty-Nine," he said in his deep voice, always baleful, toned with doom. The other showed no pleasure, no expectation of reward. But the Griffin opened another drawer and took from it a crisp currency bill for a hundred dollars. "I am not ungrateful for good workmanship," he continued with the tinge of mockery that was always in his lightest utterance. "Send this to your family. You may write them. Naturally you will attempt to give no information, though there is none you could extend that would be of any value to those who—who do not appreciate my activities. Give the letter to Quantro, who will attend to it. That is all. You may leave the model. Go."

Twenty-Nine left, his misery relieved, not so much by appreciation of the gift from the man who held him in thrall, owned him, body and spirit, beyond all ransom, as thankful in the knowledge of what the money would do for the family he had renounced.

The Griffin gazed after him sardonically, anticipating the eagerness of those relatives, of wife and children, changed to bitterness as they read the barren lines, charged with blank despair, the money, precious enough, cast aside like the fairy gold that turns to withered leaves.

"I think," said the Griffin aloud, softly, purringly, "that we can now get in touch with our friend Manning."

III

MANNING CAME out from the showers in the down town gymnasium where he kept himself in training, his lean body glowing from the brisk rub down with a rough towel after his game of handball. The lithe muscles played beneath the smooth, tanned skin, showing a little too prominently. He was too gaunt, body and face.

The grizzled trainer, owner of the place, regarded his favorite client with affectionate anxiety. Manning had started out to fight the Griffin under cover, but the Griffin had himself exploded that in a congratulatory letter to Manning the day after his appointment. Publicity could not be avoided. The trainer surmised the strain, the danger Manning incurred, and he feared he was in danger of going stale.

"You're wanted on the telephone, Mr. Manning," he said. "Take it in the booth. Better put this over you."

He draped a big towel over Manning's shoulders as the latter stepped toward the booth. Already Manning felt the premonitory vibrations that warned him of a message from the Griffin. He had never received one here before, but he knew too well that the Griffin kept himself well informed of Manning's whereabouts.

For a split second he hesitated before he took down the receiver. He knew what he would hear—the confident announcement of another murder, another prominent and useful citizen to be sacrificed to the death-lust of the madman. A wave of weariness and depression submerged his soul; he fought through it. There had been so many failures, so many almost victories. He had caught and destroyed the Griffin's agents, but none had ever given the slightest clew to where they might find the Griffin's lair. This time, surely, he would succeed. The very laws of nature could not justify the continued triumphs of this malignant destroyer of civilization and progress.

The Griffin's deeds palsied the city, alarmed the nation, broke down the machinery of justice, threatened finance, encouraged crooks, and advanced the reign of terror that seemed to threaten the greatest city in the world.

Manning heard music, the strains that always came to him when the Griffin spoke through the telephone. He fancied he could hear the strum of barbaric drums, the blare of strident trumpets, the clash of cymbals and the high wail of strange, stringed instruments. It might have been the celebration of some savage Tartar raid, prefacing horrible orgies. It made his flesh creep.

Then came the devilish chuckle of the Griffin before his deep voice followed:

"I fancied I should find you here, Manning. I have found the intimate study of the habits of those in whom I am interested a great source of success. I understand you are looking a bit drawn. I trust you are not allowing your misfortunes in our Game to weigh upon you. I rely upon you to be always at your best."

The music had died away. Manning did not answer. There was no use. He wanted to know, to strive once more to get to grips with this insane assassin.

"You know my hatred of hypocrisy, Manning, how I despise those blatant prigs who fancy themselves demi-gods, philanthropists. So, I have decided to eliminate a man who boasts that he conducts a forum where the truth is told and the cause of the downthrodden championed. Bah!

"You should know his name without my telling you. John Fremont, head of the chain of sheets he calls newspapers. We will give them something worthwhile publishing, the demise of the owner and dictator of the contemptible rags."

Manning's eyes narrowed, his jaws clamped down.

John Fremont, whose publications from coast to coast fearlessly published news that was clean, exposed all graft, defied all who tried, by threat or deed, to silence them. Fremont, the man who stood for true American citizenship.

"You have pad and pencil?" the mocking voice went on. "Or perhaps you will not need it. The date is Thursday, which is the thirtieth and the last day of the month. This is Monday, which gives you ample time, my dear Manning, to make those elaborate precautions of yours that have, hitherto, not proved eminently successful.

"I shall not tell you any exact hour. Some time between midnight on Wednesday and the same hour on Thursday. This provides the element of suspense and adds interest which I hope you will appreciate as I do. Considering Fremont's position in the Fourth Estate, there will be no question about adequate publicity—for both of us, Manning, both of us."

Then there was nothing but the mocking laugh, once more the faint music and, Manning could have sworn, the scent of burning amber in his nostrils. He had known that perfume often in his Oriental travel. He could not be mistaken.

His face was haggard when he emerged from the booth. To the hovering trainer he looked years older.

"You're not ill, Mr. Manning? Nothing I can get you? No bad news, I hope. I've got a bottle of good Scotch."

Manning summoned a smile, knew that he was only grinning in somewhat ghastly fashion. He was not an abstainer, and he felt he needed a drink.

"News I hope to turn to good account, Mac," he said. "Not altogether unexpected, not altogether pleasant. I could stand a drink. Thanks."

In his mind's eye he could see the flaring headlines announcing the death of Fremont, latest victim of the Griffin, the news that Gordon Manning had once more been worsted. It was not so much the personal element that affected him, though he would feel the blame of that, for the whole of the resources of the regular police force had failed ignominiously, time and again, before he had been called in. No, it was the dread of a failure that would take off a brilliant, honorable man whose stand and whose force did much to restore and maintain public confidence in the belief, none too vigorous these days, that the right must prevail.

Fifteen minutes later Manning was weaving through traffic uptown in his powerful roadster. He was an expert at the wheel. He did not waste time in telephoning, knowing Fremont was a hard man to get access to, with a corps of secretaries who warded off any but definite appointments.

His card and his personality broke through the outer guard

at the offices of the *Clarion*. The man he finally met was eminently competent, as were all those close to the big newspaper publisher. His glance at Manning's face was comprehending.

"It is something important?"

"Vital."

Manning's grim emphasis brought a corresponding gravity to the features of the secretary.

"Mr. Fremont is not very well. It is not serious, a bad cold from which he is recovering. The doctor persuaded him to stay at home for a few days. He is at his country place on Long Island."

"I shall go there immediately," said Manning. "I want to see him personally. It is not a matter to be discussed otherwise, at present."

Manning was entirely himself again. The responsibility stiffened him, invigorated him, stimulated his keen wits. He was once again the stern, efficient, uncompromising officer of Secret Service, reckoning odds, but facing them.

The other nodded.

"I will give you a pass," he said. "We are obliged to constantly protect Mr. Fremont from cranks and more dangerous enemies, especially since his signed editorials on Communism. I take it this may be an even greater peril?"

"It may be," said Manning, tersely.

"You could not get through without the pass and my telephoning ahead," the secretary went on. "We must establish your identity there. We consider him efficiently guarded. We have taken every precaution."

"I am sure of it," said Manning, a little wearily. He was also sure that the Griffin knew all about the guarding of Fremont, at home and abroad, very likely knew all about his indisposition though there had been no news of it.

He unfastened the links of his right-hand cuff, rolled up his sleeve, and revealed a tattooed star in red and blue. There was a well healed scar in the middle of it, not readily visible.

"You might fake the tattooing," he said, "but not the scar. A bullet went through it once. Tell them to look for it if any one giving the name of Manning, looking like me, dressed like me, talking like me, driving a similar car, claims my identity."

IV

THERE WAS no question as to the efficiency of the protective methods employed at Quiet Acres, Long Island, John Fremont's country home. The name of the estate seemed to have been bestowed upon it in a hope that had not been entirely fulfilled. There had been sabotage in the press-rooms of the chain of papers from time to time, and threats had been made against Fremont himself, so that he had been forced, much against his will, to employ bodyguards.

This had been exploited in his columns, occasionally, decrying the conditions that obliged a citizen who was upholding law and order to hire men to protect himself.

Aside from his anti-Communistic editorials, Fremont, of late, had been insistent that the Federal Government condemn the manufacture and sale of weapons, save under the most rigid regulations. This stand had brought threats of reprisal from the racketeers.

Much of this Manning recalled, more or less thoroughly, as he drove to Quiet Acres. Fremont might be dubbed an altruist, but he was honest and he was on the right track. It was no wonder that he should have enemies in high places, as well as low, who sought to destroy his efforts by his elimination. And now a far subtler foe attacked. There was a high fence of woven wire about the entire estate, surmounted by angled strands of barbed wire. In addition, this was charged with a powerful current nightly, only one of many precautions that Manning was to be shown.

Back of the fence there grew a luxuriant and well-trimmed hedge, so that the wire was not visible from the house, a stately Colonial mansion in excellent preservation, partly restored. Its portico was columned and, seen from the main gate beyond the wide stretch of perfect lawn, shaded by magnificent trees under which was shrubbery with occasional flower beds, the place had a quiet dignity that matched the name Quiet Acres. It seemed an ideal spot for a man who was a thinker, as well as, perhaps, a dreamer, to retire for rest and recreation, or to use for the working out of his problems.

But it was in reality strongly fortified. There was a massive gate, of wrought iron set between posts of granite, with a small lodge just inside, designed to conform with the main building. The driveway curved in a wide sweep with one diverging road to the rear, to the garage, the greenhouses and kitchen offices. This was the only entrance.

Manning brought his car to a halt, seeing the gates closed. A man in quiet livery came out and spoke through the gate. Manning saw another lounging in the open door of the lodge, caught sight of others at its windows, half concealed by curtains and window boxes. Unless he was mistaken, he observed also the muzzle of a gun, screened by the flowering plants.

He gave his name and the information that his arrival had been telephoned ahead by Wentworth, Fremont's secretary. The man was polite.

"A Mr. Manning was expected," he said. "Could he identify himself?"

The man in the doorway gave an order and the gates opened, evidently controlled by a lever within the lodge. Twenty yards up the drive, a chain was swung across it. Manning was invited to drive in, slowly. The guard came from the doorway and looked at the scar in the tattoo mark carefully.

"We have to be careful, Mr. Manning," he said. "I know of you and I imagine that your coming might mean special care on our part. We admit no one who is not well known to us by sight without rigid identification. The tradesmen and the men they send for deliveries are never changed, and they come only at regular intervals. I am in charge for the Hinkley Agency."

Manning nodded as he fixed his cuff. "You can't be too careful," he said guardedly. "I know your agency—an excellent one. I am glad Mr. Fremont had the matter attended to so thoroughly."

"It wasn't exactly his arranging," said the other, plainly glad of the opportunity of talking to a man so high up in his own profession. "I understand he objected to it strongly, still objects, but he was overruled by his friends. He's a fine man and should not be allowed to run risks. We haven't had much trouble, none serious. I guess the racketeers know pretty well what they must expect if they fool around here. They'll get a hot reception. The voltage along that fence after dark is the same as they turn on in the hot seat at Sing Sing.... Okay with the chain," he called over his shoulder.

Two men came from the lodge. Manning saw the bulge of shoulder guns.

"We've got six men in there, night and day," said the agency detective. "Six more about the grounds. There are flood lights in the trees that make the grounds as light as a Tom Thumb golf course. Three men in the house. The servants have all been with Mr. Fremont a long time. They're devoted to him. There is an alarm signal to the lodge. Private wire to State Police Headquarters. I don't think much more could be done," he added, his face a little anxious. Gordon Manning might have come on a purely private matter, but the shrewd operative did not think so.

Another man came to the door.

"We've telephoned the house, Mr. Manning," he said respectfully. "Mr. Fremont is expecting you. If you'll leave your car in front, it will be taken to the garage."

It certainly seemed as if Fremont was efficiently safeguarded, Manning mused as he drove on. But he knew the Griffin was capable of penetrating better defenses than this. He himself had surrounded houses with guards only to have them passed by some subtle method that no efforts on Manning's part had been able to prevent.

The butler matched the residence. A powerful man, though elderly, his demeanor perfect.

"Mr. Fremont," he said, "is awaiting Mr. Manning in the library. You have no bags, sir?"

"None."

An under-butler, in the same quiet livery, who had been hovering in the background, retired as the butler ushered Manning to the beautiful circular stairway that swept upward about the hall. Manning's keen gaze suggested that this second man was one of the inside guards, doubtless qualified enough as a servant and also in the other capacity. There was an air of alert efficiency about him that denoted more than the ordinary employee.

"Mr. Manning, sir."

The library was on the second floor, a paneled room hung with some fine, old portraits, furnished in Colonial manner with rare pieces that might have graced a museum, but seemed eminently in place here. There were books along one wall and in recesses, a fireplace Adam might have designed. Everything was in harmony, in period.

Fremont rose from his desk chair to greet Manning. He showed signs of weariness, or recent illness, Manning thought. A man of ordinary stature who gave the impression of bigness. A grand head, white-haired, a florid complexion, piercing eyes, the forehead of a philosopher who was also a seer. His greeting was cordial.

"Wentworth said this was important," he said. "I can guess what it may all mean. That madman, the Griffin, has chosen me for his attentions?"

Manning went straight to the point. Evasion with a man like Fremont was ridiculous.

"So," said the publisher. "It might be expected. I am a man of peace, desiring peace for others, Manning, but it seems that peace is not a thing generally wanted. I am hampered and surrounded by guards even more than the Chief Executive in this

Land of Freedom of ours." He smiled whimsically. "Have you seen the precautions my friends have surrounded me with? They appear to me more than adequate."

"Let us hope they are," said Manning, gravely. "I have seen them, but they do not entirely satisfy me."

"You say that the Griffin makes an essential point of acting upon schedule?" said Fremont. "I can understand that phase of a mind diseased. Also the truth of your suggestion that if he should fail in any detail it might mean a complete collapse. Let us see if we cannot compass that. You see, Manning, being threatened is nothing new to me. I am able to sleep nights in spite of it, and carry on days. I am not a fatalist, but I do not believe in worrying. My friends do that. I have affairs that seem to me more important, that fully occupy my mind. Even my death would not entirely neutralize my projects. I have been working against that contingency recently."

He touched the papers on the desk before him.

"I have at least two days ahead," he continued, still with the hint of hidden humor, to Manning the revelation of true bravery. "On Thursday, we shall see what we shall see. What are your suggestions?"

"I want to be with you personally, from midnight on Wednesday to the same hour on Thursday," said Manning. "I have some matters that must be attended to, but I should like to come here Wednesday evening and not to let you out of my sight until the time limit expires. In the meantime, if you are under medical treatment, be extremely careful of what you take in the way of medicine, of your food. Doubtless that is watched. I believe that the Griffin is aware of that. I do not think he will strike in any such fashion, but—"

"I understand," said Fremont. "As a newspaper publisher, I have not missed many of the details of this lunatic's methods. Manning, I do not underestimate him. Neither do I underestimate you. He has a madman's genius. All genius is perhaps a trifle mad. But, this time, you and I may rid the world of this monster. Let us take up his challenge. Come here, by all means. I shall enjoy you as a guest. And I will obey instructions. In the meantime, it is getting late. Will you not dine with me to-night?"

Manning agreed, glad to get the chance to study Fremont's habits, as, no doubt, the Griffin had done, and not so closely as he now had the opportunity to do. Fremont was a delightful host, his conversation brilliant and illuminating. That such a man should be disposed of by such a creature as the Griffin was insupportable.

Before he left, Fremont showed him over part of the house. Manning noticed, if Fremont did not, that they were seldom out of observation. Silent servants appeared and vanished on supposed errands. It was not that they mistrusted Manning; they were fulfilling strict orders.

"This house," said Fremont, "is ancestral, if we of America may talk of ancestors. But it has been in the family for several generations. I have no children of my own. I have never married. But there will be a Fremont to leave it to. This furniture"—he laid his hand almost caressingly on a splendid highboy—"is old and beloved."

He mentioned the clock in the hall as he saw Manning to the door, the butler discreetly and unobtrusively present.

"Not a grandfather's, but a great-grandfather's, of my own. It has wooden works and is a bit erratic. It needs regulating all the time, but I would not part with it."

Manning admired the case of mahogany inlaid with sandal wood, the fine columns set with brass, the sonorous tick. It gave off a wheezy warning, and then gonged the hour. Fremont patted it.

"Man-made, and outliving man," he said. "Keeping the record of what man calls time."

Manning stepped outside. His car was waiting. As the guard at the lodge had said, the close-clipped lawn was as bright, almost, as day. There were no shadows. Light poured down from the powerful electric lamps in the trees. A mouse could not have crossed without being seen.

Patrols showed as he drove on to the gate. They carried submachine guns.

It looked on the surface as if there was no danger to the owner of Quiet Acres, but Manning was not at ease as he drove on through the night, back to Manhattan, so to Pelham Manor where his own house stood with his little corps of faithful Japanese.

There was a letter waiting him. Envelope and enclosure of heavy gray paper, the ink deep purple, the writing extraordinarily bold. Sealed with an oval of heavy scarlet on which was embossed a griffin.

Brought by a boy on a bicycle who seemed to be a district messenger, in uniform. Manning knew better. He knew the Griffin's attention to details, the devilish cunning that made his crimes so eminently perfect.

There were only a few words:

My dear Manning:
Fremont is well guarded, as you have found. An interesting man in many ways. Nevertheless, at the hour appointed!

No signature, only the clever sketch of a griffin's head.

v

THE DEEP voice of the clock in the hall, Fremont's great-grandfather's clock, that had ticked away the lives of so many in the generations since its wooden works were assembled, chimed.

They counted the strokes. Manning glanced at his wrist watch to confirm the news, welcome, yet to him, almost incredible.

Twelve.

"And it is true to the minute," said Fremont triumphantly.

"It was regulated yesterday by the only man on Long Island who understands these ancient timepieces."

Manning nodded. It was too good to be true. But his own watch corroborated the time.

The Griffin—for once—had failed.

Fremont got to his feet, flicked the ash from his almost finished cigar.

"We seemed to have foiled him this time," he said. "I thank you just the same, Manning, for your company. It has given me also a sense of additional protection. You had no sleep last night and I did, due to your presence. Now let us turn in." Fremont added laughingly: "The bolts and bars have all been attended to. There are watchmen on duty in the house as well as outside, but there is one thing I always attend to, the winding up of the clock downstairs that has just announced midnight.

"The witching hour, eh, Manning? It's growing old, that clock. You have to haul up the weights gently to wind the cord on its wooden wheels. But it is faithful. I'll fix it and then we'll go to bed. Your vigil is over."

Manning got to his feet. There seemed to have been some slip. The Griffin had never failed to be exact in his predictions. "Somewhere, between midnight Wednesday and midnight Thursday," he had boasted. It had been a boast. Midnight had struck, and yet....

As he followed Fremont downstairs, he took out his automatic, examined it. The vibrations of evil that affected him when the Griffin telephoned, and at other poignant moments, were with him now.

He saw the light from outside through the fan-shaped light above the heavy door. There was a light in the hall.

Fremont's shadow and Manning's own were flung fantastically on the wall as they descended the circular stairway. The clock ticked on. Seven minutes past the hour when Manning looked at it.

Seven minutes beyond the hour appointed.

He looked at the lock, the bolts, the chain on the door. All in order.

Fremont opened the door panel of the clock that showed the iron weights at the end of their suspending cords.

He pulled on one, drew up the weight. The wooden machinery creaked a little.

He pulled up the other, standing in front of the ancient timepiece. It reached its limit and then there was a click, a sharp explosion, a burst of fire and Fremont staggered back, his feet tangled in a rug, falling, his throat torn away by a slug, his hands clutching at it as he toppled, his vertebrae smashed, the spinal cord severed—life gone before he struck the floor.

At the same moment all lights went out, within the house and without. All was pitchy darkness. Manning heard footsteps coming.

There came three knocks on the door, on the brass, Colonial knocker.

He answered the challenge. With his gun out he slid back the bolts, unslotted the chain, sprang the lock. It took time and when he finally opened it he saw nothing but the ray of a torch far across the lawn, the beam of an electric flash, joined by others, coupled with shouts.

Lights now in the house. Other torches, a lamp, the butler and another man, bending over Fremont's body.

Manning did not see them. He was shouting across the lawn, proclaiming himself, looking in vain, as he knew he would, for some sign of the Griffin, of his agent, whoever had knocked upon the door.

The lights were still out, the current would be off from the fence. He stood on the lawn, furious and inadequate as the guards came racing up.

The Griffin had again scored. Fremont was dead. But—it was beyond the appointed hour!

Manning turned to go into the house. There was something

strange attached to the brass knocker. Something scarlet, scarlet as a gout of blood.

The red seal of the Griffin!

V I

THE BUTLER, grief distorting his face, called Manning. It was the telephone. And Manning had expected it. The Griffin's voice, his mocking laugh. Manning controlled himself to listen. There might be yet some clew.

"Manning? You see, my friend, you failed again. It was just a question of studying habit, Manning. I know enough of yours to kill you whenever I wish. Not yet, I think. You still amuse me.

"Fremont was fond of that great-grandfather clock of his. Had a man come to regulate its works once every month. Wound it himself.

"Well, the man came yesterday. He was quite easy to impersonate. A rather striking personality, not meaning any pun. Looked just like the theatrical idea of a Swiss watch and clock expert. So did my man, Manning, so did my man. I saw the double myself, listened to him speak. The make-up and the accent were excellent.

"The lights going out and the knocking on the door, were, I admit, a trifle melodramatic. You must humor me there, Manning. You remember the knocking on the gate in Macbeth? Effective. And it gave me a chance to set my final seal on the performance. The current at Quiet Acres comes on a leased line from a main power transmission that is not hard to eliminate.

"As for the actual cause of death, that was a little device that I myself suggested. My pseudo Swiss left the clock wound up, as he always did, and you may be sure he handled the weights carefully. But—the next time Fremont handled them—which was to-night—you know what happened."

"After twelve o'clock," said Manning. *"After twelve o'clock,* checked by my watch, which is correct. You failed after all. *You failed!*"

If he could taunt the Griffin sufficiently, augment his madness to a frenzy, the death of the publisher might not have been entirely in vain.

He heard the Griffin's chuckle.

"My dear Manning, you have overlooked something. By that watch of yours, doubtless, it is twenty-one minutes after twelve, but not by solar time, Manning, only by Daylight Saving."

The voice ceased. Through the receiver there came only a faint dying sound of exotic music.

*Manning Traps the Messenger of Murder—
and the Hours of Doom in Which the Griffin
Promised Death are Almost Over*

T HE MYSTERIOUS, unrecognized residence of
the Griffin was built upon the summit of a wooded knoll
entirely owned by the monster who chose to be known only
under his fabulous *nom de crime*. The Griffin—an apt symbol,
this mythical creature, half lion, half eagle, ready to rend with
beak and claw, to swoop or leap, and to destroy.

Save for the outward appearance, the house was practically
a fortress, impregnable, almost, to all but artillery fire. It was
less than fifty miles from the towers of Manhattan, twenty
minutes of flying time, an hour and a half by motor or train.
Yet, so remote was it, so cleverly did the Griffin carry out his
comings and his goings, that few people knew the place existed
at all.

The trees were thick enough, and the house so cunningly
placed in a natural depression, that summer or winter, it could
not be seen from the infrequently traveled road. The drive that
led upward to the evil aerie was masked. It seemed merely an
inconsequential lane, a wood road, perhaps, or a way for cows,
from and to pasture.

Deep in the bowels of the knoll, the Griffin had his underground laboratories. There the men who were his slaves
labored—men no longer known by name, but only by number,
serfs to his despotism. They came from all ranks of life, carefully selected, every man an expert in his particular profession
or trade.

They never saw the outside world. And every one of them, however much he might long for liberty, knew that freedom would only lead to another type of imprisonment—and disgrace for their loved ones. There were none of them but had committed crimes, none but were hunted, few for whom rewards were not offered. Men of infinite capacity, but weak. Out of their weakness the Griffin forged the links for the strong chains of his own machinations.

They hated him, but they feared him more. He held them at his mercy, and they knew how slight a thing that was. Now, as he passed among them, clad in a long robe of black brocade, his face covered with a yellow, shining mask that clung without revealing his identity, like some scabrous outer skin that was ready to be sloughed like the skin of a serpent, they surrounded him with the emanations of their hatred, their desire to rid themselves of his unholy thrall.

Yet, even if they had been able to destroy him, even if they could have won their way out of the crypts where they toiled, they knew their lives were proscribed.

The Griffin knew what they felt, and in his almost maniacal mind he rejoiced in it. Behind him, close, watchful, always hoping to be called upon, there came the dwarf, the Caribbean from Voodoo Land, squat, mute, and deaf; a fantastic figure in turban and raiment that would have suited some freak at a medieval court.

His long arms, immensely powerful, though they showed no more muscles than those of a chimpanzee, allowed the knuckles of his hands to reach to his knees. In his sash he carried a long knife, razor-edged. His shoulders and torso made up for his diminished legs. His head was oversized, his eyes held cunning and cruelty, and he was the personal bodyguard of the Griffin, ever aching to be allowed to play the butcher. He looked like the familiar to a wizard, and, in his clinging mask and sweeping robe, the Griffin might well have passed for the necromancer.

There were strange lights and shadows in these corridors and chambers, curious sights and sounds and smells. The odors of chemicals, of heated metals, of electric energy. The source of the general illumination was invisible, but it was ample. Here were men working over small furnaces whose glare enhanced their set, drawn features, the faces of men who had lost hope. Now and then some livid ray would flash out from electric contacts. This would be a workshop with these nameless craftsmen toiling over some diabolical conception of the Griffin, to be used in his fiendish plans against society, the world at large.

He walked quietly, his dark eyes glittering through the slits in his mask, observing all. Some of the workers cringed at his approach, while others glanced furtively and caught the roving gaze of the swaggering dwarf, eager to find excuse to annihilate, to kill.

The Griffin passed on, through this labyrinth hewn from the living rock, equipped so elaborately as to its mechanics, a dungeon in its living quarters.

He came to a vaulted place where a dog cowered, chained, fearful of the surroundings. A slave in brown denim overalls that hid his number—17—on sleeve and back, black numerals on a white label, stirred as the Griffin entered. Number Seventeen was elderly, not perhaps so old as his surroundings made him appear, but bald almost to entirety, deep lines in his tired face, his deepset eyes gleaming.

"You are ready?" asked the Griffin in a voice that sounded like a bell-stroke on a temple gong—a voice of doom.

"I am ready," answered the man. "The dog has not been fed. It is hungry. I am not sure of the results until the experiment is made. The constituents of the lethal dose are new to me, and you stated that it was imperative they should be so compounded that all traces would be absorbed and disappear."

The Griffin chuckled. It was the cluck of infinite derision.

"I like always to leave them baffled," he said. "To show them that their analysts, their toxicologists, are purile. Also, there is

*Flickering in the television
mirror was the Griffin's face.*

the satisfaction of removing all clews. Even if they had me—the Griffin—in their hands, they could prove nothing. I should laugh at them. Knowledge—that is what we seek—the knowledge that is Power. So," he added abruptly, as if he regretted his talk, "go ahead, show me."

The orbs of Number Seventeen dilated their pupils, contracted them. He looked at the Griffin almost murderously. His glance seemed to say—"would this were you, instead of the dog."

The famished beast seized the hunk of meat that was flung to him, smeared slightly by a white substance like ointment. It gulped down the flesh hastily and then terrific tremors took possession of its body. Writhing, convulsed, foaming—it died, with the Griffin watching its slightest motion with sadistic pleasure, though a frown slowly gathered on its features that wrinkled the half transparent mask.

"You must perfect this," he ordered. "Whatever I might enjoy the more, it must not be said that the Griffin is not merciful in his executions. I want the last result to-morrow, at this hour. You understand?"

II

GORDON MANNING, ex-officer and distinguished agent of the Intelligence Department in the late war, left the down town gymnasium where he kept physically fit and walked with swinging strides toward his office suite.

There, on the outer door sign, he was announced as a consultant attorney and did, in normal times, so act. Now his whole energy was concentrated on unmasking the Griffin and delivering him to justice. Single-handed, he hoped to track down the unbalanced fiend whose whole diabolic pleasure was murder—track him down alone, after the whole civic force had failed.

There were times when Manning almost admitted failure himself. Thus far he had been worsted by the cunning of the insanely clever evil genius who believed he held a grudge against civilization and those who advanced its progress. But Manning was not without some clews by which he ultimately believed he would conquer in the strange duel.

It was literally a duel. The Griffin had deliberately challenged him to contest in what the Griffin called a game. He had been the first to congratulate Manning on his appointment, though this had been a closely veiled affair. He went further and named the victims he had, so far, counted, even going to the length of naming the days when they would be disposed of.

The Griffin's succession of crimes had roused not only New York, but the whole country. They had affected the stock market, besides threatening the very foundations of civic existence. Manning's pride was in arms, aside from his keen responsibility as a citizen. He had himself been jeopardized a dozen times and the Griffin, in his devilish cunning, had struck to undermine Manning's resources and his manhood by placing the woman he loved in danger.

It was not easy to ignore such things, on top of the Griffin's constant triumphs. The result showed in Manning's face, in the extra leanness of his body. He fought against it, against the constant threat and strain of another pronouncement by the Griffin of his next coup.

It was close to the end of the year. New York had just experienced its bitterest day on record. It was still close to zero, though the weather showed signs of change. Throughout the United States and most of Europe the weather had been unseasonal. There had been one flurry of snow and then an icy aftermath. Even on Broadway there were streaks of ice along the pavement and the street. The apple vendors, the unemployed, shivered by their boxes and placards.

Manning crossed the street just at the changing of the light from red to green for north and south traffic. Vehicles anxious to make their destinations started up and Manning quickened his steps. A woman, burdened with bundles that proclaimed her Christmas shopping, slipped on a film of ice, dropped a package and tripped over it in front of a truck, coming on like a juggernaut with its clutch released to high speed.

The driver, through his cab window, did his best, his eyes goggling at the impending catastrophe. Onlookers held their breaths or expelled it in cries of alarm. The woman seemed doomed. No one ventured to rescue her save Manning, who dashed in front of the machine and grasped her, half lifting her by sheer strength as he leaped for the curb, thrusting her to safety, sprawling himself just beyond reach of the lurching truck.

Her bundles were scattered. Traffic was held up. A police officer came hurrying up as other now officious and eager persons collected the packages, crowded around rescuer and rescued. The woman was dazed, sitting up. Manning got to his feet and slid through the gathering throng. That was the fashion of the man. Only his supreme coördination could have pulled it off and now, with a split trousers knee beneath his overcoat, he hurried to his building, keeping the damage out of sight, mounting to his suite on the ninth floor. He had other clothing there, and once in his private office, he changed.

Deliberately, he took a drink of excellent Scotch, knowing his pulses were unsteady, his condition not normal. The issue between him and the Griffin was having its effect on him.

The Griffin called it a game, but it was one in which he had all the advantage of the first move, the initial planning and preparation. It would have unnerved a weaker man. To Manning it served to summon up a determination that was growing almost desperate, that not merely challenged patience but called for all his intelligence.

He had got so that he was tuned in to the Griffin's activities. He had a prescience of when they were about to culminate, and to-day he felt a hunch that the Griffin was once more about to strike, to choose some outstanding and useful man and mark him for doom that Manning might not be able to prevent. The responsibility was enormous, almost overpowering, to be the man to guard against a madman's uncanny cunning and dia- bolical resource.

Manning sipped his highball, looking out to the towering buildings beyond his office window, the peep of river and bridge that proclaimed the industry and genius of Manhattan. Yet all this was threatened by one fiendish maniac. Even as he gazed his telephone rang with a curious vibration that told Manning that the Griffin was on the other end of the line where with an ingenuity born of himself or those who served him, he had managed to so synchronize the impulse of the wire that it was useless to try and trace the call. The Griffin controlled many methods that ranked high in science. He was no ordinary an- tagonist and he was motivated with the instinct of a devil.

Manning did not avoid the issue. He had past reason to believe that the Griffin knew that he was present. The man had infinite resources.

"Manning?" The deep voice, like the sound of a temple gong tinged with mockery, boomed through the receiver. "It's almost a month since I've called you. Have you been expecting to hear from me? The stars in their courses have controlled me."

Manning said nothing. He was there to hear. He had guessed that in the Griffin's madness there was a streak of mysticism, that the man supported his machinations by some outside aid like astrology.

"But my divinations evolve, Manning. The game is on once more, the pieces set. This time it is one of those pseudo-scientists who seek to set the world ahead, not knowing that I am far in front of them. You know Ezra Farnett, who prates of telepathy, of thought transference and vision, when he does not think he is a musical genius. Ha, ha!"

The mocking laughter rang in Manning's ears, and back of it he could hear faint strains of exotic music.

Ezra Farnett!

A genius! He was of world-wide fame for his enterprise in science, particularly regarding the projection of sound and sight; known also as a musician extraordinary whose compositions had been termed occult, whose harmonies stirred and stimulated the soul. He stated freely that, to him, music was the complement to his scientific exploration and energies, that it inspired and hastened his discoveries. A curious being, Ezra Farnett, unique and masterful, a blend of the practical and the dreamer.

And the Griffin, in his strange complex, his hatred of all those who accomplished, who stood for advancement, had chosen him for sacrifice.

"It is still two days from Christmas," the deep voice went on, a voice that was one of Manning's few clews to the Griffin's identity, a voice he could never fail to distinguish. "That is a pagan festival which certain cults keep holy. We will let it pass as hallowed. A time for gifts, which reminds me, Manning, that your own life is too valuable, or at least its efforts too interesting to me, for you to risk it on behalf of a woman out buying Christmas presents."

This was far from the first indication of the Griffin's watchfulness of Manning's moves. It was an espionage that made Manning feel belittled, that was probably employed by the Griffin with such an idea in view. It was the Griffin's boasting statement that murder should be an exact science, that the ordinary killer used his own crude methods, whereas, by carefully studying the habits of an intended victim, one could devise a method that was infallible. Manning had no doubt that, for all his talk of the stars, the Griffin had held Ezra Farnett under close observation for days, if not weeks, plotting his devilish deed.

"I shall kill Ezra Farnett sometime between midnight of the thirtieth and the same hour on the thirty-first. He will not live to see the New Year. You see, my dear Manning, I do not even concede you a chance of saving him. You will play your best, I know, but you are no match for me. I marvel, sometimes, at your continuing to play the game as you do.

"It will be a fitting elimination. Warn him, Manning. Protect him, to the best of your ability. And protect yourself. You may need to. There are times when you weary me and to-day is one of them. So use your wits, you will need them all," he concluded sarcastically.

The voice ceased. The strange music that hummed through the receiver as Manning replaced it on its stand seemed to linger in the room while Manning sat with his face grim, his jaw set hard, his face lines graven deep, staring out of the window, striving to conjure up some plan by which to come to grips with the Griffin.

He sat there while the early winter twilight came sifting down upon Manhattan and its towers began to gleam with a myriad lights. He was still in his chair, in the dark, when his secretary came in before she left for the day.

III

IN HIS circular chamber at the top of his house the Griffin sat silently chuckling. In front of him, on the heavily carven desk, there was a bronze disk suspended. He had been talking in to it, to the man he loved to bait—Gordon Manning.

Quantro, the dwarf, stood behind his master's chair.

The fantastic music rose and fell, murmuring about the curved walls of steel, covered with golden tapestries, walls that showed no inlet or outlet, no means of ventilation or lighting. Yet the air was pure, tinged with a faint incense of burning amber, the light was clear and steady.

The Griffin beckoned with uplifted finger and the ever watchful dwarf came before him. The Griffin spoke to him in swift finger language, using Spanish for the brief words.

An opening showed in the wall as the Griffin pressed a button. There was a lift there into which Quantro stepped, descending in the silent mechanism on his errand to the laboratories.

A few moments passed. Then the bronze disk gave out a note. The lift was rising. Out of it came the man numbered 17, Quantro back of him, watchful, suspicious.

"Well?" asked the Griffin. "Where is it?"

"I have not finished it. I will not prepare it in that fashion. It is the act of a devil. A horrible treachery. It means you intend to kill a man, to fling him into eternity, unprepared. It is murder. I will not be a party to it."

The Griffin began to laugh. His eyes glittered back of the mask slits.

"You should have been a preacher, Seventeen," he said. "To fling a man into eternity, unprepared? What is eternity? What preparation will serve a man after he is dead? What did you think I wanted it for—to kill more dogs? You fool. If you will not put it up as I bid you, others will. And as for you, who disobey me...."

"Others will *not!*" Seventeen suddenly shouted. "You are bound for eternity yourself!"

He whipped out from his overalls a chemist's spatula, ground to razor edges, and leaped at the Griffin in a frantic frenzy and a desperation born of an endless degradation.

An uncouth sound broke from the lips of Quantro. It was like a yelp of satisfaction. The Griffin had not moved. He stood with arms folded in his black brocade, the leprous mask in place.

Swift as Seventeen had been, Quantro was swifter. He sprang high into the air as if catapulted. His fingers, at the end of one long arm, viced about Seventeen's wrist, dragged down the limb with a gorilla's irresistible strength. There was a crack of snapping bone. The arm hung useless, the spatula on the floor. With inhuman ferocity Quantro drew his own long blade from his sash and plunged it again and again into the vitals of the unfortunate wretch, kneeling over him when he fell, striking still, growling and yelping like a hyena over a still warm corpse.

The Griffin watched with his glittering eyes. Only when the puddling blood threatened to reach one of the rare rugs with which the room was furnished did he put out a foot and stir Quantro, who looked up with bloodshot eyes and slavering lips. The Griffin's imperative gesture sent him reluctantly away, wiping his knife and his hands on the fall of his sash.

The Griffin touched a spring. An opening appeared in the center of the floor in front of his desk, widening like a camera's diaphragm, revealing a tubular shaft. Into this the Griffin spurned the wasted body of Seventeen, with his foot consigning it to oblivion. It would be a good object lesson to those other of his slaves who would see it before they disposed of it. The penalty of disobedience.

"They all lack imagination, even the best of them," the Griffin muttered as he picked up the spatula and examined it. "The fool was a chemist and he uses this. Now, if he had thrown acid he might have scored. Number Nine will be the one to complete my device."

He turned to Quantro, spoke once more to him in panto-
mime and digital talk, patted him on his turbaned head as he
passed, as he might have patted a dog who had just performed
successfully, and seated himself again at his desk to await the
coming of his slave.

The music swelled and diminished. The Griffin seemed in a
reverie, toying idly with a griffin in gold-bronze, couched on a
tablet of black onyx, until the bronze disk gave out its sonorous
note once more. In response the Griffin's features, beneath the
mask, were like those of some Egyptian monarch, hawkish,
imperial, and compelling. His lips were thin under the high-
bridged nose, his cheek bones high, his jaw lean, the whole
assemblage harsh and cruel. At times his eyes seemed to give
out strange lights, now crimson, then the lambent green of a
wolf's, the tawny glare of a lion's. They played there like flickering lights of Hades gleaming in Stygian caverns, hinting at
madness.

It was Manning's conviction that if, some day, the Griffin
should fall down in one of his murderous plans, the shock and
disappointment to his grandiose dementia would be the complete unseating of all the machinery of his brain, eccentric, but
as yet invincible.

The diaphragmatic opening to the shaft had closed automatically. Now the lift revealed itself once more and a man
shambled out ahead of Quantro, a white slave whose hands
were stained with chemicals, whose hair had almost vanished
and whose eyes were dull. Here was an instrument who would
not revolt.

IV

THE LAST day of the year was heralded by New York's
heaviest fall of snow for a score or more of years. It snowed
all night in banks and drifts that men and machines labored
vainly to dispose of through the day. Wild, icy winds from the
rivers swept and eddied and spiraled high amid Manhattan's

towers. Traffic struggled hard on land, abandoned the task on the water, where the snow blew in blinding blizzard bursts and the gale wailed and blasted.

The dwelling place of Ezra Farnett was part of a modern and exclusive caravanserai uptown, on the West Side. It was built about a quadrangle. A drive surrounded shrubs, now mounds of snow, and a frozen fountain. The quadrangle was entered by two arches. Ezra Farnett's doorway was beneath one arch, his apartment was duplex and looked out both on street and inner court.

There were watchers under the arches and in the quadrangle, watchers supplementing the regular employees of the place. These latter evaded their bitter duties, but the others, who had been changed twice since midnight, challenged the storm. They were heavily clothed and heavily armed. The fury of the gale that, at times, rushed about the quadrangle like a whirlwind, flinging the snow like foam, called for special alertness. The windows were caked and frosted and crystaled so that the lights shone dimly out.

Within, Ezra Farnett and Gordon Manning sat in the studio that was both library and music room. Manning had taken every possible precaution. He had examined the apartment, gone over the grand piano lest the Griffin might have managed to place there some infernal machine that would explode when certain chords were inevitably struck. That would be characteristic of the fiend, sure that Farnett would play some time during the twenty-four hours the Griffin had set as his life-limit.

But Manning found nothing. Farnett's two menservants were Flemish, devoted, incorruptible. Eighteen of the twenty-four hours had passed. Six now remained. There had been no poison in the food, no attack from some hidden assassin.

But it was a night of nights for murder.

The studio was on the second floor, the windows were fastened, as well as rendered opaque by the snow; there was no way to reach them, and there were four trusted men without.

Equally, the doors were barred, those that led outside and those that communicated with the rest of the building.

It was a man's dwelling, well but not too luxuriously furnished. There were many books and a few good paintings. One carven frame contained a curious inclosure. It was a small oblong of metal, like a mirror of steel. It covered a grating through which entered certain wires, behind which was a contrivance whose intricacies were too much for Manning, though he knew its use.

It was a television transmitter that also carried sound. Farnett had not displayed its use to his guest and protector. The static was unfavorable. During the afternoon Farnett had rested. He had slept also between one and five in the morning, slumber induced by an opiate, largely at Manning's request. He was no longer a young or even a middle-aged man, though still intellectually vigorous.

He knew, as did all New York, of the Griffin's diabolical deeds, and somewhat to Manning's surprise, took his warning philosophically.

"I am infinitely obliged to you," Farnett said. "But I wonder if I would not be almost as much obliged to some one who would painlessly, quickly dispose of me? I have accomplished some things and I have paved the way to what others must inevitably finish. Your Griffin does not know how spent I am. He confers on me the compliment of imagining me his enemy because, in his perverted brain, he resents all rivals, hates genuine progress.

"My brain can still conceive, and does, but my body is tired out. I am close to seventy. One cannot renew human cylinders and furnish spare parts. I get tired—too tired even to play. I must limit myself to an hour a day at the piano. I shall play for you to-night, during our vigil. I hope, for your sake, that you may circumvent the Griffin, or even, through my departure, capture him. The man is not responsible. He is evidently a lunatic, suffering from the sins of his forbears, probably, with tissues that cannot stand the strain of his faculty of imagination. A mentality run *amok*.

"He takes long to strike. Maybe the storm has disrupted his plans and thus your idea that failure will result in his own disintegration will be proved. *Selah!* So be it. It is all on the knees of the gods—and there are no gods. Divinity lives within ourselves alone."

A clock chimed. It was seven o'clock. The old year was passing fast. Dim murmurs of the fury of the storm manifested themselves when even the thick plateglass, set in steel frames, rattled. A fine film of frost had formed, or drifted in, between the junction of the window panes. Dinner was served. Oysters, a soup of real turtle spiced with sherry, a curried fowl and a bottle of red Beaune, artichokes, no sweets, but Cheddar cheese and Napoleon brandy with the coffee. A man's dinner, in a man's house.

Farnett ate little. Manning did not do much better. He did not mistrust the meal, but he was convinced that the Griffin was not frustrated by the weather, that already he had planted somewhere his instrument of death, that all was devised, prepared, and that even now the Griffin was waiting, in full content, for the fulfillment of his scheme.

He glanced at the television plate and it seemed to him that something flickered over it, vague and uncertain, as if a projection sought to register itself against outside resistance.

Eight o'clock. Four hours more. Manning had not slept. He felt no fatigue. He was girded against the onslaught of the Griffin that might manifest itself at any moment, *must* do so within two hundred and forty minutes, or fail.

Farnett finished his coffee in which he had placed the century old brandy, burned in sugar.

"I shall play for you," he said. "Then I shall lie on the couch here until midnight, with you, my friendly guardian, watching me. After that you can rouse me and we will congratulate each other. I shall live on and the Griffin, perhaps," he added whimsically, "will be like the little leprechaun who huffed and puffed, and huffed and puffed until he blew up with mortification."

Under the magic fingers of Farnett the piano became, to Manning, a hundred instruments. He heard the devil-drums of barbaric lands, the shaken sistra of ancient Egypt, the cithara of medieval music, lutes and flutes and Andalusian guitars. Panpipes and deep-toned trumpets, calling to battle, challenging. Rattling gourds and bawling conches as wild hordes swept on to rapine and loot. Music of love, pagan and divine. High inspiration, the paeans of the dead dynasties of gods and demigods, the shrill pipe of sybils, the rolling rhythm of martial strains.

He knew now what Farnett meant when he declared music an inspiration, a vibrational urge to those attuned to cadence. The piano, like a horizontal harp, sang to him of his own ambitions, of his longings for love, for achievement. It evoked anew the desire to open the world, like an oyster, with his sword. It spoke of combat and of peace. It ended in soft, lingering chords.

Farnett sat on the piano bench, exhausted but elated.

"So it finishes," he said. " 'So fleet the works of men back to the earth again; ancient and holy things fade—like a dream.' How it storms. To dream and not to waken, only to dream once more the vision is accomplished. Good night, Manning. I'm tired. I'm glad to have known you. I have heard of you before, of course, in war as well as in what we call peace, the period between wars when men rest and sharpen their weapons for the next encounter. And still, some of them, too many of them, keep on killing. Like our friend the Griffin. I don't want to see another war. Man. *Homo sapiens* he calls himself. The wise one of the genus who devotes his brains to the art of destroying his kind. With the wild ape still in him. Well, there is no end to wars and the making of wars. The Four Horsemen are grooming their wild steeds, saddling up. Good night."

V

T HE HOUSE phone rang. Farnett answered it.

"Something wrong with the steam," he said. "They want us to shut off the radiators for half an hour until they trace the leak. The engineer seems to think it's in this section of the building. He says, and truly, that this is no weather for steam valves to misbehave. He's coming up."

Manning nodded. It all seemed natural enough. But he knew the Griffin. This was no night for outsiders to appear, however plausibly. His hand slid to where his automatic nested in its shoulder clip.

A knock sounded and Manning answered it. There was a grizzled, elderly man in overalls, carrying a box of tools. He had a red scar on his right cheek that looked like a scald. He touched the peak of the cap he wore.

"Evening, Mr. Farnett. Sorry to disturb you. But it's a nasty night and we don't want the heat to go wrong. There's a blockade somewhere. Air in the valves, I reckon. It won't take a minute or two."

Manning had taken his seat again. He seemed to look at the blank oblong of steel in its metal frame, Farnett's television producer.

The engineer fiddled with the valves, turned them off.

"Your rooms are warm," he said. "They'll keep you comfortable till we fix things. Can I go into the bathrooms?"

Farnett yawned, nodded. The man knew where to go. As he disappeared Manning leaned forward.

"You recognize him?" he asked.

Farnett smothered another yawn.

"Oh, yes," he replied. "It's Sissons."

"Excuse me," said Manning.

He strolled to the bathroom. Sissons straightened from where he had been testing the register.

"It's not here," he said. "I'll just take a look at Mr. Farnett's bathroom upstairs. But I think the trouble's in the next apartment. It's vacant. They're gone South for the winter."

He disappeared, carrying his tools. Manning kicked off his shoes and followed him. He entered Farnett's bedroom, on the upper floor of the duplex, halted. The engineer was in the bathroom. Manning gave him a minute, and then glided to the open door.

He saw the man standing over the toilet bowl, the hot water running. There was a cabinet back of it, with a mirrored front. In the mirror Manning saw the man squeezing out something into the bowl—a metal tube, labeled.

He had no business doing anything like that.

The next second the man saw Manning. He dropped the tube and started to whirl as Manning leaped.

Manning saw his hand slide down. The overalls were not intended for the quick handling of a gun. Manning did not use his. He jumped and got a wrestling grip. The engineer's apparent age shed itself as he strained against the hold, but Manning was too quick and expert for him. Manning got him in a hammer lock and threw him. The man's head connected with the tiled flooring of the bathroom and he relaxed, unconscious.

Manning gave him a swift inspection before he turned to the basin. In it was a tube of well known toothpaste, partly squeezed. Another on a shelf inlaid in the tiled wall. They were duplicates, or would have been when the fake engineer had finished squeezing his to seem the same as the other.

Here was a deadly device—of the Griffin. Frustrated this time.

Manning held no doubt that analysis would prove the tube the fake Sissons meant to substitute was filled with deadly, swift-acting poison.

He put it away safely in his pocket, the cap replaced, then stooped and with a moistened towel wiped off the artificial scald on the man's face. He lifted the gray wig, and his face grew grim and earnest.

He had one of the Griffin's tools, unhurt save for perhaps a slight concussion of the brain. The tiled floor was hard. The man breathed stertorously. Manning felt his pulse. Then he looked in the cabinet. It was a deep one and well stocked. There were two unbroken packages of medical bandages.

Deftly Manning used them to securely tie up his prize. It did not take long to truss the killer's tool.

Manning left him there. He could keep. This time they would hold the man, give him a real inquisition, an improvement on any police third degree. They would wrest from him all he knew of the Griffin's actions and whereabouts. Manning was in no mood, nor would he be, to show any mercy in his mode of questioning. Too many valuable citizens had been killed, too often had he been frustrated by the necessary slaying of an emissary. But now he had one at last, alive. Others had refused to talk, this one should not.

Manning had traveled in many lands. He knew strange, savage ways to torture, to break men down. He felt exultant.

He found Farnett divested of his outer clothing, lying down on a lounge beneath the television tablet.

"What happened?" he asked feebly. "I heard some sort of a commotion. Tell me, Manning."

Manning told him briefly. He was worried about Farnett. The man did not look too well. His eyes were dull and his cheeks were sunken.

"Haven't you got some tablets to take?" he asked. "I think the main danger is over. Take it easy."

"I'm cold," said Farnett, drawing his dressing gown closer. "It was just a fake about the steam. Turn it on again. I'm cold. There are some strychnine tablets upstairs, in the medicine cabinet, but I don't need them now. I took some digitalis I keep handy."

Manning turned on the valves. The steam came readily enough. He fixed the cushions under Farnett, who now seemed responsive to the drug he had taken.

Halfway up the stairs Manning felt a curious sense of dizziness. He had not been himself of late, with the strain of his warfare with the Griffin, and he fought it off. His fight with the pseudo-engineer had been short but severe.

He wanted to search the man before he called up headquarters. He found it hard to breathe, his heart was pounding, but he mounted the stairs and found his man, still seemingly out, on the bathroom floor.

Manning started to search him. He found a gun and then a small cardboard box. He opened it, with a hunch as to what was inside. His hunch was justified.

Seals! Heavy crimson paper, gummed on the inside, bearing the symbol of the Griffin. The killer had been instructed to fasten one of them on his victim. And Manning might find them useful later.

As he looked at the seals, the room seemed suddenly to revolve about him. He lifted himself from his knees and then felt the strength go out of him. He could not get air into his lungs. Something entered them, but it was not oxygen. He fought to rise, but could not. The last thing he heard was the hissing steam.

VI

MANNING CAME to, panting. He thought he was back in the war. Some alarm was ringing. Gas! Gas!

Where was his mask? He was strangling. But not going to quit. A light glowed faintly overhead. Electric? What....

Nothing short of the invincible purpose with which he had pursued the Griffin, his absolute determination to annihilate this fiend, could have got him to his feet.

There was a vital spark within him, born of his will, that whipped his dying senses.

Gas! Gas without question. But this was not the trenches. A hospital, with the tiled walls and floor? No! They had no hospitals like that where he had fought.

He saw the lax form of the engineer in his overalls—not a uniform—and his sluggish memory was spurred.

There was a window to the room and he thrust it up, gulping at the cold air, the driving snow.

He had to stoop once more and he did it, as a diver does, holding his breath, shutting off the radiator valves through which the deadly gas might still be coming. The same in the bedroom, then downstairs. The wild wind blew the curtains out straight, the white flakes rushed in. It was freezing—far below freezing, but better that than death.

He was too late.

Farnett lay stretched out on the couch. His low vitality had succumbed. The Griffin had triumphed after all.

Had he?

Manning, assured that Farnett was beyond recovery, utterly collapsed under the deadly fumes, raced back to the bathroom.

There was clear air there now, plenty of oxygen, but the Griffin's aide, like Farnett, had not been able to assimilate it. Unconscious from the flying mare, his lungs had not been able to help his beleaguered body. The man was dead.

Manning went slowly down the stairs, ready to call up headquarters, to report another failure for himself, another victory for the Griffin.

He paused as he entered the room. The television plaque was beginning to glow.

As Manning gazed, a vision materialized upon it. The picture of a man, masked with something that effectually disguised and yet half-mockingly revealed him.

He heard a voice. The voice of the Griffin, that he had heard so often—too often—and knew so well.

"I had two strings to my bow, Manning. I am not sure, at this moment, which one sped the fatal arrow. Perhaps the toothpaste, perhaps the cyanogen. But I time these matters. By now I am sure that Farnett has joined 'the great majority.'"

For once Manning lost control, looking at the mocking vision on the plaque, regarding the stiffening form of Farnett. As if in a dream, he heard himself hurling invectives at the portrait that was now gradually fading.

"Here's hoping, Manning," sounded the voice of the Griffin faintly. "Some day we'll get to grips. Meanwhile, your oaths are not too fitting. This *is*."

Through the plaque, now only vacant metal, there seemed to come a strain of music. Wherever evolved, it was plain enough in that room of death.

Chopin's Funeral March. *La Marche Funébre.*

THE GRIFFIN'S DOUBLE CROSS

In the Heart of a Fortified Laboratory,
the Griffin's Tool Threatens Manning
with Death from a Jar of Germs

THE BROADCASTING stations had said good night through their suave-voiced announcers and the silver gongs had chimed. Hundreds of thousands of radio owners were prepared to tune off for the night when suddenly, unannounced, there came on the air the deep notes of a booming voice in words whose portent was so startling, so arresting and sinister, that the ears of half a nation strained to listen, thrilled with horror.

There were others who heard with hatred, with anger, with chagrin at their own past and present impotence to still that booming voice for ever. Men, many of them, who had tried in vain to capture the owner of the mysterious voice, the arch-fiend who had terrorized Manhattan, who had murdered more than a score of prominent, useful citizens, heard the words with a shudder.

A maniac, the speaker was, beyond a doubt, and one possessed of infinite resource and cunning, primed with the deviltry of Eblis. A magician who by some method, was sending his fateful, grandiloquent message abroad.

"This is the Griffin speaking."

There was a short pause in which strange, exotic music could be faintly heard. Then a chuckle, diabolical and exultant, as if the sender was enjoying the shock he knew his five words had caused.

The assurance, the conceit of the man was astounding. It was not the first time he had sought publicity to satisfy his grandiose dementia, his colossal ego.

"I make no apology," the deep, confident voice went on. "I would clear up a misunderstanding. I have been described as a menace—even as a monster. I am a philanthropist. There are those who seek to rid the world of me in return for my having eliminated others who, with their insane theories, their pretentious humbuggery, their false morality, have clogged the path of the world's true progress.

"I expect no recognition, no meed of praise, no statues nor tablets to my memory. Rather, I may be execrated. I do not pose as a martyr, nor do I intend to meet the fate of one. I pit my wits against the pseudo-intelligence of others, and laugh at the efforts of a perverted police system. What I do, I do for my own satisfaction.

"My task is far from ended. The stars in their courses are with me in my enterprise. Them I consult before I strike. You will hear of me before long. I have a list of those who must be removed. Their fates are decided, the days are appointed. They will be warned. Let those who think they can circumvent me make their endeavors. The ancient, mythical creature whose symbol I have taken, half lion, half eagle, armed with beak and claws, able to fly and leap, was worshiped once, at Cnossos and elsewhere, as a deity. I make no claim to deity. But it would be easier to pluck the flaming star, Aldebaran, from the firmament, to halt the rhythm of the universe, than to thwart my high endeavor.

"*This is the Griffin.* Good night."

Silence, and then the malicious chuckle once again, as if to stress the mockery of his final greeting. Again the strain of music, slowly dying out, gone.

The air was void of sound. The violent crackle of static followed, ceased, as a late program from a night club came faintly in with the latest jazz. It had no listeners. Men and women looked at each other with pallid faces, dry-lipped, their eyes fixed as if on something unseen and infinitely malignant, a flying, invisible monster that soared on widespread wings with outcurved claws and open beak, seeking its human victim.

The Griffin was abroad.

I I

IN HIS library, in his own house at Pelham Manor, Gordon Manning, special agent, ex-intelligence officer in the Great War, whose mission was the capture and destruction of the Griffin, turned off his radio. His face was haggard with responsibility, graved with lines of effort that, so far, had only met with failure.

The colossal insolence of the Griffin left him untouched. He knew the man to be crazed, possessed of the idea that he must avenge some injury he had suffered, perhaps unjustly. Even as the violent maniac is endowed with super-human strength and cunning, so the inflamed brain of the Griffin conceived plans beyond the scope of a sane person.

He had agents, linked to him by some mysterious bond, slaves who did his bidding, made his schemes possible. They were men skilled in science and mechanics. Manning had met with them. More than one he had killed. Others had committed suicide. From none of them had the slightest clew been gained that led to the Griffin or to his hidden aerie.

Slowly Manning refilled the pipe that had gone out. The Griffin would strike again. At any moment he might communicate with Manning in what the Griffin chose to call a game. Jeeringly he would give Manning the name of his next victim, set the very day of attack, defy Manning to prevent the crime.

Manning had traveled far, seen many strange things. He knew that magic was merely the phenomenon of the unknown. He had witnessed the weird rites of Tibetan priests, of mahata-

"*There's trouble—
more than I
can handle!*"
said Sloane.

mas, shamans, and South Sea Tahungas. He did not believe in the supernatural. There was nothing that could not be explained.

Yet his subconsciousness, reacting to atavistic fears of the days when his forbears lived in caves or trees and shivered at the ways of wizards, was, for a brief moment, flooded with a sense of the unreal.

Automatically he quoted, half aloud, from Poe's Raven.

Be thou gone, thou thing of evil,
Be thou beast, or be thou devil;
Take thy beak from out my heart
And thy form from off my door!

The sound of his own voice roused him. He gave a short laugh as he stood to his full, lean height and lit his pipe.

Quoth the Griffin: "*Nevermore*"

he paraphrased, as he stood in front of his fireplace, where logs smoldered.

"Some day we'll clip your wings, my mysterious friend," he said. "Trim your talons and prune your beak. Stuff your hide and place you on exhibition. Some day you'll slip, and I'll be there to watch for it. Some day, some time, perhaps the next."

His clean cut features were grim as he stood there, the amber stem of his pipe close clipped between his teeth.

A Japanese servant entered, silent and deferential.

"There is nothing more to-night, Tomaki," said Manning. "Thank you. You have locked up?"

Tomaki hissed with indrawn breath.

"Everything is lock," he said. "I go to look, make sure. There is knock on door. I get Matsumi. We open, quick. There is no one there."

Poe was still in Manning's mind.

Darkness there—and nothing more.

"Never mind, Tomaki, I was just quoting," he said. "What did you find?"

The Griffin had his stronghold; this was Manning's. There was no darkness outside his door, day or night. Extra light flooded the path from the gate, two hundred feet away. There was no shrubbery, no place for a man to hide. At the side, leading to the walled garden, topped with tearing spikes, and to the garage, were strong metal lattices with locked entrances. Yet some agency had been there, delivering a message. And he knew from whom.

Tomaki was holding out a letter on a silver salver. The envelope was of heavy, handmade, gray paper, the inscription in bold script, the ink purple.

Gordon Manning, Esq.

Manning turned the envelope over. It was sealed with an

oval of scarlet wax that held the impression of a griffin's head and neck.

"That's all, Tomaki," he said evenly.

Slowly he broke the seal.

I I I

THE GRIFFIN sat enthroned in his high, carved chair behind his massive desk, like a semi-deity, and an angry one.

Behind him stood his bodyguard, Quantro the dwarf. Stunted and distorted of figure, grotesque of costume, he looked, in his turban, long robes, and sash, as if he belonged to some medieval court. A long, keen, unsheathed knife was tucked into the sash—the knife he ever itched to use. Deaf and dumb was Quantro, child of the Caribbees, born within the shadow of voodoo.

The chamber was circular, built all of steel. Rich rugs were on the floor, golden tapestries covered the curving wall. The lighting was screened. There were no windows, but the circulation of air was perfect.

The vague perfume of burning amber, the faint strains of barbaric music, suggested wild dances on a moonlit desert, dancing girls whirling in a savage saraband.

In front of the desk stood one of the Griffin's slaves, men who were little better than living robots, save for their specialized brains. They had been picked for their abilities to carry out the mad schemes of the Griffin. All of them were men outside the law and had been promised a refuge that turned out to be a prison.

The man, nameless, known only by a number, was a gaunt, harassed figure in stained overalls, his fingers dyed with chemicals, his face deep-lined with despair, pallid and unnatural from working over retort, crucible, and test tube, shoulders bowed, eyes dull.

He had not been successful with his latest formula. The result had not pleased the Griffin. Number Eight awaited judgment, penalty. He had no longer a soul to be seared. He had concocted poisons before, knowing well enough that they linked him with murder. But he had a body to be tortured. He still clung to life because of the pittance—with an occasional bonus when he pleased the master—that was sent to his dependents, denying them knowledge of his whereabouts.

The Griffin owned what there was of him. Freedom meant the inevitable capture and penal servitude where he could not earn the little that kept his wife and children from destitution.

The terrible eyes of the Griffin, with the red light of madness in them, glittered through the slits of the mask he wore, a covering of clinging stuff, golden, clammy in appearance, like goldbeater's skin. It seemed like a skin that was being sloughed off, still adherent, repulsive as a leper's face, horrible, sinister. Through it his hawklike features showed, distinct, but sufficiently disguised.

His voice was deep, unmuffled by the mask. It was not unduly harsh. It did not match his flaming eyes.

"You say, Number Eight, that you fear even your final result will not come up to my expectations?"

"I am afraid not," said the man, tonelessly. "The potion is tasteless, odorless, untraceable. It will be instantly absorbed by the tissues. No autopsy can detect its use."

"It is not your function to discuss any possible use to which it might be put," said the Griffin evenly, though the fire in his eyes waxed like the fire-play of an opal. "You assured me in the beginning that your formula would prove successful. I do not like to have my plans go awry. To what do you attribute your failure?"

"I am not certain that it is a failure. The last solution has yet to be tested. I was about to try it, on one of the dogs, when I was summoned."

"Exactly," said the Griffin, placidly. There were animals for experimental purposes kept in his deep underground cellars.

"But you have not yet answered my question. Suppose this solution, like former ones, fails to kill instantly, produces extreme anguish while life lasts, wherein did your formula err?"

"The formula was correct," said Number Eight. "I would stake my reputation—"

"Your reputation?" asked the Griffin, mildly enough, but with a mockery in his tone that brought a flush to the man's face.

"My *life,* then," he retorted with some show of spirit. "Not much of a wager," he added bitterly. "But all I have. The error is not in the formula but in the materials. Three of the drugs are rare, imported from Saigon. They may have been adulterated, or deteriorated, a wrong species of one of them may have been substituted. Like digitalis, different types of the same genus produce varying effects on the heart, though with the same general attributes."

"I see. Well, let us trust the test is satisfactory. I am sure you have worked hard. You have been useful to me. So, I did not summons you to criticize you unduly."

The Griffin rose, somber, dominating in the long robe of black brocade he wore and crossed to where a cabinet whose pedestals were griffins conformed to the curve of the wall. He took from it two silver chalices and a silver flagon, handled and elaborately chased.

From it he poured two measures of liquor, spicy, the deep amber of Tokay in hue. He offered one to Number Eight, raised the other.

"I drink your health," he said. "Honor me by drinking mine."

Number Eight gazed at him with a curious hesitation, as if he found some irony in the suave speech.

"Tut!" chided the Griffin, gently. "You are afraid? Then I will drink first. To your health, Number Eight!"

He drained the shallow goblet, smiled as Number Eight followed his example and suddenly fell writhing to the floor, his face gray with anguish, his limbs cramped, his belly a pit of molten agony.

The Griffin watched him. Quantro stepped forward and gazed with malicious glee, the pleasure of a wanton child who enjoys the throes of a tormented animal.

It did not last long. No organism could sustain the racking torture that twisted the poor wretch. His body was still contorted, his face a thing of horror, when at last he died.

"You wagered your life," said the Griffin. "And you lost, because you failed. I do not brook failure. You have upset my plans," he went on, his voice quickening to fury. "To hell with you!"

He turned and beckoned to Quantro, then touched a button that caused an opening to suddenly appear in the floor, swiftly widening, as the diaphragm shutter of a camera opens. Into the steel chute the dwarf, displaying enormous strength in his long arms, shot the twisted body.

The Griffin poured himself another measure of the wine, careful to see that the air hole that had released the poisoned liquor through a second outlet in the curved lip was closed. It was but a common conjuring trick, a little elaborated, but he had used it before to like purpose and it intrigued him.

"I deal swift death upon occasion," he said aloud, as he set down the chalice, "swift and violent, but never lingering. It is not artistic. He would have liked to see *me* writhe, the craven slave."

He began to pace the floor where the opening had closed.

He had intended this latest poison for his next coup. Now he must change his arrangements within a fixed time, and it annoyed him to be thwarted.

Gordon Manning believed that if the Griffin once failed, his tremendous ego could not sustain the blow and he would go stark mad. Now, at this check, Quantro cowered. He had chuckled over the death of Number Eight, he quailed now before the storm he sensed brewing in his master.

But presently the Griffin chuckled also. Quantro could not hear it, but he felt the change.

"It will be amusing to see how Manning takes this," the Griffin said.

He took his seat again, made sign to Quantro, who brought a Turkish hookah. The dwarf lit the bowl of hemp-treated tobacco as the Griffin set the crystal mouthpiece between his lips, and the smoke flowed upward through the rose-scented water.

Presently he pitched his voice to a certain note and spoke into the bronze disk that stood on the desk, suspended between pillars. It was through this he had broadcast his challenge to the listening world an hour before.

The sensitive diaphragm responded, translating his words into a vibrant sound that, in turn, was changed to an order underground, the order for the Griffin's meal.

Quantro stood by, tasting each dish, smacking his blubbery lips. The Griffin watched him keenly. Some of his slaves might conspire in their despair. He took no chances.

With his liqueur he relaxed. Quantro removed the remnants of the meal, descending by an automatic lift that opened in the wall. The Griffin was left alone, to his sensuous music, his incense and his thoughts.

"Manning will have read my letter by now," he said softly, his low voice like the purr of a satisfied tiger. "He will be on the alert once more. And, once more, it will be checkmate for Manning. This second plan is far better than the first."

He took up the pipestem again, inhaling the fumes of *bhang*.

IV

BELMONT IS the name, my dear Manning. Raymond Belmont. The fool who thinks himself a wizard—who would pit himself against the adamantine rulings of the stars, who seeks to change the ordained course of life through his pitiful discoveries and medicaments.

There is the stake for our next game, Manning—the life of Belmont. I, who am elect, who have read the heavens, know

that his course is ran on the nineteenth of this month, somewhere in those divisions of time that men use to divide that
which is indivisible, in the twenty-four hours between two
midnights.

It is ordained. The astral forces may not be halted. Do you
take up the gage?

Manning read the letter over again the morning after he had
received it. Night had brought him no special counsel.

He could see plainly enough that the Griffin's enormously
inflated egoism was increasing. Now his astrological studies
had convinced him he was the chosen arbiter of Fate, appointed to carry out the destinies he imagined written in the stars,
casting the horoscopes of those he divined were to be eliminated. In his warped brain the idea had become fixed that men
like Raymond Belmont interfered with the decrees of preor-
dained existence because they helped men to live happier, longer
lives.

Belmont was a scientist who had devoted his time and his
great wealth to the investigation of diseases whose sources were
obscure. He had filtered germs that had eluded research, created
serums to destroy them. His worth to mankind was incalcu-
lable. His foundation treated cases unable to otherwise obtain
treatment. His loss, at the very zenith of his powers, would be
staggering.

And the Griffin, in his arrogance, with his kinked brain, had
selected him for destruction.

Belmont was a recluse, pursuing his studies and experiments
on his estate on Staten Island, remote from the world, surrounded by his staff. He was never interviewed, and gave out
his priceless discoveries only when they were perfect. It would
be difficult even for Manning, with all the influence he could
command to get through to him. But it had to be done.

Belmont, on a far higher scale, believed himself to be appointed for one purpose. He was the born healer. He would be
inclined to scoff at the threat of the Griffin, if, indeed, he had

ever heard of him. In some ways he was particularly vulnerable to the attack of this monster.

Yet he must be warned, be protected. This was the seventeenth. Manning had none too much time.

He found it impossible to get through to Belmont personally. They had no mutual acquaintances. The secretary who answered the telephone at Belmont's place seemed to have been chosen for his ability to keep out all interference. Nothing that Manning could urge elicited anything further than the information that Belmont was engaged in a most important laboratory experiment.

"I'll pass on what you say," said the man finally. "But the orders are final. There is no occasion to worry. No danger of anything happening to Mr. Belmont while we are looking out for his safety."

The telephone was shut off on this last statement, nor could Manning reconnect. There was nothing to do but make a personal visit, exhibit credentials, and try to impress on Belmont's aides the very real danger. Belmont's house was his castle, and he seemed to have stout protectors, but Manning knew that the Griffin had penetrated the most subtle of defenses before.

V

HIGH WOVEN wire on steel poles, topped with strands of barbed wire, surrounded the barren grounds of Belmont's place. There was no attempt at gardening, no shrubbery or trees, merely lawns through which wound the roads and paths.

At the only gate a guardian stood outside his watchbox, surly and reticent and suspicious of all comers. Two savage looking police dogs were beside him. He challenged the military looking man who drove up in a powerful roadster.

"You can't come in without a pass. You got to have a pass of some kind. Got to make an appointment."

"My name is Gordon Manning. I am a special agent of the

police. Here is my badge. I must see Mr. Belmont on a matter that is vital. It may mean life or death."

His manner had some effect, coupled with the sight of the gold badge.

"I'll send your name up to Mr. Henderson," said the guard grudgingly. "If he wants to see you, all right. You don't look like a crank, but I've got my orders. Folks use all kinds of dodges to get inside. You got a card?"

He took the oblong of pasteboard, put it into a small manila envelope and attached that to the collar of one of the dogs. The intelligent brute did not wait for a spoken order but ran toward the main house, barking as it reached it.

"A smart dog, that."

The surly watchman made a grimace that was probably meant for a grin.

"They beat boys, or any other messenger," he said. "They don't loiter. He'll come back on the jump with your answer."

The door had been opened and the message removed from the dog's collar by a youth. The dog remained outside while the door was shut again. A few minutes passed, then the clever animal came bounding back. The watchman read the return message.

"You can go up," he said grudgingly. "Mr. Henderson will see you. Leave your car outside. The dogs won't bother you."

Belmont's secretary, Henderson, had been chosen with regard to scientific affiliations, but he was naturally far from a fool, and the perpetual horde of visitors had made him wary.

"It is impossible for you to see Mr. Belmont, Mr. Manning," he said, gazing at the visitor through horn-rimmed glasses, a good deal like an anxious owl afraid of the disturbance of its nest. "He is engaged in the final development of some most important experiments."

"There are some things even more important than experiments," said the other. "Mr. Belmont's life, for example. Did you ever hear of the Griffin?"

The pupils of the secretary's eyes dilated behind the lenses. "You mean—" he gasped.

"I mean that Mr. Belmont's death is prophesied by the Griffin. You know what that means. And you may have heard of me."

The secretary nodded, his perturbation too great for words. Plainly he had heard of Gordon Manning, or read of him, and the crimes of the Griffin. But he was not too credulous.

"If that is the case," he said. "I must naturally do all I can to help protect Mr. Belmont. You will pardon me for asking, but how do I know that you *are* Gordon Manning?"

The other nodded.

"It is well that you are cautious," he said. "I have, of course, come prepared to identify myself. However, I would suggest that you take the most obvious means to satisfy yourself. Call up police headquarters in New York—Spring 3100. Ask for Chief Commissioner Netley. He is likely to be in at this hour. If not, get one of the deputy commissioners. They know about this threat, and while they leave the protection entirely in my hands, they will understand your natural hesitation and can arrange with you some mode of absolute identification. If you do not mind, I will wait here until that is completed. I should prefer not to leave the premises until the time limit set by the Griffin."

The secretary bowed and asked him to take a seat, offering him a cigar, which he smoked placidly while Henderson obtained his connection.

He talked at some length into the phone, with a gradually increasing satisfaction.

"I got through to Commissioner Netley himself," he said finally. "He is sending over two men. I imagine they will arrive on the next ferry. They will bring with them an official photograph of Gordon Manning, and his finger-prints. The commissioner says that he is sure you will be glad to have the comparison made. I can easily arrange for the finger-prints to be taken here, in our laboratory."

"That is quite satisfactory to me. I congratulate you, sir, on your carefulness. I presume that the commissioner told you I should want to take full charge?"

"He did. I shall be very glad if you will, after—of course—the identification is made. I am, in a way, the watchdog of Mr. Belmont," the secretary added with a nervous laugh. "We have our own guards, but I am not accustomed to cope with such emergencies as this. Perhaps, while you are waiting you might like to look around a little. There are certain portions of the equipment that may be shown, if you do not mind conforming to the regulations. They call for a guard to accompany all visitors."

The guard turned out to be a man in a uniform much like that of the State police, with puttees and Sam Browne belt, a holstered gun at his right hip. The inspection took some time. On their return to the secretary's office Henderson advanced genially.

"Everything is ready, Mr. Manning," he said. "The commissioner did not wait for the ferry, but sent over a special launch with two officers from the Identification Bureau, with a motor cycle. They are waiting for us."

The identification was complete. The photograph was unmistakable. The finger-prints that were taken tallied precisely. Henderson showed relief, offering an apology for his caution.

"Don't mention it. I'll take over, if you don't mind. The real danger begins at midnight to-night. But, from now on, kindly have all visitors referred direct to me. I should prefer to use these two officers to guard the gate instead of your regular watchman. Not that I have anything against the man. He was very efficient, but, if I am to be responsible I must handle things my own way. It will be easy enough to get leave for them to remain here."

One of the officers saluted.

"It is not necessary, Mr. Manning," he said. "The commissioner told us to stay under your orders."

"Then you can take over the gate immediately. Six hour shifts. I don't care who goes out. But I do care very much about who comes in. I may send for additional guards."

"It is quite in your hands," replied the secretary. "I shall arrange for you to see Mr. Belmont."

"Thank you. It will be very necessary. I shall take pains not to disturb him, but I am going to be close to him myself for every moment of the twenty-four danger hours."

V I

IT WAS two hours later when another roadster drove up to the Belmont gate. The driver got out, and the police officer who was acting as watchman saluted briskly and greeted him.

"We've been sort of expecting you, Mr. Manning," he said.

Gordon Manning returned the salute. He did not know the officer, but that was natural enough, with the ever increasing size of the force. He was a little surprised to find him on the gate, and credited the man he had telephoned to as having taken their talk more seriously than he had thought.

"Who ordered you here?" he demanded.

"Special orders from the chief, sir. They sent us over here in a launch so as not to lose time. We're taking six hour shifts between the two of us. I understand it's the Griffin again, sir. I hope you get him this time."

Manning nodded curtly.

"You can send my name up," he said.

"That's all right, sir. I've got orders to admit you—and no one else—unless you give fresh orders."

Manning was ushered into a room to the right of the hall inside the door, fitted up like the reception room of a clinic. An inner door opened and a man entered who was evidently no underling. His hair was close clipped in a pompadour, his face clean shaven. His mouth was a straight line, his eyes small but piercing, and his nose outstanding and arrogant. He was well tailored, his manner precise, but confident. To Manning, old army man himself, he suggested the soldier and the officer, with a touch of the Teuton, though his speech showed no accent.

He was affable without being friendly.

"Sorry to have kept you waiting, Mr. Manning," he said. "I know your mission and appreciate it. Know you and your reputation. Mr. Belmont is engaged in a most delicate, intricate conclusion to experiments over which he has worked for years. It promises a satisfactory ending—but he must not be disturbed. That, I am sure, you can understand."

"I've come to see he is not disturbed," said Manning.

"That we also appreciate. But we are quite capable of protecting Mr. Belmont—even from this man who calls himself the Griffin. I have taken extra precautions. You see, Mr. Manning, Mr. Belmont is a genius. It is his brain, rather than actual chemical reactions, that brings about his triumphs. He may stay in the laboratory for thirty-six hours—he may roam about the house, even the grounds, like a sleep-walker. He must not be annoyed, must not come in contact with strange persons, even if they are here to protect him. His thread of thought must not be broken. He will be watched, continually. But I cannot allow you, nor any of your aides, to augment our forces."

"How do you know you can trust *them?*" asked Manning.

"They have all been here for years—none less than two. They are devoted to Mr. Belmont. Again, we appreciate your efforts, but we feel sure we are entirely adequate."

"I don't," said Manning bluntly. "I can't force myself inside your grounds, or your house, but I *can* make sure no one else enters. There I shall use my authority. Mr. Belmont's safety is vital, but is not altogether paramount. This fiend, who styles himself the Griffin, is a universal enemy. In the name of the State I must make every attempt in my power to apprehend him. On your part, I expect you to join forces with me."

The other considered.

"I will stretch a point," he said finally. "I will permit you and your men to throw a cordon about the house and the buildings. I will admit you within the wire. Within doors *I* am responsible. I have full charge of such affairs as Mr. Belmont's executive manager."

"It is a fair proposition," said Manning, seeing he could do no better. He knew Belmont was hard to handle. At least he had gained a valuable concession. "Give instant orders that the place is closed to every one else, save myself and those who enter with me."

"You relieve me from the awkwardness of my position," said the other. "Now, I must hurry back to Mr. Belmont. He may miss me. He is sometimes erratic, even intolerant. But the question of his safety is as close to me as it is to you, Major Manning."

He gave a brief bow which struck Manning as a slightly false note. He was not altogether sold on this intimate executive of Belmont's. He believed him German, of a military type. But then Germans were preëminently scientific. Belmont was not the kind to consider racial prejudice.

After all, he could assemble such a corps of picked men that not even an exploring rat could get through. He could not get in to personally guard Belmont, who would be busy completing his experiments, doubtlessly fully protected, but he could surround the place with men who would challenge on sight and shoot in the same breath—and shoot straight. He himself would command them.

VII

IT WAS four o'clock in the afternoon of the nineteenth. Gordon Manning had been awake for nearly twenty-four hours, but he did not feel the need of sleep. He had thirty men with him, twice as many as he had felt were necessary to thoroughly patrol and guard the small estate. They took watches of eight hours apiece straight, and split the central eight into dog-watches.

The big chimney belched smoke. Important work was

forward. Manning did not relax his vigilance for a moment, even in the bright October sunshine. There seemed little to fear on the face of things, but he knew the Griffin was abroad.

The duel was on. So far, the Griffin had always won. With every fresh encounter the tension grew tauter.

All was serene. Blue sky and white clouds added the final note of peace. But he had known the Griffin to strike from the air itself. Or he might tunnel up like a mole. His methods were subtle, but they were sure. And never the same. The Griffin had never duplicated his mode of killing. Always he held the advantage of previous strategy, the study of the prospective victim's habits. And then, he limited the time of action to twenty-four hours. It meant to Manning an almost breaking-point strain for more than fourteen hundred minutes, eighty-four thousand seconds, each one fraught with imminent danger and disaster. It was no wonder the lines in his face were graven deep.

Even his exceptional nerves were strained to their last degree of endurance. He had to use all his will to keep from getting jumpy. It seemed to him that an inner voice, a hunch, warned him to take instant action. He had long since come to regard his so-called hunches as a distinct biological phenomenon, logically based upon the subconscious working out of various impressions recorded there.

He instinctively distrusted the man who had obstructed his original plan of stationing himself by the side of Belmont through the whole threatened period.

The man was forceful, doubtless eminently capable, but—

The lines of an old quatrain came into Manning's mind.

> *I do not like thee, Doctor Fell,*
> *The reason why I cannot tell;*
> *But this I know—and know full well,*
> *I do not like thee, Doctor Fell.*

Belmont's house had always been difficult to enter. It was natural enough that a man engaged in abstruse and intricate problems, especially when solution seemed at hand after many failures, should wish to be absolutely free from any interruption or annoyance.

But—the Griffin would know his ways. It was the Griffin's boast that the ordinary killer moved largely on impulse, lacked imagination, used obvious means and weapons; whereas he— the Griffin—studied a victim's habits, found the weak points, devised ingenious ways to take advantage of them.

During the day various men had left the premises, supposedly at the end of their work. They could go, but they might not reënter on any pretext.

All seemed peaceful, but Manning's uneasiness increased. He seemed to feel the Griffin jeering at him, knowing his protection limited, playing one of his infernal tricks.

Manning came to a final resolution, to insist upon seeing Belmont himself, if only at a distance; to know that he was safe, and then not to lose sight of him. If necessary, he would help to guard him with the executive manager, but he would be on hand himself!

There was an armed guard outside every working building, apparently a regular precaution against intruders. These would not let him through. His pass related only to the grounds. He would have to go to the house.

On his nod four of his men strolled behind him, forming his interference, should it be needed. The door was opened by a youth whose attitude was belligerent.

"You can't come in," he said. "Nobody can come in to-day. It's special orders from Mr. Manning."

"Whose orders?" asked Gordon Manning. Instantly he saw through the infernal chicanery of the Griffin. A plot ludicrously simple but efficient. Foolproof. His face showed no sign, though his eyes narrowed.

"Manning," the youth went on. "The guy who came out from headquarters yesterday morning to take charge until to-morrow. You're acting under him, ain't you? You talked with him?"

Manning concealed his impatience. Even now a deadly fuse was sputtering, at any second an explosion might take place, if the mock Manning knew of this move of his.

"I'm not exactly under his orders," he answered. "But I've got to see him again, right away. Something has happened. Where is he?"

The Griffin's cunning had forestalled Manning, knowing his habits too, knowing Manning always spent the hours of danger with the threatened man. He had simply sent a man on ahead with forged credentials, the telephones controlled by his method of synchronization in case they were used to check up on identity.

And this agent, this murderer of the Griffin's employ, had been close to Belmont all day, was with him now, would strike at his own convenience!

"Where is he?" he repeated. "Jump to it, my lad. This is serious."

His will beat down the youth's opposition.

"I'll find out," he said.

"You needn't call him," said Manning. "Just find out where he and Mr. Belmont are, right now. That's all."

The lad went to a house phone, put the question.

"Know where Mr. Manning is? I've got a message for him. It's important, see?"

Manning waited. His men were on the porch, idling there but ready to follow him on signal.

"They're both in the culture room," said the lad, at last. "Where they breed germs."

Manning opened the front door, called in his four men.

"Show us where that is," he said.

A man came hurrying in, wearing horn-rimmed glasses, excited and distressed.

"What's all this?" he demanded with some show of authority. "I'm Mr. Henderson, Mr. Belmont's personal secretary."

Manning jerked his head impatiently at him.

"Well, *I'm* Gordon Manning," he said. "The *real* Gordon Manning. The man you've admitted is a fake. He's here to kill Mr. Belmont, not protect him. These men and my others outside are all Manhattan detectives. The two officers that first arrived are fakes also. All agents of the Griffin. Now, get out of my way before murder's done, if it hasn't happened already."

They stood back, aghast. There was no challenging Manning's force, his real authority. Henderson gasped like a landed fish.

"My God?" he faltered. "What have I done?"

"Nothing," snapped Manning. "You've been fooled, like the rest of us. Here, my lad," he added, addressing the youth, "take us to where they are."

They passed through various offices where clerks and stenographers were at work, staring at them as they passed, but not alarmed. Henderson had practically collapsed at the thought that he had, however unwittingly, betrayed Belmont. There was a covered walk from the house to the culture room so that Belmont could visit it at any hour. At the end of the walk there was one of the uniformed guards. He challenged them with an imperative order to halt, his hand on his gun.

There was not time to argue. Manning respected the man's attitude, but he had to get through.

"I've got a pass," he said, fumbling in his vest pocket as if to produce it.

"Why didn't you say so? Let's see it."

What he got to see was Manning's fist, shot out in a sizzling uppercut. The man went down and out. Manning took possession of his gun.

They were not through yet. The culture room was the heart of Belmont's citadel. There, of all places, he must not be disturbed. There he performed his miracles, nursed or destroyed the strange germ forms that were the enemies of humanity, but might be made to serve it.

There was a narrow corridor ahead of them with a steel door

at its end. This had a narrow observation slit in it, closed from the inside with a slide. It gave Manning an idea. The false Manning would hardly have had time to acquaint himself with the features of the guards. The man just knocked out, still unconscious, was about the same build as one of the men with Manning. He could treat the Griffin with some of his own medicine.

VIII

"**P**UT ON that chap's coat, belt, and hat, Sloane," Manning ordered. "Keep the visor of the cap well down. Doherty, you stay and watch this man when he comes to. Hold him. Ready, Sloane. Come on then, all but Doherty. Knock on that door, Sloane, and if any one answers don't let him get too good a look at you. Tell him there's trouble outside. It may work."

Manning and the others crouched while Sloane played his part.

The slit opened. Only the eyes and nose of the man inside showed, but these were the unmistakable features of the one who had represented himself as Gordon Manning.

"What is it?" he demanded sharply. "Why have you left your post?"

"There's trouble—more than I can handle," said Sloane. "You're in charge. You better tackle it."

"I'll come. Go back and wait for me."

Manning prodded Sloane and the quick witted Irishman played up.

"Very good, sir," he answered with a salute. He swung on his heels and marched away as the slit closed.

The door of heavy steel opened slowly inward. Through the widening gap Manning distinctly heard a groan. The three flung themselves at the door, forcing it back. Manning was the first to leap through.

He glimpsed shelves and benches that bore a gleaming array

of glass jars filled with strange contents. He saw a body lying on the floor at the far end, looking like a rag-stuffed dummy. Then he saw the killer, coming out from behind the door, a glass container in his hand. His eyes gleamed.

"You came too late, Manning," he said. "I am not such a fool as you think. Keep back. If I break this jar all of you will die within the hour."

It might be a bluff, it might well be truth. Manning temporized.

"You too," he said.

The other laughed. "I would much rather die now than wait until you send me to the electric chair."

He held the container aloft, dramatically, at full length of his arm, ready to hurl it.

His back was toward the open door. Sloane had returned. And the killer had overlooked that incident. Sloane caught Manning's eye and gave a slight nod, unseen by the murderer. Then he sprang and caught the wrist of the hand that held the jar and now essayed to throw it.

All he could do under Sloane's viselike grip was to toss it. Manning was waiting for it like a crack first baseman hoping to retire the other team. He caught the container with its deadly contents deftly, and set it down on a shelf while the rest secured the killer, who fought furiously.

Manning looked down on the face of Raymond Belmont. Not only did it bear the seal of death, but on the forehead was the scarlet cartouche, the oval of heavy paper embossed with the seal of the Griffin.

Belmont had been stabbed in the heart with a poniard, the silver hilt of which protruded from his breast, driven home between his ribs by an expert's hand.

"I could take no chances of interference, Manning," said the captive. "What do you propose to do with me?"

"A great many things you won't like before you go to that

chair," said Manning grimly. "I want to find out all you know about the Griffin."

"You mean torture, I suppose. Why not try a bribe? Suppose I told you all you want to know, could I escape the chair? Go free?"

"I can promise nothing," said Manning sternly.

The other laughed, lightly at first, and then with a growing hysteria.

"Too late, again," he gasped when he had managed to somewhat control himself, his eyes streaming. "I couldn't tell you where the Griffin lives if I wanted to. I don't know. None of us do. We leave blindfolded, through winding tunnels, and the bandages are not removed until we travel a long way in a car. The same method prevails when we report back—if we *do* report. It looks as if you will have to send me to the chair after all. Let us go. Have you no handcuffs ready? I trust you do not mind if I straighten my clothes somewhat. At least my tie?"

The two who had been holding him had released him, watchful and alert. His hand went to his disheveled pocket. They had handled him vigorously and cloth was torn and buttons gone. He wore a pearl stickpin, which had a safety catch on its point.

This he coolly released and then, his hands well down in front of him, he suddenly jabbed the pin deeply into his wrist before Manning could prevent. Blood spurted from a vein, the poisoned pin fell to the floor. The action of the venom was fast, a faster poison than the poison of a king cobra.

He seemed to shrivel, a faint rattle in his throat before he was gone, beyond all earthly reprisal.

There was a telephone in the culture room and Manning picked it up. He had to communicate with the authorities concerning Belmont's death, the death of the Griffin's agent, his own failure. It was not a pleasant thing to do, but it had to be faced. Once more the Griffin had triumphed.

And then he head the Griffin's own booming voice speaking. Mocking, with a faint strain of music over in the background.

"My dear Manning. I have been expecting to hear from you. The pitch of your voice is easily picked up by my own private televox apparatus. Telephones these days are really quite unsatisfactory in some ways, but very satisfactory in others, to those who know how to handle them.

"I have told you how carefully I study the ways of those I wish to eliminate. I have also studied *yours*, Manning. It was really absurdly easy to impersonate you, to synchronize the Belmont telephones, to represent Commissioner Netley and establish my men ahead of you. The advantage, you see, of making the first move in our game. Quite laughable, Manning. You still amuse me—and you will hear from me again."

"One of these days," Manning muttered, "I shall amuse you no longer."

He gave an order to Sloane.

"You and Doherty get that fake officer at the gate. There's another one somewhere round. Get them."

But he knew, even as Sloane and Doherty hurried off, that the two would have gone. They were minor actors. But their escape was the final straw that brought something like a groan from Gordon Manning. He stiffened, straightened.

After all, the Griffin was not supernatural. Some day, he would slip.

Manning's mouth was like a closed trap, his eyes glinted, his fists closed as if he felt himself at last at handgrips with the Griffin. Those grips, once made, would not be loosed.

J. ALLAN DUNN has adventure in his blood. He has wandered across the globe, led on by restless curiosity; he has poked into the world's strangest corners, he has sailed into unknown ports. He is always looking for the new and the mysterious.

He's been an artist and a rancher, a miner and a horse wrangler, a pearler, a windjammer's skipper, a war correspondent, a sugar planter, a prospector and an author. In the course of his travels he has been pretty well shot through with lead and steel; and he's enjoyed bubonic plague, cholera, and some of the other choice fevers that come out of the tropics.

Mr. Dunn was born in London, England, of Irish parents. That's probably where he got his magical gift for story telling. He went to Oxford University, and then spent several years traveling through Europe and along the African fringe of the Mediterranean. One day he sailed to India, and, returning, went back across the Equator to South Africa.

He felt the lure of western horizons about that time, and took a steamer for the United States. He finally hit Colorado and tried his hand there at mining and ranching. Hard luck trailed him, however; probably it was fortunate, because Dunn pulled stakes and looked for new worlds. Down, in New Mexico he lived through enough thrilling experiences to satisfy any ordinary man for a lifetime.

He decided to withdraw momentarily from an adventurer's

career, and joined the Salt Lake *Herald* as a reporter. But the Spanish-American war broke out about then, and J. Allan Dunn couldn't resist the lure of danger. They sent him to Cuba to cover the war.

In tropical Cuba he discovered that a war can be more hard work than glamour. He had to hike twenty-two miles every day between the battle front and the cable office in Siboney, where he sent out dispatches to the papers. There was only one cable going out of Siboney, he relates, and the war correspondents used to toss for turns. Unlucky ones had to sit up until three in the morning to get their stories through.

When the war was over, wanderlust took Dunn to California and to Honolulu. Tall tales of fortunes in pearls in the South Seas sent him down there. Pearling, he discovered, was a lottery. "I lost," he admits, "but I had a good time."

He explored New Guinea, that strange land north of Australia where head hunters still roam and death waits for the white man who is bold enough to pierce into the cannibal-inhabited interior. Dunn came out with his head, and his life, happily. He bought a barkentine and sailed up the Yangtze-kiang, and about then another war broke out and gave him an excuse to wander in another strange country.

That was the Russo-Jap war. He covered it for the duration. His side-kick was Jack London. J. Allan Dunn traveled with another man the world well remembers, when he was in the tropics—the famous Richard Harding Davis.

Dunn has made many unique business adventures. Among other things, he has prospected for gold in the Klondike and tried to run a sugar plantation in Hawaii. The only thing that ever paid him, he says, is writing. He has written almost two thousand short stories, numberless novelettes, and between twenty and thirty serials.